Mrs. Shaw

MODERN
African
Writing
from Ohio University Press

Ghirmai Negash, General Editor
Laura Murphy, Series Editor

This series brings the best African writing to an international audience. These groundbreaking novels, memoirs, and other literary works showcase the most talented writers of the African continent. The series also features works of significant historical and literary value translated into English for the first time. Moderately priced, the books chosen for the series are well crafted, original, and ideally suited for African studies classes, world literature classes, or any reader looking for compelling voices of diverse African perspectives.

Books in the series are published with support from the Ohio University National Resource Center for African Studies.

MUKOMA WA NGUGI

Mrs. Shaw

A NOVEL

OHIO UNIVERSITY PRESS   ATHENS

Ohio University Press, Athens, Ohio 45701
ohioswallow.com
© 2015 by Mukoma Wa Ngugi
All rights reserved

Printed in the United States of America
Ohio University Press books are printed on acid-free paper ⊗ ™

25 24 23 22 21 20 19 18 17 16 15   5 4 3 2 1

Library of Congress Cataloging-in-Publication Data
Mukoma wa Ngugi.
    Mrs. Shaw : a novel / Mukoma wa Ngugi.
        pages cm. — (Modern African Writing series)
    Summary: "In the fictional East African Kwatee Republic of the 1990s, the
dictatorship is about to fall, and the nation's exiles are preparing to return.
One of these exiles, a young man named Kalumba, is a graduate student in
the United States, where he encounters Mrs. Shaw, a professor emerita and
former British settler who fled Kwatee's postcolonial political and social
turmoil. Kalumba's girlfriend, too, is an exile: a Puerto Rican nationalist like
her imprisoned father, she is an outcast from the island. Brought together by
a history of violence and betrayals, all three are seeking a way of regaining
their humanity, connecting with each other, and learning to make a life in a
new land. Kalumba and Mrs. Shaw, in particular, are linked by a past rooted
in colonial and postcolonial violence, yet they are separated by their differing
accounts of what really happened. The memory of each is subject to certain
lapses, whether selective or genuine. Even when they agree on the facts —
be they acts of love, of betrayal, or of violence — each narrator shapes the
story in his or her own way, by what is left in and what is left out, by what is
remembered and what is forgotten"— Provided by publisher.
    ISBN 978-0-8214-2143-7 (hardback : acid-free paper) — ISBN 978-0-8214-
4515-0 (pdf)
    1. Africa, East—Fiction. I. Title.
PR9381.9.M778M77 2015
823'.92—dc23

2015007879

Dedicated to

Thomas Sankara,

Ruth First,

and Maurice Bishop,

who died so we may live only to be betrayed again, and again.

Acknowledgments

With deep gratitude and debt to Carmen McCain, to my wife, Maureen Burke, and to my father, Ngugi Wa Thiong'o, for their deep reading and criticism of the early drafts. Also deep gratitude to Nancy Basmajian, Laura Murphy, Gillian Berchowitz, and Ghirmai Negash for making a home for Mrs. Shaw at the Ohio University Press Modern African Writing series. To my agents Gloria Loomis and Julia Masnik—here's to many more. Thank you!

Contents

Kalumba—Escape into Exile

The moment Baba Ogum opened his eyes, he realized he was going to get shot. And he would die. Baba Ogum realized it even as his body continued to obey his earlier command to stir, even as he read the warning—*be still*—in Kalumba's frantic eyes. In the same sharp flash with which you realize, a moment before your hand lets go, that you are inevitably going to drop a glass of water, and it will break, Baba Ogum realized he shouldn't have opened his eyes, he shouldn't have flailed his arms, groping to find where he was—he should have kept his eyes closed and his body limp. He should have remained dead, and because he had not, he was going to get shot. Their eyes locked. One pair a few seconds from death managed a sad familiar smile that said *I will not betray your hiding spot*. The other, the hidden pair, promised in exchange that they would never let go of what they were witnessing.

What had brought Baba Ogum to this point? A conscience and a Bible—short and to the point. That just about summed up his life. He had not been surprised when they came for him. He had in fact anticipated just a routine questioning, a few inconvenient hours and he would be on his way. But in extraordinary times, he was learning, nothing remains predictable for long. There had been a coup attempt—he should have taken extra precautions.

At the beginning Baba Ogum had been reluctant to speak to the flesh. His calling was to make good Christians. But as starved, bruised, and battered bodies walked into his church every Sunday, he could tell that the faithful were losing faith in both worlds. They had long ago lost faith in the world of Bata Shoe Company and Goodwill Tea Plantation where most of them worked. And now the better world of the faith was losing its luster. Faith feeds on hope. To preach to the flesh was a pragmatic choice.

As he lay there just a few seconds from dying, his first sermon flashed through his mind. His congregation walking in dutifully for two hours of escape before returning to their real worlds, and he, his heart beating into his chest, reminding himself that today he had to speak to their flesh—and that in the process he would be making powerful enemies. He chose the sermon carefully, just like any artist with a canvas, each stroke an understatement that resounded outside of its colors to become amplified in the minds of the audience. A good artist suggests, he told himself, and so he started.

There is Judas and there is Peter. Judas betrayed Jesus for thirty pieces of silver, with a kiss. And Jesus told Peter, "I tell you, Peter, before the cock crows this day, you will deny three times that you know me." And so it happened that after Jesus was captured, Peter, though he'd vowed to follow Jesus to his death, instead followed in the footsteps of Judas the traitor, denying Jesus three times. Not once or twice, but three times. There is Judas and there is Peter. Judas betraying, Peter denying. Let me ask you, whose sins were greater? The one who betrayed or the one who denied? In our times, whose sins are greater? Those that betray us for the thirty pieces of silver or the pious that stand by, denying the injustice of it all? We, the people, are the body of Christ; the State, Judas. Need I tell you who Peter is? Go home—you have much to do.

This, his shortest sermon, would become in time his legendary trademark—a haiku that a few days later developed into an epic in the minds of the people. After he thundered out the words *Go home—you have much to do,* his congregation looked confused as they left the pews only to stand outside the church. He followed them outside, with his hands raised, as if pushing a big tide back into the ocean. He thought he had lost the people, but the following Sunday his church was overflowing. When he walked in, even before he said a word, he received his first-ever standing ovation. He became the only priest in Kwatee Republic who received standing ovations one week after his sermons and always before the new one.

After that his haiku sermons, as they came to be called, rarely lasted more than ten minutes. The people came to be recharged, and as soon as their batteries were ready, they went back to the streets. His congregation kept growing; his sermons, easily memorized, were whispered across the nation. Sooner or later, his priest's cloak would lose its power of protection, and between going to hell or staying in power the rulers would take their chances. Better to reign over hell on earth than to serve in heaven, and so they started coming after the priests. Baba Ogum was a victim of this newfound faith in the now.

Kalumba had been running for hours through carnation farms, large tea plantations, and at last a dense forest full of thick wild berry bushes with sharp thorns that were cutting into his skin. His lungs were about to implode. Each heartbeat, a resounding thud of pure will, sounded spaced out, lonely even, as if at some point the distance between each heartbeat would grow longer and longer until only his body, devoid of life, would be left running. His chest heaving, he stopped.

Earlier he'd had to abandon his rucksack, his survival kit of two books, roasted goat meat, a pair of expensive black dress pants, a white shirt, and newly polished black leather Prefect shoes—the trademark of Bata Shoe Company. After rummaging through the rucksack, he removed a passport and with a bemused look, as one does before handing it to the customs official, he stared at his black-and-white photo. In the moonlight he imagined it more than he saw it. In it he was wearing his high school light blue shirt and black blazer, even though he had finished sixth form just a few months before. He was young and life was in front of him—this was before the dreadlocks that now wet with sweat kept slapping against his face, before the politics. He looked at the photo again and thought how he looked like his father when he was about the same age, how they both looked tortured even before their innocence was lost. There was no going back, so he crumpled the passport into his back pocket. Into his left front pocket he slipped a few thousand shillings and into the other, transcripts from primary school through university, which had looked out of place in his large sweaty hands in the middle of a forest. Realizing that he would not be hungry for a long time, he discarded the bread.

His only other possession was an army flask. With its strap broken he had to carry it by hand, and it became heavier and heavier even though now empty. Earlier, the sound of water hitting its insides had seemed louder than it actually was. His temples throbbed, and he felt like his blood would break through the thin skin. He had been fascinated by how quickly the rings of vapor from his breath dissipated into the cold air, but now the only thought in him was to make it to the meeting point. The mist would soon lift as the morning sun began to heat the earth. Soaked in sweat, his T-shirt and jeans clinging to his body, he thought just how unprepared he had been for this moment. He would be better off running in his nice trousers and shirt—they were lighter. He would be better off running without a shirt, but a quick look at his bare arms, sliced in a thousand places by thorns and dry branches, convinced him to leave it on. He did not mind the pain as sweat drops rolled into the thin red crevices. It kept him feeling alive.

It was almost daybreak. He started running again knowing he would have to stop soon and rest. For the past two hours, unable to move any faster, he had been running at a crawl.

He was beyond tired, but he wanted to live. When he came to a stream, he paused and drank some water. It was very cold, even though the sun had now revealed itself fully. He contemplated filling the water bottle halfway to keep it light and then realized he had to fill it up all the way. He still had a long way to go. He looked around the stream. He hadn't come as far as he'd thought. Even though he had been running for five or six hours, he hadn't come that far—not with fences to climb over, maize and napier grass plants cutting into his skin, and tea plantations arranged like a maze. When he was young, he and his friends would sneak out of school to come and play here. What used to be an hour's drive had taken him all night.

He knew exactly where to stop. Meters from the stream there was a massive baobab tree, branches contorting high into the sky like muscular arms lifted in prayer. They would sometimes smoke stolen cigarettes here. He was running back into his childhood. The tree's massive trunk had been drilled hollow by time, and it looked like a hut without a door—one supported by thick roots that ran in and out of the earth. He sat in the hollowness, a silent witness of generations, and it in turn embraced his battered body. He was hungry and wished for the food he had thrown away. For generations, his ancestors had prayed and sacrificed to their god here. He and his friends had joked that it was thieves and the hungry who answered the prayers by eating the meat left for sacrifice. He wondered whether, if he looked around, he could find some cured meat, a bone that he could crush to find marrow preserved over many generations.

For the past few hours, he hadn't thought about his father, Sukena, relatives, and friends . . . how they would take his flight, and how they would cope with the harassment that would follow. He wondered if his father would think his exile was a selfish act, like suicide. But he had to trust his father's judgment; he would be relieved that his only child had escaped. As long as Kalumba was alive there was hope. Sukena—he would miss her. He felt his heart beginning to give way, so he let his mind wander to Ogum, the dead preacher's son and his best friend. Ogum had grown up in the same area as Kalumba; they'd gone to the same schools, and even though they had enrolled in different degree programs, they'd been admitted at the same time and would have graduated on the same date, except that Ogum had been suspended for one year after being involved in a strike against higher tuition fees.

Ogum spoke fluent Lulato. Only in Africa would speaking your own language with fluency be an achievement, they joked. In addition to Lulato, he also spoke the national language of the Kwatee Republic, English, and Kyukato, Kalumba's language. It was people like Ogum—who had lived in other cultures in addition to their own—that deserved to be leaders. But neither the Lulato nor the Kyukato trusted him, and therein lay the stupidity of the whole thing, Kalumba angrily thought. To understand other cultures was to be diluted, to be compromised. It was to be dirty.

He painfully dragged himself from where he was sitting to lean against the inside wall of the baobab tree. He wondered, after all the sacrifices made at this tree, if the culmination of their magic would save his life. And as the warmth of sleep came over him, he felt safe and protected.

Kalumba dreamt that Sukena had given birth to a little boy with no stomach, always hungry and always crying. The boy's crying morphed into loud voices and army trucks and helicopters circling above the baobab tree looking for him. He felt the heat of a bright light in his eyes. He wasn't dreaming. How had they found him? He opened his eyes to find blinding sunlight streaming into his eyes. He closed and opened them again. The sun had found a hole through the tree to launch its invasion. He was relieved. But just as soon as he felt safe, he heard agitated voices, screams, and then machine-gun fire that sounded like thousands of people clapping loudly at a rally. He crawled from inside the baobab and looked toward the stream. On the other side, he saw soldiers laboring to pile dead bodies on top of each other in a wide but shallow grave. It resembled a first dig to lay the foundation for a house. They were stacking the bodies such that heads locked against feet until they rose into the sky—a funeral pyre. Kalumba, well hidden by rocks in the long grass, felt vulnerable, as if he were out in the open. From where he lay, he could see the thin but determined blanket of blood flowing down the banks and into the stream, dividing the clear stream upward from the downstream water thick with redness. Some of the dead were in army uniforms, and others were clearly civilians. He could not make out the faces, but he knew they had to be members of the movement. These were the activists that he, together with Ogum, had not been able to reach to warn. He lay there transfixed, a reluctant witness, as immobile as the baobab tree. The soldiers lazily started moving back into their trucks with their guns slung on their shoulders like machetes or hoes, tired farmers leaving the field for the evening. The smell of gasoline made its way to where Kalumba was hiding. He saw one soldier fumbling in his pockets like a smoker looking for matches. It hit him— they were going to burn the bodies and bury the remains. As the soldier searched his pockets, Kalumba noticed that one of the bodies was still alive. A man was stirring. At that moment, their eyes met. The man in the pile of bodies was waking up as if from a nightmare, disoriented. He was starting to grope around when he seemed to remember what had happened and understood why there was a pair of eyes hidden across the stream frantically telling him to be still.

The soldier paused for a second, contemplating whether to burn him alive or shoot him. He dropped his lit match and in a small act of mercy drew a pistol, marched toward the man, and shot him twice in the chest. Kalumba imagined the man feeling his body getting heavier and heavier as it pressed against the other dead bodies.

He recognized the man. It was Baba Ogum. In fear and anger, Kalumba bit into his arm so that the pain smothered the scream rising in his throat. Another matchstick made contact. Flames rose, lapping furiously against a soft wind as they came to life. Baba Ogum, already fading into his death, disappeared in the flames. The soldiers left. The smoke from burning flesh plumed straight into the sky. Kalumba looked around. It was a beautiful day. He thought about how lucky he was to have a full container of water. Then he doubled up and started vomiting. He had just witnessed a massacre and the assassination of Baba Ogum. Kalumba was taking flight, taking the pictures of the dead with him, but he had done nothing to help them. Instinctively, he grasped the paradox of the witness. The witness was always a coward, always less than the martyr. The witness testified because when called upon, he or she chose not to die. The witness testified in order to keep the ghosts and the guilt at bay. Kalumba should have died with Baba Ogum.

He wanted to do something—go by the fire and say a prayer—but instead he crawled back to the baobab tree. He noticed he was bleeding heavily from his stomach. He must have crawled over something sharp, but he could hardly feel the wound. His body was entering into a numbing state of shock. Soon he could see the memory of Baba Ogum's eyes full of despair and fear, a grimace as the bullets entered his body—but he felt nothing. He lay inside the hollow tree for hours.

Perhaps this massacre was the culmination of generations upon generations of sacrifices. Massacres and genocides: how much can a people endure? He thought back to the thousands killed by the British during the uprising that finally gave way to the first independence. The kidnapping and assassination of Mr. Shaw—a vicious and determined British intelligence officer—by the independence movement, followed by a heavy-handed response by the British, then overwhelming resistance and the British giving in. And now they were at it again. Was this the culmination? Death as a constant no matter who led the country? Kalumba retraced his flight.

A soldier, who was probably also in that pile of bodies, had come to his home the night before, unarmed and alone. Even without a weapon he had a soldier's arrogance about him. Kalumba wasn't scared. A few months before, he would have been; soldiers and dictators rule through the threat of violence, symbolic and real, and the uniform without the gun is the same as one with a gun. It was like colonial white skin—whether it carried a Bible or not, the most important thing was the wrath of the army it threatened to visit upon the souls that refused to be harvested, or those that rebelled. Over time, white skin became the army itself. But he had not felt afraid of the soldier. He had experienced everything but death at their hands, and short of killing him, there was nothing more they could do.

But that was Kalumba the victim and survivor. Kalumba the witness wondered if this held true anymore. There was more to be afraid of, like people who conduct massacres in the middle of a beautiful day as carelessly as if they were on a lunch break. "Look," the soldier had said to Kalumba, "I . . . we do not want to see more people dead. Especially the young people, and even though we anticipate more trouble from the likes of you, what we call professional agitators, this is our country and you are needed. Protect yourselves and your friends. We shall deal with each other later. Like men . . . eye to eye. If you do not leave tonight, there is a chance you will be dead by morning."

The soldier gave Kalumba the List, and just like that he left. Perhaps he had been one of Kalumba's torturers, an assassin doing one act of penance, or perhaps he was just being pragmatic. But no matter, the soldier had saved his life. Kalumba did not doubt him. He had felt the vise tightening. He had already been arrested and tortured. After his release, he was being followed. He was sure that their house phone was tapped. Several politicians, moderates, nationalists, and radicals had been disappeared. He understood that something big was about to happen, with that same instinct that informs soccer players in a tight match that their opponents are flagging, or with which soldiers sense that tides are turning in times of war.

He felt that the culmination of all the right and wrong moves had brought history to a point where decisions had to be made and something had to give. It was victory, exile, or death, but things could not remain at the cusp of a violent explosion much longer. It was not the movement that Kalumba belonged to that had made the first move. It was a section of the army, and the dictator had exacted his price. He and those like him who were part of the Second Independence Democracy with Content Forum, or SIDCF, were going to feel the full effects of whatever had just transpired.

After the soldier had left, Kalumba looked at the List. Baba Ogum's name leapt out at him. Like most names on the List, it had been written hastily. They were not even typed but written in pen or pencil, then photocopied. There were some names that had been carelessly cancelled out, but he could not make them out. He wondered if that meant they had already been contained or had won reprieve. The ones he could make out, like his, were names of activists he knew to be alive. The names were written in different hands. He became very angry. Here on a piece of crumpled paper were people's lives. How many antigovernment speeches earned an assassination? How many rallies? How about silence when asked to sing? How many silences add up to your name on the List? He called Ogum first on his cell phone and ten minutes later from a neighbor's phone a few houses from where he lived. He told Ogum that his father was on the List and gave him the names of others Ogum could easily reach.

"Comrade will know what to do," Ogum said, referring to the leader of the Second Independence. The Leader was without protocol. He believed in a leaderless movement and carried the paradox lightly, often joking about it. He knew most of the movement members by name and they in turn trusted him. "I would not worry so much about your father. Just give him a heads-up," the Leader said, his voice betraying no anxiety. Baba Ogum had been in this situation many times—he was popular and he was a priest. For activists like Kalumba who were less well known, who had already been thrown in jail and tortured, being on the List left flight as the only option. For in the scale of ever-increasing sanctions, being killed was the logical step after detention and torture. So they called everyone they could, and it was only afterward that Kalumba went back home to prepare himself for flight. Neither they nor the Leader knew that a coup was being planned. Had they both known that one would be attempted shortly after the soldier came to see Kalumba and it would fail, and that the government would take that opportunity to try to weaken the opposition by blaming the coup on political activists, they would have urged Baba Ogum to be extra cautious or take flight. The soldier who had saved Kalumba's life was probably dead. Baba Ogum was dead, as were those whom the government had managed to round up, those that Kalumba could not recognize in the mass pyre.

The sun seemed to be fading, like the day was nearly gone, but it was only smoke from the fire. The smoke reached the tree. It swirled angrily looking for a place to escape and, finding the small window that earlier had streamed sunlight, funneled through it. His eyes misted. He was crying. The shock was wearing off, and the pain that comes with thawing overwhelmed him. Though wide awake, he registered nothing: not the pain, not the burning bodies outside, not the torture he had endured a few months ago, not even his father, who by now would be worried. He shut down completely. When he woke up from his catatonic state, it was dark. Even though he did not know it at the time, he swore to himself that he would live. A wounded animal, limping and stumbling, he continued his journey toward exile, a survivor and a witness.

Ogum heard a rustling noise and jumped up from where he was sitting. His eyes took a few seconds to adjust well enough to make out a silhouette pushing through the old wooden door. It took a long time for the door to open. The silhouette walked in, feet dragging along the dusty floor. Ogum fumbled in his pockets for a match. He struck it and held it to the lantern. As he did so, he heard a gasp and a shuffle toward the door. He knew this could not be Sukena. He whispered Kalumba's name, and as the light from the lantern filled the room, the silhouette turned around.

When he saw Kalumba, he knew something had gone terribly wrong. Thin prickly blackjacks, green leaves, and even little twigs were embedded in Kalumba's long dreadlocks. He looked as if he had been swimming in a river of blood, and as he shuffled along, he left little drops of blood on the sawdust-covered floor. He was doubled over, holding his stomach with one hand, the other hand holding a bloodied water bottle. But more shocking than his appearance was the expression on his face. His normally jovial face, alive in debate or jokes, was gaunt, as if it had wilted.

And Kalumba's eyes, Ogum saw later as they talked, alternated between disbelief, fear, and outrage, sometimes vacant yet full of anger, with slivers of shame and flashes of exhilaration for being alive and safe. He seemed to be experiencing a thousand emotions rapidly—emotions that were intense, sharp, and without relief. It was a wonder that he was not on the ground paralyzed. The light from the kerosene lantern, not quite a bright white and not quite a bright red, almost yellow in fact, painted everything in the room a sickly orange. That it rapidly pulled shadows long and short as a sharp wind blew through the cracked walls made matters worse.

Ogum, after calling out Kalumba's name, had not said a word. He pulled out a dusty wooden chair for him to sit on. Kalumba numbly looked around. This woodshed at their old primary school was their alternative meeting point in case of complications. And with the failed coup attempt, there were many complications, including roadblocks and a list against which every person's ID was being checked. All their plans had changed. They could no longer bluff and bribe their way through the airport. There was too much at stake now for the corrupt immigration official or state security officer to let them pass. At that moment Sukena walked in. Kalumba tried to stand up as she walked in, but he was too drained.

She gently motioned to him to remain seated and walked over to him. She looked at Ogum, but he just shook his head. Kalumba reached out and held on to her. Since the beginning of his ordeal, less than twenty-four hours ago but seeming like an eternity, it was only when he saw Sukena that he thought he might be okay. He'd known things would be safe when he had walked in and seen Ogum, but it was Sukena's presence that made him feel he might be okay. The last part of his journey to the school had been painful. He had never felt so much fear in his life. Not even when he was arrested for the first time. Seeing the executions had broken him. To get to the toolshed, he'd had to walk through the open soccer field; otherwise he would have had to double back and climb the fence behind the school.

Had he known his legs would be shaking as he walked across the field, or that his heart would be pounding so hard that it would make him think he was going to die and his chest would tighten like a fist in terror, or that he would feel so vulnerable and lonely as he waited for a warning to stop and then a bullet in his brain that he would wish for death, or that the dull moon would feel like a spotlight on him, perhaps he would have changed his route. But he had made it, and Sukena was here. He started crying, at first slowly, with sobs that heaved both him and Sukena, who, standing, was holding him to her stomach, rocking back and forth.

Then he started wailing anguished wails that were so low she felt them without hearing them. They got louder and louder until she thought the wails would rip them into pieces. Sukena knew she had to do something or they would all crumble to the floor. Nothing had prepared them for this— driven by ideas, she knew they had to feel the cost in their flesh and minds. But for the past few months, each day had come with little surprises: Kalumba's arrest and torture, his amnesia about the torture, and, more, the fear that they would be next. Self-preservation and empathy do not go hand in hand, and she had felt herself growing more and more distant from Kalumba. She couldn't tend to his wounds fully, and the guilt of feeling that she loved him less kept growing. And now here he was, wailing like a little kid and risking their arrest.

Taken by surprise, Ogum watched helplessly as Sukena thrust Kalumba back, then took one step back and slapped him so hard that he spun on the chair, which swiveled on one leg, hesitated for a moment, and then came crashing down, taking Kalumba with it. The slap took Kalumba by surprise and quieted him down. Sukena stood him up, then seated him on a plastic pail of dried-up red paint and explained how they would get him out of the country as she reached down and removed red ochre from her bag, lying on the dusty floor. As if she had done this all her life, she began kneading it into his dreadlocks. Its richness fought the smell of kerosene out of the woodshed. At times she would treat them one lock at a time, lifting each up as if she were sewing with thread, and with the heels of her palms worked the ochre in. She massaged it into his roots in sharp quick rough movements. For Kalumba the red ochre was a relief as it lodged deep into his scalp, a cool gritty healing potion.

When it was all worked in, she stood up, took the lantern, and held it to his face. It would need time to solidify, but they had to move soon. She told him to take off his shirt and trousers. She poured some water from Kalumba's flask onto a cloth and scrubbed the blood off his face, chest, thighs, and legs. She unwound a long green wrapper holding her own locks in place and wound it around Kalumba's back and stomach to stem the bleeding from the wound. From her bag she removed a long flowing red cloth. She draped it over one of Kalumba's shoulders and under the armpit of the other, leaving the shoulder bare, and then let rest of the red cloth fall to his ankles. She checked through his jeans pockets and found the passport, school certificates, and money. It was risky to be without a form of identification, but it was even riskier for Kalumba to be caught with his passport on him. With Kalumba on the List, they would be shot dead on the spot.

She stuffed everything back into the jeans except the money, which, using a corner of his cloth, she folded into a knot. She stuffed his bloody clothes into a corner of the shed. They would come back for them when it was safer. She gave him six amulets, made of what seemed like a million tiny beads in a rainbow of colors, to put on each wrist.

Finally, to complete the ensemble, she gave him a calabash. It was full. He opened it. It contained warm fermented porridge. As he painfully lifted it to his lips, Sukena watched him. He almost resembled a Samasi warrior, but without a bow and arrow, a spear, or a fighting stick he would not pass . . . but only if a Samasi cop stopped them. But then again, such a cop, in disguise as well, would not peer too closely. In a sense Kalumba's disguise was perfect. To everybody else in the country, the Samasi wore red cloth and wove their hair in red ochre. They were not seen. And when seen they were wished away because they reminded the Africans of cultures sold to the European, of tilling in his garden, of working as maids, of copulation to provide child laborers and later generations who managed his bank accounts and his estates.

Also, the police would not expect an educated African, even a radical one, to go this far. What would the Samasi think of her disguise? She did not have time to ponder—Ogum was already insisting that they move if they wanted to get to the border before dawn. Kalumba attempted to say something but instead only managed to stare at Ogum with large frightened eyes. "My *ilkiliyani*," she said, "let's go." Perhaps he wouldn't have started to follow her outside had he known she called him her junior warrior, she thought to herself.

Before they got to the door Kalumba gestured for them to stop. "Your father, Ogum, your father is dead," he said, placing his hand on Ogum's chest. Ogum did not move, but Sukena and Kalumba heard a sigh escape him as he stiffened up. Kalumba tried telling them about the massacre by the stream on a beautiful day, how he had been woken up by gunfire, how the baobab tree had sheltered him, about sacrifices and black smoke and how the soldier who had given him the List was also probably killed. He spoke too fast and it came out jumbled. They did not follow him logically, but it had been a strange day and they understood him intuitively—his body told the story, the cruel laceration across his stomach as if the earth had tried to cut him open as he crawled to the stream.

Ogum remembered Kalumba's eyes alternating fear and vacancy, and Sukena the hysteria. Kalumba was out of breath. He stopped talking, and then the words that had been stuck somewhere inside him loosened. In one quick flood he told them everything. He folded the pain back into his body and slowly absorbed it into his flesh. He did not say a word. Sukena embraced him, trying to contain him, trying to soak in some of his pain. He was shaking. His tears glistened against her dark cheeks. "I am so sorry," she kept repeating to Ogum. Kalumba was now sitting down again. Feeling responsible for Ogum's grief, he could not embrace him. It was as if a grenade had been thrown in their midst, creating destruction and rifts between solid friendships.

"We have to get Kalumba to the border—there is nothing more to be done," Ogum finally said. He snuffed out the lantern and followed his companions out, closing the door behind himself. They walked to an old Datsun pickup. Kalumba noticed the number plates—KVG 750. It was his father's car. It was good that he was once again able to record details, he thought to himself absently. They put him in the back. That was how the Samasi were transported.

In spite of Sukena's confidence, the first checkpoint was nerve-wracking. They did not know what to expect. The police officer who flagged them down was armed with a machine gun, a pistol, grenades, and an army knife. They were not relieved to note that handcuffs weren't part of his arsenal. He was not here to place people under arrest. A senior police officer, he was bureaucratically polite when asking for Sukena's driver's license and Ogum's ID. He checked their names against the List. As the flashlight moved through it, Kalumba could see that it bore the same careless marks as the one he had received from the soldier. The police officer walked over to his car to radio in their names. They could hear a squeaking voice telling the police officer to be more thorough: Ogum and Sukena were known radicals, and the car they were driving belonged to a suspect's father. He came back and handed back to Sukena her driver's license and Ogum his ID. The one thousand shilling note she had tucked in with her license was still there. He ordered Sukena and Ogum out of the car and carefully patted them down. Then he fished through the glove compartment, under the long leather seat, under the mats, and even inside an unused cigarette ashtray that sat on the dashboard. Kalumba knew he would not pass this level of scrutiny.

The officer walked to the back of the Datsun pickup, hand dangling slightly above his pistol as if in a Western movie. With his free hand he checked under the spare tire. He signed for Kalumba to stand up. He looked under where Kalumba was sitting. Then he walked to his car and spoke something into his radio. They heard the squeaky voice telling the officer to let them go since they were not on the List. He walked back.

"Protect your father," he said to Ogum, to the surprise of everyone in the car. "It's too late," Ogum said. "He died this afternoon." The police officer shrugged. From somewhere in the thickets by the roadside, they heard two gunshots. "A great preacher . . . Save yourselves," he said, his voice trembling. Three other police officers emerged from the darkness, led by bright flashlights, one crossing out a name from their list. They started to walk toward the pickup. Before they reached Kalumba, Sukena, and Ogum, the police officer–turned-savior beckoned for them to get moving. When they reached the spikes he signaled with his flashlight for them to stop. He walked over to the driver's side, reached in to the dashboard where Sukena had placed her driver's license, and pulled out the one thousand shilling note, making sure to brush his hand against her breasts. He walked to the back of the pickup. "We have to eat," he said as he waved the one thousand shilling note in Kalumba's face. "Stay gone, asshole," he whispered. And he waved them off.

They drove in silence, afraid that words if spoken would become too heavy—grief would stall the car. Soon, they were four or five kilometers from the border post. It was not safe to get any closer. Kalumba would have to get off here and find a suitable place for crossing. The border post was usually no more than a stall with a thick and heavy nylon rope that cut across the road, but it was still not worth the risk. With the coup attempt, there were bound to be soldiers. It made sense for Kalumba to cut through unmanned areas. It was here that the colonialists had divided the Samasi in two and put each half on one side of the border. In some places, borders had created enmity between families by giving them different names. But not here. As a consequence, the border had no meaning. The Samasi did not even pause; it was their land, and they had not drawn any lines around it.

Ogum remained in the driver's seat as Kalumba and Sukena climbed out of the truck. They hugged and held on, each for a long time trying to burn this last moment, before the interruption of exile, into their memories. And when they both felt that it was imprinted on their skins and on their breath and in their memory, they let go. But just as soon as they let go, Sukena reached out to embrace Kalumba again. She thought about their love, how he was so broken up that when she held him, she could feel the fissures of strained skin.

"No promises," she whispered to him as Ogum signaled her it was time to go. Ogum did not look at Kalumba or say good-bye. "I have to go look for my father's ashes," he said and started the car. As an afterthought he leaned out through the window to say something and then changed his mind. He was angry at Kalumba but did not know why. Maybe it was his grief trying to find a face, he told himself.

Kalumba stared back at Ogum guiltily, expectantly even, as he rolled up the window. He knew something had irrevocably broken and it would take all their strength to mend it—or this grief would destroy them a day at a time. The fight for their friendship would be for their very own lives.

~~~~~~

Kalumba stood still for a while and watched the furious ball of dust and light roll away, then started for the border. He hadn't been walking for long before he noticed headlights haphazardly and busily digging holes into the night, sometimes all but disappearing, then reappearing as the approaching vehicle dipped in and out of the pothole-filled road. He stopped, hoping for more words that would soften the day's events. He wanted to embrace Ogum and apologize for his father's death. No, he wanted to console Ogum. He wanted to tell Ogum that he too had been killed together with his father and that exile would kill him again. He wanted to offer Ogum his own life in place of his father's—or something that would lessen the pain. He wanted to make promises to Sukena, promise to marry her, to come back within a week, to liberate the country single-handedly, promise her anything that would fill the silence that he too had felt had been steadily growing between them.

When he could peer through the ball of dust, instead of the old pickup, what he saw hurtling toward him was a massive 4×4. He started to panic, thinking that he had already been spotted. But when it screeched to a halt beside him, he found that it was full of white tourists. They wanted to take photographs of him, but he signed that he wanted to be driven in their motorcar to the big city across the border.

"Probably to buy cattle," one of them said. "Well, let him hop in," another said. They did not put him in the carrier cabin at the back. They squeezed him into the back seat.

"Yo! Mr. Samasi, can you teach us to say hello? How—do you—say—hello?" they asked him, gesturing wildly. "Ogum probably knows Samasi," he thought to himself. "Molo," he said in his language. They didn't know he was speaking Kyukato, and if they did, they didn't care. They repeated after him in chorus, "Molo."

"Why do you people kill lions? Do you know I once dreamt of hunting a Samasi hunting a lion? Man, he doesn't look too good—perhaps the hunt didn't go too well." And thus their journey continued, pausing only briefly to show their white skin and their one Samasi to the soldiers at the border post. They too had escaped the coup.

Soon they reached Kiliko town. Camera flashes tore into his eyes as his companions took what felt like a thousand photographs of him. The townspeople, who would be described in a postcard to America as composed of natives in bright tribal costume and administrators with suits that had browned and bruised collars, went about their business, as did some tourists with cameras and long hair. But some of the other tourists crowded in as if on a kill and snapped a few photographs of Kalumba.

Thinking about being in the United States, he wondered if he would ever come across a calendar of himself, the Samasi Lion Killer who was just tame enough to take photographs with tourists, or if he would someday walk into someone's home and find his photographs adorning walls. But for now it did not matter. Like his disguise, white skin had saved his life. He had made it out of his country barely alive. But he had survived, dying but still alive, and for now that was enough to work with. Exile would not be a form of death—he would make a meaning and life out of it.

2
Ogum's Internal Exile

To another, Jesus said, "Come, follow me." But he answered, "Lord, let me first go and bury my father." And Jesus told him, "Leave the dead to bury their own dead; but as for you, go and proclaim the Kingdom of God." Jesus was a man of action. When our children demand Justice and Freedom, we have to be decisive. We must be a people of action, Baba Ogum had once preached in a haiku sermon. It was with a great sense of irony that Ogum quoted the sermon to Sukena when they were debating whether to reveal the massacres to the whole nation or accept the deal with the Dictator that promised an end to further political persecution and a level playing field.

"He did not mean, 'Let the truth bury the truth,'" Sukena responded. But ten years ago, a few days after his father's death, it had made political sense. When the Leader suggested that they use the massacre for leverage, the movement leadership was split into two. One half argued that the Dictator would without a doubt be understood as a criminal and even his Western supporters would have to demand that he be tried for crimes against humanity. But the Leader and the other half argued that freedom should not come at the cost of tearing the country's fabric apart. The Dictator would commit more crimes in order to hide older crimes, more assassinations would follow, and he would do whatever it took to remain in power. The only protection from being tried for crimes against humanity would be remaining in office till he died. There was one catch, though—those in detentions would not be released, nor those in exile asked to return. The Dictator did not want to appear weak. The Leader argued that with no further persecution they would have the Dictator out in no time. It was to their advantage, too; they would rally the people around freeing those in detentions and allowing the exiles back—"We shall have many Mandelas," he said. The Leader's argument carried the day, and those like Sukena who disagreed were bound to the oath of secrecy that followed.

For Ogum the decision had been easy. His father was already dead. If his death was going to bring the Kwatee nation closer to liberation, then some good was coming out of it. In his own logic, he even decided that his father would have done the same had it been Ogum who was killed. But he had not counted on the pain that would follow as he helped his mother search for a husband he knew to be dead. He couldn't tell her—the risk of her going public was too high. Mama Ogum knew that something terrible had happened to her husband when he did not come home that night.

When Ogum came home she enlisted his help—they first went to the church, but Baba Ogum wasn't there. They visited several police stations, then hospitals and finally the morgues. They called his friends and relatives, but of course no one knew where he was. With the coup attempt, they all said they were afraid for him. Ogum, in pain, watching his mother's grief, suggested that perhaps he had gone into exile. Mama Ogum said that nothing was missing in the house and he would never leave without telling them. But nevertheless once the idea entered her head she found hope in it. Every time the phone rang, she answered hopefully until slowly she came to terms with the reality that he was probably dead somewhere.

Ogum at first felt like he had betrayed her too. It helped that he met movement members who would thank him for his sacrifice, it helped with the grief, but as months went by his comrades moved on to other things, and Sukena, who never really agreed with him, was not a source of great comfort, and so his anguish became private, something that only he knew and that ultimately he could not share with anyone. He started to resent his mother and her stubborn mourning, and he spent less and less time at home. When he was at home, he avoided being in the same room with his mother. And as his anguish became greater, finding out who had betrayed his father, who had added Baba Ogum's name to the List, became more and more important. The more he thought about it, the more his anguish found solace in the idea of finding someone to blame.

That was ten years ago, Ogum was thinking while on his way to visit Baba Kalumba, as he turned to the left when he came to the main road that ran a few hundred meters from his house. Behind him was his neighborhood—all large beautiful colonial houses. The house where he had grown up and now lived up had previously been owned by a colonial. It had five bedrooms and servant quarters at the back where three servants—a maid, a gardener, and a cook—lived. The garden was elaborately manicured, and the bougainvillea that climbed on the trees seemed to be an unusual bright green.

The stream that ran close to the primary school that he and Kalumba had attended, the same stream by which Kalumba had found shelter during the massacre, ran through his backyard. Years later, Ogum's mother had told him that shortly after the coup attempt the stream had run red for several hours. Though she didn't know it, Ogum thought, her husband had paid one last visit to his family as his life emptied into the stream.

Ogum walked by Memorial Primary School, the best in the area, which catered to the local elite. Next to the school was the Memorial Golf Club, where Baba Ogum had been a member. It had taken Ogum a long time to reconcile his estate-living, golf-playing father with the religious figure so many people revered—before his death, they had argued about this a lot. How could Baba Ogum fight for the people when he underpaid the workers who looked after his house and caddied for him on the golf course? Past the golf club was On Time Police Station, as it was derisively called by the poor. For the local elites, however, the police were on time whenever they dialed 999.

By now, Ogum had come to a crossroad. If he took a right, he would wind up in the tea plantations. The plantations needed slave labor now as they did before independence, and if he turned left he would soon come to the village that supplied it. Straight ahead was a stub of a road—a dead end. He turned left, passed the rich shopping center, and found himself in front of Our Lady of Mercy Primary School. It was a run-down school filled with run-down children belonging to parents who worked in the tea plantations. Sukena had attended primary school here. Kalumba's father had been the headmaster, though Kalumba had attended the more prestigious Memorial Primary School. Ogum hoped to remember to ask Kalumba's father about this when he got to his house.

Ogum paused at the bus station but decided to keep on walking. He loved walking to Kalumba's house. The walk from his house to Kalumba's was like watching history, the past and present etched into the landscape, scarred like the people who made a life off it. It was a huge photo album that recorded the people's tragedies and triumphs, deaths and rebirths; it pulsated with the lives of the people living in its contours. When judgment day came, God would also call the earth as a witness to condemn or exonerate humankind.

A few hundred feet from the bus stop was Our Lady of Mercy Hospital. Like its namesake, it catered to the poor. The wealthy went to personal physicians and, when terribly sick, went to hospitals in Europe or South Africa. For the elites, the whole of Kwatee was a business transaction, a place to be farmed and mined, and they participated in nothing outside of golf and nightclubs and other monuments to their opulence.

They could not even invest in a decent hospital that might benefit the very workers who made their leisure possible. Every town, no matter how small, must have a slum where its excesses are stored. Ogum's town was no exception. Up on a steep hill, midway between the estate of Ogum's childhood and the village where Kalumba's father lived, opposite the clean post office and the dairy cooperative where large-scale farmers in large trucks and peasants on beat-up black mamba bicycles alike brought their milk, Harlem glared back both threateningly and in accusation. Nobody knew why it was named after the Harlem of New York. But in this Harlem, a volcano erupted every night, to which at least one life would be lost. Drugs and cheap alcohol lethally mixed with embalming fluid, car-battery acid, and hopelessness lit the volcano. Sometimes the alchemists of the lethal cocktail *changaa* put in too much battery acid, which eroded the insides of the drinker until he died from the inside out like a dog poisoned with ground glass mixed in with its food.

At other times it would be too much embalming fluid, which left the drinker blind. In great irony, the residents of Harlem were preparing themselves for death. But almost always the mixture burned skin, and *changaa* drinkers who had survived could be identified by flaming red lips—black actors in blackface in the minstrel show they called life. On judgment day, whom would God hold responsible for Harlem? The residents quick with a knife or those that sent and kept them there?

Ogum lifted his eyes off the photo album to nod a quick hello to a young couple. Clearly they were on a date: The man was dressed in a clean but cheap black suit and plastic black shoes made to resemble real leather shoes. The woman was wearing a heavily flowered nylon dress and imitation high heels. They were holding hands, talking animatedly about something and only breaking from their laughter to say hello to Ogum; then they veered off into Harlem.

Past Harlem was the town proper. It did not consist of much—a market area where the poor came to sell their produce and where the elites from the Memorial area came in sunglasses and suits to haggle for cheaper prices. But the town itself was forever growing upward, slowly, hesitantly, but always. The tallest building in town, ten floors high, had taken twenty years to build, two years for each floor. There was always some building without a roof. On other days Ogum found resiliency in the constant building, but today, on a religious interpretation of the landscape, Ogum thought that the town was like the tower of Babel, forever doomed to incompletion.

Past the market and behind the town was land that had belonged to Kalumba's grandfather, but at independence instead of being returned to him, it had been given to a colonial chief who still wielded considerable power. When they were young, Baba Kalumba often took Ogum and Kalumba there to remind them that colonialism, like any good parent about to die, made sure that its children would be well looked after. "When you fight for a second independence, shoot the little bastards," he had always said, much to their alarm, as squatting, he filled his hands with the dry red soil that he could never take with him.

It was slightly past midday, and the hot sun felt like a huge magnifying glass following Ogum as he walked. He came to Kamuingi village, where Sukena had grown up. He tried to imagine an ash-scaled little girl with mucus running down her nose, wearing a dirty dress that had once belonged to an older cousin. He could never reconcile this image of Sukena, captured in a photograph that she carried in her wallet, with Sukena the activist, the fierce Sukena of a gapped smile, long dreadlocks, tight jeans, and slender hands that whirled when she was explaining something or rested on her hips, arms akimbo, when she was angry.

Kamuingi village was densely populated. If residents of Harlem were an army of workers, the residents of Kamuingi village were an army of farm laborers. The trucks that took the milk to the cooperative early in the morning, once emptied, continued on to Kamuingi village, where they packed in as many of the villagers as they could. Once full, they carried the people to the tea and coffee plantations, where they sprayed DDT, made sure the soil floors underneath the trees were clean, and harvested coffee beans and tea leaves. They worked from seven in the morning till six in the evening, when they got paid just enough to keep them alive until morning. Thus they lived, working hard but living poor in mud houses that did not keep the cold away at night, that leaked and once in a while, for good measure, washed away in the rainy season. And just as in Harlem, the residents of Kamuingi tried to find life, or perhaps lose it, in *changaa*.

It was not that they didn't struggle to live the life they imagined for themselves and their children. They had made attempts to organize themselves. The villagers had started a people's theater group. Its leaders were jailed or exiled. They had tried to begin gathering the money they earned and buy a bus and compete in the transportation business. That too had failed, because local politicians, who also doubled as businessmen, thwarted their plans. They had tried saving up and taking out a collective loan to open food stalls in the town and close to the factory, but their idea had been stolen by the same local politicians who thwarted their other business ventures.

Once, they had even elected one of their own into parliament. Politicians normally gave the residents money for *changaa* and cigarettes in exchange for their votes. But the young man had handed out boiled pieces of maize, cobs divided into four parts. This single act, which reminded them of Jesus and his feeding five thousand people with two fish and five loaves of bread, gave them hope. But soon after he got into parliament, he found that he could not operate without money. He couldn't attend the expensive dinners in expensive hotels where deals were made. He couldn't afford to make a large enough contribution to the president's favorite charity to get his attention. He couldn't give bribes for contracts. Without money, he found that he was largely useless. He sold his voice and never spoke for the villagers again.

And yet the residents of Kamuingi were not resigned. There were those that drank embalming fluid and those that prayed for them. But they all woke up loving their children and went to the plantations hoping that their children would not become like them. They returned each evening loving their children, hoping that in time they would open up more crossroads for their little crossroads to follow. When Second Independence Democracy with Content Forum came into their lives, balancing fear against their poverty, they left the churches and *changaa* shacks and joined the movement en masse. Baba Ogum's church had been in Kamuingi. Now Ogum could admit to himself that his father had had a lot to do with the residents joining the SIDCF. But back then, when his father was still alive, he had wished that the Kamuingi residents would burn the church as an act of revolution. Ogum kept walking.

He was almost at Kalumba's father's house. He walked past the end of the village and down into a deep trench that resembled a dried-up river valley; blood belonging to freedom fighters had fallen here. The trench was like a long deadly meandering snake tearing deep into the earth. This opening in the earth was not natural. Residents of Kamuingi had been forced to dig around their village when what they called the Last Great Uprising started. It had been dug mostly by women and children, because the men had been carried off into deprogramming camps. The trenches had long spikes in them so that anyone who tried to leave or enter at a place other than at the fortified main entrance was impaled. What now appeared to be a natural ridge, pleasant to look at, that broke the monotony of the landscape was nature's way of healing trauma. Perhaps without the constant jarring reminder of an internment that was yet to be broken, the villagers could at the very least slept better at night.

Ogum finally crested the ridge, and before him he could see the road that would take him to Kalumba's home. But he decided to take another route that would take him past a small muddy pond. Tons of soil and gravel had been thrown into the formerly vast lake to make way for an expressway between the capital and the second-largest city. The soil and gravel had sucked the water out of the lake, leaving an ancient hippo herd without nature's protection. As the lake had shrunk, it had choked the life out of them. They had eventually starved to death. Their massive jaws remained, popping out of their thin skeleton frames, hundreds of the white jaws stretching for over a mile. The road demanded constant sacrifices. Dead dogs and donkeys in all stages of decomposition were spaced out almost evenly. People too died here. This gluttonous road that could have been an angry river was always hungry.

Ogum veered off the expressway. He turned from the tarmacked road into a narrow *murram,* one that itself became a grass path into an orchard of plums, pears, sugarcane, bananas, and avocadoes. The smell and sounds of the terrible highway behind him were lost in the heavy musk of syrupy sweetness of fruit and rushing wind making formless music. The orchard opened up to a small wooden house. He knocked on the door, but there was nobody home. He walked up a thin garden path until he came to a man and wife planting maize. He greeted them and asked for permission to continue walking up the small path to Kalumba's father's house. They were surprised that he spoke Kyukato so fluently, but he explained that he grew up in the area. He offered to help. They turned him down. "If you have grown up in the area you should know you don't walk into someone's home empty-handed," the wife said. "Why don't you go and pick some fruit to take to Baba Kalumba. And some for yourself to take to your parents so they won't think badly of us," she added. He laughed and agreed with them. He walked back to the orchard.

―――――

Ogum did not find Baba Kalumba in the house; he was at the back tending to Mama Kalumba's grave. Ogum noticed the date on the tombstone. Today was the thirty-fifth anniversary of her death. She had died a few years after independence when Kalumba was still a child. Baba Kalumba tended to it like a farmer to his crops. Like the kind neighbors who were digging holes and planting maize—it was a duty that was also love, a familiar love that is yet another detail. Ogum made his presence known with a quick hello. Baba Kalumba acknowledged him and continued working.

Waiting for him to finish, Ogum walked back to the house, entered the kitchen, and filled a green plastic pitcher with orange juice. He found some leftover beef stew, heavy with red onion, green and red peppers, and tomatoes, and he ate it without rice. It always surprised him that Baba Kalumba cooked so well. He found two chairs, put them out on the verandah, and sat. It was now late afternoon, and he knew that Baba Kalumba liked to watch the sun set.

Had he taken the other road after leaving Kamuingi village, Ogum would have passed by the home of Baba Kalumba's neighbor. A revered goat slaughterer and brewer of Kyukato traditional beer, he was invited to every celebration in the area. Soon, with Kalumba's return, the man would be in heavy demand.

Ogum was here because of Sukena. They had started going out shortly after Kalumba had left. Even though they told themselves that they did not know how it happened, they knew exactly how and, more precisely, why. They both wanted it to; they were in love. He couldn't remember a time when he was not in love with her, even though he knew this couldn't possibly be true. How could he not be in love with Sukena? Sukena of the gap-toothed smile? How could he not have loved Sukena, the full-time freedom fighter and part-time lover, as he liked to tease her? His love for her was the absolute against which he measured everything else. He knew that if she asked him to put aside everything else for her, he would. But he also knew that was the one thing she would never ask of him. Meeting at a crossroad called Kalumba and having found common cause in a deep love for each other and in their hatred for the Dictator, they should not be surprised that their journeys, once parallel, had collapsed into one.

Baba Kalumba soon joined Ogum on the porch, asking him about the fruit in the kitchen. Baba Kalumba said he didn't understand why his neighbors insisted on giving him fruit when he had his own, but they both knew it was more of a gesture than a gift. They sat quietly for a while. Ogum made the first move, thus revealing his strategy.

"Your wife, she died such a long time ago and yet you have never remarried," Ogum said, half questioning and half accusing.

Ogum knew he could, from the time when he was young, get away with making such statements and asking direct questions. Perhaps it was because he was always welcomed as an outsider, or maybe it was his character that gave his tone the amount of respect needed to remove the sharpness of such questions. Kalumba also asked questions that way, so it might have been generational. But Kalumba came across as being brusque whereas he appeared conversational.

"I never thought I should. I had offers. I fucked around for a while, but when it came down to it, I just didn't take another plunge." Baba Kalumba, perhaps because of having to be careful with language as a headmaster, had acquired the unsettling habit of speaking what he meant after his retirement. Or maybe he was just comfortable with Ogum, who had become his surrogate son and a good friend. "I did think it might be good for Kalumba to have a woman around. But I never did it."

"Do you think it has something to do with having lost your wife?"

"You read too many psychology books at the university. Weren't you supposed to be in history? I did wonder if I was afraid I might lose someone close to me again, but I don't think that was it." Baba Kalumba shifted in the chair, so that instead of facing the sun he was facing Ogum.

"Just because you are aware of a possibility doesn't rule it out . . . psychologically speaking. We expect the truth of something to reveal things we don't know. The new knowledge becomes the truth. But sometimes it's the opposite . . .

Truth is often what we already know, old and stale. The second telephone ring that confirms you are actually hearing a phone ringing," Ogum answered. He cleared his throat and reached for some more juice.

"I am not trying to demean your psychology, young man, but I think I know my situation. In any case, what kind of a doctor makes a diagnosis without examining the patient?" Baba Kalumba said defensively.

"Why didn't you remarry?" Ogum asked again.

"Guilt," Baba Kalumba answered. "The irony . . . By her dying, our marriage was saved. So I tend to the grave of the wife I no longer loved." All the while as he spoke, he was looking at his hands. Ogum already knew this; Kalumba had told him about his father's intention to divorce his wife. Baba Kalumba's was a strange guilt, one resulting from an unconsummated betrayal, obstructed by the death of the victim. So he mourned her even though he did not love her. He could not forgive himself, and so his mourning could never turn into healing. Only if she had remained alive could he have suffered through his betrayal and forgiven himself. His guilt, Ogum understood, through an objectivity that Kalumba could not have, was a selfish act.

"But that only makes you a widower, surely you understand that? People remarry," Ogum offered.

"Ogum, how am I a widower? That would be a lie," he said angrily, glaring at Ogum. "Too much guilt," he added, completing a thought that was running in his head. "If you dig deep enough, you will find that past a certain age we all become guilty of something . . . from just living, Ogum, just from living." Then he fell quiet.

He stared down at his hands, as if they were guilty of pushing his wife's car off the road into a ditch. He knew it was an accident, but the guilt . . . He then lifted his gaze so that he stared into the sun halfway down in its descent, as if he wanted to go to its hell with it. Then he turned and looked around at his farm and became the same headmaster who had sat Ogum and Kalumba at the Ping-Pong table for history lessons.

"But tell me, why are you here?" he asked Ogum.

"Sukena. I would like your permission to marry her." Ogum was brief and to the point. Baba Kalumba valued that quality in him. He was quiet for a minute or two, then said, "But Sukena is not my daughter." He was not going to make it easy for Ogum.

"Baba Kalumba, I know. I need your blessing because Kalumba will not give us his. He never writes back. Ever since Sukena and I became serious, I have e-mailed him at least once a month. No answer, raindrops in a desert. It's getting tiring, but I do it," Ogum explained.

The last phone call Baba Kalumba had received from Kalumba was years ago. Kalumba was drunk, and his father could not make out what he was saying, so he hung up. To his father, it was as if exile had killed Kalumba but his ghost kept appearing, asking to be appeased.

"You and Sukena should have come to me sooner. People have been talking. People say you stayed behind because of her . . . that you stole her from him. Then they say that our two peoples do not mix well. What makes me angry is that those who have not visited my homestead since Kalumba left are the ones who are talking. These are people who would not have kept him safe for a night. But both of you should have come to me first." From his tone, Ogum could not tell whether Baba Kalumba was angry at him or not. The feeling that he and Sukena had committed a terrible crime came back to him. He tried to speak and explain that they couldn't have come earlier because they themselves were in pain and conflicted, but Baba Kalumba interrupted him.

"Ask for his forgiveness," he said.

"But we haven't done anything wrong. All we have done is fall in love. How can we apologize then?" Ogum protested.

"Because it is the way things are done. Haven't you caused Kalumba, your very own brother, pain? Haven't you caused me some sleepless nights? Even though you didn't mean it and no court on earth would find you guilty, you should ask for forgiveness from Kalumba. And he in turn will forgive you, knowing that there is nothing to forgive."

"An empty gesture?" Ogum asked in disbelief.

"No. It's a ritual. Ask your brother for forgiveness. You and Sukena have each other; he has no one. You ask for forgiveness because he is your brother whom you haven't wronged," said Baba Kalumba, each word uttered with force and conviction.

"You sound like my aunt. How far do you extend this forgiveness? The colonizers, their gatekeepers, the Dictator, and his cohorts—if they ask for forgiveness can we give it to them?" Ogum asked, feeling like he was sitting by his aunt's feet letting words and ideas wash over him.

"They have done wrong. They cannot ask for forgiveness before giving penance—return what you stole and the form of penance will be determined. If you have actually done something wrong, you don't ask for forgiveness. You begin your penance by correcting your wrong to the equivalence of the original sin." Ogum could tell that Baba Kalumba was easing into the conversation as they entered the world of the abstract.

"An eye for an eye?"

"Let me put it this way; returning what was stolen makes everyone see once again. The aggressor is no longer blinded by the guilt of theft and fear of revenge, and the aggrieved is no longer blinded by the constant need for revenge," he said, smiling.

They continued talking on like this, just enjoying the lightness of the dialogue until they both realized it was getting late. "Come, take the fruit basket. It's getting late; let me walk you to the bus stop," Baba Kalumba said.

On the way to the bus stop, they visited briefly at every home. They drank more tea and ate more bread than they thought possible. They had tea without sugar in some homes and in others without milk, while in others all the ingredients were in excess. In some of the homes, they ate full meals of chicken and chapati. In other homes they ate boiled maize and beans tossed in salt and in some homes goat stew. They listened to all sorts of jokes, some tasteful and others tasteless, and they told and listened to stories and the day's politics. Finally they emerged from the last home ready to burst at the seams, waddling along. But the job had been done. Ogum had been seen with Baba Kalumba. That would quiet the gossipers.

They went by the area drunk who was passed out, lying face up a few meters from his house. He never quite made it inside, though from the look of his clothes it was not for the lack of trying. His elbows were bruised and his trousers caked at the knees from trying to crawl home from where he fell. He carried with him the tragedy of a soldier who dies a few feet from safety. Baba Kalumba turned him over to his side to make sure there were no ants around. Ever since *changaa* had become lethal, in addition to being robbed and beaten senseless, drunks were being eaten alive by ants. The ants went into their ears, anuses, mouths, and eyes and left in their wake badly disfigured bodies. But there were none around this man, and so Ogum and Baba Kalumba walked on.

By the time they were done with their little odyssey the sun had dipped past the horizon. Darkness surrounded them. The wind was picking up the dust in greater and greater loads as the bus tore it from the *murram* road until Baba Kalumba and Ogum were engulfed by the cold dust. Before the bus limped to where they stood, Baba Kalumba turned to Ogum.

"Your father . . . It has been very hard on you. People like us do not know how to let go," Baba Kalumba said. It was a statement, and Ogum did not know whether to say anything in return.

"You are my son, Kalumba's brother. If I had to choose between Kalumba and you, I would let both of you die if both of you couldn't live," Baba Kalumba said fiercely. "What happened to him over there? What is killing him?" Ogum could feel the anguish.

"Baba, I do not think it is about what happened to him there. It is about what happened to him here. He saw some things we are not supposed to see. You are right. Past a certain age we all become guilty of something," Ogum replied. "History just caught up with him . . . with us all. But he will be okay."

"It's good that you try to keep him alive by writing so often. Even if he doesn't write back, he reads and feels connected," Baba Kalumba said.

Ogum wanted to say that Kalumba was selfish, but he did not know how he could say it lovingly. Instead he reached out and embraced Baba Kalumba. There was a story he now felt he had to tell Baba Kalumba about his son, the kind of story one would tell at a funeral or to a grieving parent.

"When we were in standard five, Kalumba kept losing his lunch to a bully—a much bigger and older kid. So every day Kalumba lost his lunch, and every night he dreamed of revenge. Then it came to him. He found some sleeping pills and ground them into his lunch. When the bully came for his food that lunchtime, Kalumba asked him if he would like to play hide-and-seek, and if he found us, he could have his food and mine as well, and what's more we would watch him eat our food as our stomachs grumbled. As was the custom, he was to count to fifty as we looked for a place to hide.

"But as Kalumba had told me earlier, he believed the bully would open his eyes (fearing a trick—we had just been taught in our history class how the missionaries came and when the Africans who prayed with them opened their eyes their land was gone) before he reached ten and therefore would see us run to the high end of the soccer field where grass was the longest. That is exactly what happened. He found us and roughly grabbed our lunch boxes. He looked at Kalumba's, a delicious goat stew, and mine, a not-so-appealing maize and beans, but he did not care. He ate the two meals together, dipping my maize and beans in the stew, and per the deal, Kalumba and I watched.

"The bully was woken up in the middle of night by a search party in a forest of lunch boxes that had been planted around him. He had also defecated on himself. Worse than the beatings he received from the headmaster and his father, he became the object of ridicule of the whole school. He became known as the *sleep eater then-er shitter.*"

Baba Kalumba laughed so hard Ogum thought he had lost it. "You played dangerous games," Baba Kalumba finally said as he tried to find a straw of authority and adulthood.

The bus arrived. He hoisted his basket of fruit onto the roof carrier, and the conductor climbed up the side to secure it. As the bus pulled away, Ogum yelled, "Remember *sleep eater then-er shitter.* Kalumba will be fine!" Baba Kalumba started laughing again. His boy was a legend of sorts even before he became a man.

It was still early, and Ogum did not feel like going back home yet. But it was too late to embark on the journey to the capital city to see Sukena. He had not told her he was going to see Baba Kalumba. She would have wanted to come along, and he was not sure how she would take his having gone alone. He alighted from the bus at the next stop and made his way to Mexico 2001 Bar to remember Sukena and Kalumba before the troubles threatening to end their friendship had begun. He sat his basket of fruits on an empty booth and ordered a cold Castle—luxury of a liberated South Africa. He chuckled as he tore off the wet label but not cleanly enough, so it left little tufts of white paper on the bottle, making it look old and used. Mexico 2001 used to be Mexico '86 when the bar opened during the World Cup held in Mexico. It was the time when every schoolboy wanted to be like Diego Maradona. But after the World Cup ended, the bar had become Mexico '87, '88, and so on until it drunkenly leapt over the millennium and became Mexico 2001. He imagined that when the world ended, only Mexico Bar would remain standing, changing the year on its sign into infinity, ellipses behind the name.

He walked over the jukebox and played song number 363. Lightnin' Hopkins's "Tom Moore Blues" filled the bar. None of the few patrons turned to stare at who was playing the blues. Nothing was unusual here. From the other side of the bar, a woman heard the song playing and walked over to Ogum.

"You must know Kalumba and Sukena," she said to him. "They played this song all the time."

"Yes. He is my brother, and I have plotted against him," Ogum said. The woman laughed but did not say anything. "We went to the same school," he added. He moved and made space for her.

She sat down. "Assata is my name." She extended her arm across the table, and Ogum also introduced himself. As if on cue, the lights got dimmer, the beer a little bit sweeter, and laughter around the bar a little more careless. She noticed the fruits and asked him if he was selling them. He answered that the fruit was a gift.

"I went to the same high school as Sukena. We used to be friends, but we drifted apart a few years into university. She went political," Assata said.

Ogum nodded to say he understood. It was good that she was here. He hadn't been planning to stay for long, but now that she was here he felt in the mood to stay longer. He signaled the bartender for two more beers.

"How was she in high school?" he asked. "Sukena?"

"She wanted to become a doctor. She met Kalumba in her second year in high school. She talked of getting married and living the dream—holidays in Europe . . . the works. Strange, isn't it? How far we end up failing our dreams . . . Kalumba went into exile, and the last I heard she was in big trouble. I am the doctor. I didn't get the boy . . . though I do vacation in Europe." And looking at the Castle beer, she added, " . . . and of course Cape Town. Sometimes she would tell me that she had a crush on his friend but beg as I may she would never tell me who the home wrecker was. Oh, those were the days," she said, laughing as she poured some more beer into her glass.

Ogum didn't know what to make of this coincidence and the information it brought with it. In a sense it didn't matter. Sukena had loved Kalumba. If Kalumba had stayed, they would be married and he would be happy for them. There had always been something in him that stirred when he saw Sukena, but whatever it was, he had not acted upon it—a feeling so underdeveloped, in fact, that it did not matter. But then again, perhaps they were destined to hurt Kalumba one way or another—perhaps they would have had an affair, maybe she would have left him at the altar, who knows?

They drank a lot of beer together that night. They danced, but even to them, it appeared they were orbiting around each other, happy for the company because of what it allowed them to do—to look inside themselves—but nothing more. They danced until they were drenched in sweat and the sawdust on the cement floor was whirling around their feet. And when they couldn't dance anymore, they talked and laughed. Yet they remained strangers. And when the night was over, they walked outside hand in hand but he let her get into the first taxi and gave her some fruit to take home. He heaved the rest of it onto his shoulders and waved good-bye as the taxi sped off. He decided to walk the rest of the way home.

Even though it was late, Ogum felt the need to see his father's church. Now more than ever Ogum missed him. He should have been the one to go talk to Baba Kalumba and, when the time came, to Sukena's parents. No one preached at the church anymore. The liberationists were felled one at a time until only a few prominent ones concentrated in the capital city were left. And even though the church leadership refused to replace the assassinated preachers, Baba Ogum's congregation had remained faithful. For the past ten years, once a month they met at the church. Sometimes they recounted his haiku sermons, sometimes they roasted meat and played football and volleyball—they came to church to be a community. They cleared the road, cut the grass, and replaced panes and repaired pews when they broke.

While he was standing in front of the church, Ogum's courage failed him. Grief and the guilt of unspoken betrayal were getting heavier and heavier. As he walked away, he thought he could hear echoes of his father's sermons whispered through the trees and flowers that lined the path:

> *The Bible says—your dead will live; their corpses will rise. You who lie in the dust, awake and shout for joy. For your dew is as the dew of the dawn, and the earth will give birth to the departed spirits. I am here to tell you this: that which has lived cannot truly die. Who we are, even though buried deep down in the earth, will become light. Earthquakes break the caskets in which we bury the truth; floods wash the buried truth clean. The earth will give birth to what you bury.*

Beginning and end of sermon, shuffle of excited feet as the people, fired up, exited the church. As Ogum's father receded back into the folds of his mind, close to home, he saw a train disappearing into a tunnel. He hadn't noticed the tunnel on his way to visit Baba Kalumba. He thought of his time with Assata and how even without sex they had sucked each other dry. What was it that they had exchanged besides time? He thought that must be how exile is all the time—two orbits dancing together without touching, not even desiring and yet wishing it for remembrance. In exile, memories do not form, because nothing new happens. The train emerged from the tunnel, and its one terrible eye tore through the darkness. Perhaps exile was temporary light in a tunnel on a dark night. In the tunnel of his own exile, Kalumba could not have known where anything started or ended, being constantly without a foothold, without senses. But what about those left behind? Don't they suffer? "Everyone suffers," he said aloud to himself. "Everyone suffers." He felt grateful to Assata for allowing him to feel what was inside of him without his having to look. It was well enough to look back, but the storm was ripe and he was feeling better prepared for it. Pieces, his pieces, were falling into place.

Sukena's Internal Exile

From the age of ten, Sukena organized her life around lists. Ice cream and candy, or a new school uniform, or toys and dolls she wished for indiscriminately made it to her list. She listed things that she needed to get done, from homework to household chores that were so routine that, like breathing or waking up, they did not need to be listed. As she grew older, her list of things to get done got larger and larger, as did the cost of leaving them undone. Because they could not be accomplished overnight, her lists threatened to overwhelm her. As they became a source of debilitating anxiety, she jotted down little steps she needed to take each day to bring her dreams to fruition. An exam, a saved shilling, what to eat for breakfast, what to do on weekends were like pawns in a game of chess, part of an overall strategy that would in the long run defeat poverty, injustice, or a broken heart. Everything, from pleasure to pain, had to be eaten in small doses.

In spite of or because of the discipline the lists imposed on Sukena, she could have become anything she wanted. She could have become a scientist, painter, lawyer, musician, or writer. And because of her gender, she overcame obstacles that neither Kalumba nor Ogum as men ever came across. Sometimes it irritated her that they did not see that the cards were skewed, even as they fought for the second independence, in

41

their favor. If birth was the first step, their journey had fewer obstacles piled violently and sometimes gratuitously along the roads they took. For her, therein lay the paradox of the well-meaning like Kalumba and Ogum—there were things they simply could not see, that they remained blind to.

And then she had poverty to contend with. Kalumba and Ogum did not grow up poor; there were things they took for granted that she could not. She had to obsess about every shilling because each counted toward something she needed, whether for a pencil, food, school fees, or a school uniform. A list was not only a way to order her world but also a road map to survival. She had to fight for everything: At home growing up, she had to fight her father for an equal share of food. In the offices looking for work, she had to fend off predators who saw not even her own individual body but a generalized female body that had to be entered in order to be owned. Buses, restaurants, bars, classrooms, all spheres of her life were in one way or another affected by the roadblock of her gender.

Her father and mother, poor and working in the tea plantations, wanted her, as the eldest daughter, to stay home and take care of her younger brother and sister. The familiar story, told over a million times, happening a million more, of girls needing to stay home so that the parents can send sons to school was hers as well. But clichés are only clichés for those to whom the story is told but who do not live it—for her, she had to survive. And so she did the only thing that she could. With the help of a neighbor's son, she taught herself to read and write. She fought her mother and father. She at times refused to draw water or wash dishes and at other times would try negotiating to prove that it was possible to be productive at home while going to school. Finally they relented.

While Kalumba and Ogum began standard one at the young age of seven, Sukena began formal school at the age of nine. The war to be allowed what was hers by right but denied her by virtue of her gender had taken a toll of two years. It was, in her own words, a two-year sentence for standing up for her rights. Only, unlike a prisoner of conscience, she was nine years old. And she was lucky that her parents relented. For others it was a life sentence and at times even a death sentence.

She did not meet Kalumba, strangely enough, until they were both in high school, even though she knew Baba Kalumba, her school's headmaster. She was closer to Baba Kalumba than to her own father because Baba Kalumba had recognized her drive and encouraged her, sometimes buying her books and looking the other way when her school fees were late. Years later, when she and Kalumba were lovers, she would wonder every now and then if they were in an incestuous relationship in some way—one brought about by circumstances that orphaned her without killing her biological parents.

Her father worked all day and came home in the evening tired, seating himself in the room that resembled a living room. It had an old couch that sat unevenly on the mud floor. The mud walls were plastered with glossy magazine pages advertising all sorts of foreign goods—Ivory soap, Jaguar cars, Colgate toothpaste, vacations in Jamaica, Disneyland, Chivas Regal, red Marlboro and green Virginia Slims *you've come a long way Baby* cigarettes, and so forth. They were partly decoration and partly practical, for they kept the wind from entering through the cracks.

While her father sat in the living room, tired and quietly contemplating the walls, her mother, who worked alongside her father in the plantations, went about the business of cooking. Sukena was supposed to have prepared everything else. She was to have fetched water from the well, chopped up the onions, washed the collard greens, and cleaned whatever dishes needed washing. The house was to be swept clean every day, for as her mother always said, being poor was no reason for being dirty. It was her mother who put dinner together after Sukena did the basic preparations. They were in essence a two-woman team that kept the house running for the father and his son. This arrangement was kept until

Sukena left home for a boarding high school. It was the price she had to pay for negotiated freedom. As a child she had no choice; as an adult, on the question of freedom she knew no compromise and would not negotiate about anything that infringed on her sense of freedom. Nothing would stop her from living out her lists.

Yet in spite of it all she never felt her father was a bad man. What crime would an international criminal court judge him on? He had not killed hundreds like the Dictator, or stolen millions of shillings earmarked for national hospitals. He did not beat his wife as his neighbors did. He did not even insult her or demean her. He did not pay other women for sex as other men did and therefore did not bring AIDS to his home. He did not drink *changaa* and come home and rape his wife. He did not even beat his children, though he raised his voice and threatened violence. He was a man who believed everyone had a place in the home, and on those boundaries he insisted. "Home is the only place that should make sense" was his motto.

But if Sukena did not feel he was a bad man, she never judged him as a good man either. She got to know him better than she did her mother. He was the law, and in order to survive the law, he had to be appeased, and for him to be appeased, he had to become a known quantity. Or perhaps she never really got to know either of them. Either way, it was her father, the benevolent patriarch, the gentle dictator, who stood in the way. He never voiced an opinion against the conditions under which they worked or the circumstances that had not only brought them to Kamuingi village but also kept them there. He was one of the few people to refuse to join a theater group that spoke to a history and a world outside his domestic sphere. And when the theater group, an initiative of university professors and fellow villagers, was razed to the ground by the government he neither applauded nor felt bad. He had defined his duty for himself and he was fulfilling it— keeping and respecting the boundaries in his home.

Sukena understood that these boundaries were kept to prevent questions, for at the end of the day there remained the looming question of what they had done to deserve Kamuingi village. And the boundaries were a form of silencing. The outside world mattered to the extent that it threatened to unbalance the home he had cut and pasted from magazine advertisements. Under his tyranny, fortified by what he called Kyukato culture, they suffered. She judged him but never called him a bad man. Outside her home, there were many more like him. And many more worse than him. But she never thought of him as a good man.

It was not that her mother was passive. Like a political prisoner, she tried to serve her sentence with dignity. When Sukena got involved with SIDCF, some of the veteran members who had fought against the British and the first black government had trained them how to survive jail, since it was, they would say, only a matter of time before they started getting carted off. Sukena could recognize that survival training in her mother. Her mother had drawn lines that her father could not cross. He did not beat her, and once when he had threatened her with violence, she had shoved a knife in his face. She always stood her ground in their arguments, a technique Sukena had been taught in case she ever had to deal with a cruel prison guard. But negotiations and bribery were also part of it—cigarettes and occasionally beer or a well-cooked meal. When Sukena wanted to go to school, it was a mixture of her unrelenting war and her mother's survival skills that finally eroded that boundary between gender and education

But still, this was not freedom. If the Dictator's soldier, even when alone, drunk, and vulnerable, had behind him the whole army, her father, even when under constant attack at home from two forces, had the whole of society behind him. The church and the law were behind the man. But in addition, relatives from both sides of the family, neighbors, coworkers, and friends listened to the man before they did the woman.

As Sukena got older, she began to realize that divorce and separation were luxuries of those with property and education. Her mother had nowhere to go; she was without a home. Like a prisoner who couldn't escape, she had to find ways of staying alive within the confines of her home. Her sentence would end with her death, and she therefore placed all her hope on her children. Were Sukena's parents in love? Had they ever been in love? She could not tell, and she dared not ask her mother. Her answer, either way, would only point to a tragedy.

Sukena had loved Kalumba and now she was in love with Ogum. They were different. Kalumba was loud, given to excess, and unpredictable. Ogum was reliable and steadfast and always present. He was ambitious. He had always wanted to be a politician, one with a conscience, but a politician all the same. If their party won the elections, he would surely be awarded a position of apprenticeship in one of the ministries. Kalumba, in contrast, had wanted to retire into a life of teaching when this was all over. And for herself, she still was not sure. She wanted to travel and meet other kinds of people. Perhaps she would get a job teaching as well, save and travel, or apply for all sorts of research grants. She had finished her PhD in sociology with a dissertation on political movements and how they affect families. It was a moment that made both her parents shed tears, though she imagined for different reasons—her mother in pride and her father a mixture of pride, regret, and shame.

Sukena had then worked for a year as a consultant for an international NGO that catered to AIDS orphans, which soon ran out of funds. But now, even between jobs, her nights would often end with her narrating to Ogum all the places she wanted to travel to—Harlem, Cairo, Johannesburg, Soweto— and she would continue naming places until she would drift off to sleep. While she was not high up enough in the NGO to make a killing, she did earn enough money to start up a small eatery for her parents. They were making just a little bit more money than they did working in the tea plantations, but at least they were their own bosses. Or at least her mother had only one boss. Even though her father could cook and clean the counters at the Fish, Chicken and Chips shop, at home the boundaries between work and home remained rigid. At home he reverted to being the man and would not help around the house. But things were slightly better for her family now. Her brother was in secondary school, and her sister was waiting to get into the university. Sukena had carved out a route for her to follow.

Should she have waited for Kalumba, she constantly asked herself? But then again, how does one wait for someone without a return date? She had been determined to continue with her life, and even though she had gone for years without a lover after Kalumba's departure, it was not because it had occurred to her to wait; it was because her body was in mourning. Even though she knew Kalumba was still alive and would return someday, her body did not. It sabotaged her attempts at reclaiming her life. Once, a few months after Kalumba left, she had gone out on a date. Halfway into it she started crying, and even though she did not feel any sadness, she couldn't stop crying, and her date had walked her home.

Years later, she would laugh as she narrated the story to Ogum—how she had tried to explain to her date that she was not sad, that in fact she was feeling happy, it was just that her body was in mourning. Her date never called again, probably thinking she was crazy. Sometimes her body would refuse to wake up in the morning and she would lie there for a few hours, or her body would start trembling for no reason. The mourning peaked about eight months after he left and then abated slowly, and her mind and body became one once again. So by the time she and Ogum started making love, she had already finished mourning for Kalumba.

Sukena often thought back to the moment she first met Kalumba. She was on her way to church in her best outfit. She couldn't remember where he was going, but he was going her way. He caught up with her, and they started talking about school, what their parents did, favorite colors and music. By the time they got to church it was clear that they wanted to meet again, and he promised to come to church the following Sunday. He was not a Protestant, and it took her a long time to reconcile herself to his being an atheist. It was just the way he was brought up, he would explain. He was baptized because his mother had insisted on it, but he never used his baptismal name, Joseph. She, on the other hand, had not discarded Magdalene until shortly before she got her PhD.

As she reasoned then, she had worked too hard for the certificate to bear the name of strangers. Why should she take her name from a culture that was not hers? What kind of a god required that his children bear the name of their colonizers? She had met many Africans baptized Livingstone, Cecil Rhodes, or Delemere, but she had as yet to meet a white person baptized Sukena. It had made them laugh to refer to themselves as Mr. and Mrs. Joseph and Magdalene. When she married, she was determined not to change her name to her husband's; she had earned her name, and she was not going to lose it.

Kalumba's atheism was not like a religion, and Sukena's belief in God was not religious. She attended church every Sunday because that was the way she had been brought up. She met her friends there, and sometimes they would remain after the service for youth activities like volleyball or netball. It was also after church that they plotted their ungodly activities, like going to parties and meeting boys. But for the most part, Sukena and Kalumba's love had, from the very beginning, been serious and adultlike. They took it for granted that they would get married, and everyone else around them accorded them an adult status. Thus they could be together without adult supervision and did not have to run around hiding.

Both families approved. Sukena's father approved because Kalumba's father was a headmaster and Sukena would climb up one rung higher; Sukena's mother approved because she wished her daughter love. Kalumba's father approved because he knew Sukena from the time when he was her headmaster. He remembered how troublesome she was because she never believed anything she was taught. They had had many arguments in class and in his office, and now he welcomed more of those arguments in his home. Over the years, she would not let him down in this regard. She was always questioning him—why he did not remarry, or why he was apolitical and yet taught history. Wasn't his history living?

Had she always been in love with Ogum? Was exile that which made possible the inevitable? Perhaps if he had stayed she and Ogum would have continued as before—both devoted to Kalumba without really seeing each other. Ogum was strong, the rare combination of a warrior-politician. If his father had not been assassinated at a time when everything was in flux, Ogum's armor would not have revealed fault lines for love to latch onto. With both of them in mourning, on looking back it seemed inevitable that they would end up locked in each other's arms.

But Kalumba was gone. And now he was coming back. Older, still beat-up, broken, and perhaps even bitter. Their love was the sacrifice for their politics but they really had no choice. What they loved in each other was the very same thing that had cost them their love. Surely he could see that. Would they be able to build a friendship? She was getting a little worried about something else that was more threatening. Ogum said that others in the movement had begun talking about the List and the soldier who gave it to Kalumba. And even though he had yet to come out and say it, she knew where this was leading. Ogum suspected Kalumba of drawing up the List. There was no way of knowing. Kalumba couldn't remember what had happened. And Sukena knew that Kalumba would rather have died than betray the movement or Ogum's father. She knew it in the same way she knew she had loved him, but that would not settle anyone's doubts.

She hoped Ogum would help others see that Kalumba was not a betrayer. If he was, he would not have continued fighting after he was released and then finally went into exile. And the government would not have issued the order for his arrest and murder. More likely they would have taken him in for more questioning, using his earlier confession to make him tell them more. Or they could have leaked that it was he who drew up the list, to divide the movement. But as Ogum would say, they could not leak his confession, because they would in turn be admitting to torture; the government could have wanted him dead because he had continued fighting and, more to the point, they could never trust him. And why did the soldier pick Kalumba instead of others like Kalumba on the List? Was it because he had been assigned to take care of Kalumba, or was it because he knew Kalumba from the confession room?

She felt that Ogum, even though he never voiced it, held Kalumba responsible for his father's death. But for herself, she had come to understand that no one could have done anything for Baba Ogum. Perhaps Ogum blamed Kalumba just for being a witness. Perhaps he envied him sharing that moment with his father, Ogum being like a son who walks in too late to sit by a father's deathbed.

She was not sure where all this speculation would lead, but the movement couldn't hurt Kalumba, not after electoral victory. That would not be the best way to start the new era. And even though she wondered if forgiveness would be extended to the Dictator, she knew that others in the government would be forgiven. If this was the case, the movement would also forgive those in their ranks. But then again, Kalumba would never apologize for something he hadn't done, not even in a secret hearing. Perhaps the movement would forgive some people and forget about others. But all in all, Kalumba would be safe, especially if he returned quietly, took a teaching job, and lived what he used to refer to as a life retired from active politics.

So Sukena continued making lists. Her lists had nothing to do with the soldier's List and betrayal; hers were annotations that guided her life and charted small steps and paths up the mountain. Among other things on top of that mountain, she added marriage to Ogum. She knew that she and Ogum for the most part would live happy and contented lives. And when she left for travel or for research, he would be at home waiting for her. Her relatives pulled her aside to warn her of mixing blood. "Our blood does not mix well with other types of blood." Some even called her a traitor: "We are under siege from them, can't you see they have taken over our jobs and now they are taking our women?" It did not matter to her that they were from different ethnic groups. She would remind some of her accusers that they never had jobs to begin with and women do not belong to men. "But they belong to the race," they would argue.

Over time their attitudes had changed to a point where they had more or less accepted Ogum. But even then, he was an abstraction. Ogum was okay, he even spoke their language. It was Ogum's people who were the "problem," Sukena's relatives said. Ogum's relatives were not any better. They more or less said the same things to him. Overall, the political scene had changed, as the movement preached nonethnic politics. Even though all participants were black, they referred to themselves as the rainbow politicians to mark the multiplicity of ethnicity. As hope increased, the tensions eased. For Ogum and Sukena, in a lot of ways, their future depended on national politics. Fighting for national freedom meant fighting for a space where they could live, in which their love could flourish.

Yet, for her, even as she minded the past and the present, it was the future that counted, and she had fought for her place in it all her life. With or without Kalumba or even Ogum she would trudge on. Nothing would be allowed to stand in in the way of her dreams.

Kalumba's Diary in Exile

January 1st, 2002

Meeting Mrs. Shaw

"Hey! You there! You know what you need? A white mother."

I must be mistaken. I whirl around to face the voice. "What did you just say?"

"I said what you need is a white mother."

It's her. For a year or so now, almost every weekend I find her here. She is British. I am from Kwatee Republic—unmistakably black, African. Bar gossip informs me that she lived in Kwatee in the 1950s, lost her husband to the war for independence, taught African history at the University of Wisconsin–Madison, and, now retired, spends most of her time in bars just a few blocks from where her office used to be. I assume that bar gossip has offered her the same skeletal details about me: where I'm from, that I am in political exile and, like her, have a penchant for drink. In a year, we haven't talked, not even a hello, yet I feel that we are always aware of each other.

She intrigues me . . . very feisty. A few months back she walked into the bar, a heavy rucksack strapped around her shoulders, nearly her size. She had been touring Latin America. She produced a bottle of tequila, small and potent, *Just like me,* she said as she passed it around the bar. I lost my interest when she passed around a miniature Mayan mask made out of stone. She is unlike any other old person I have known— eccentric. She is full of energy—and even though I hate the word it is more apt to say that she is vivacious.

She is old, probably in her seventies, maybe even eighties. She is white, very thin though not frail. Her makeup does little to hide her deep wrinkles or the brown age spots on her face. Her red hair is cropped short, but even in the bar light I can tell it has been dyed. This night, she is wearing a thick red sweater and blue jeans that she has tucked into flaming red cowboy boots. I expect to find her smoking, but with a thickly veined hand she is twirling a little umbrella that came with her vodka tonic. She is telling me I need a white mother in the same way I would give a stranger I think deaf directions to the nearest bus stop or restaurant.

It is a few minutes into the New Year. It has been exceptionally quiet at Eagle's Bar. Before her interruption I was staring at the Billie Holiday photograph on the wall. It is not an original, and her uneven autograph is too glossy to have been from her own hand. The other photographs that cover the wall are all copies of a photograph of the original, too. Charlie Parker, Louis Armstrong, Duke Ellington, Miles Davis—martyrs, victims, and survivors of this country I have called home for the past ten years.

Billie's photograph—in side profile—with makeup, even in this black and white photograph, barely covering her bad skin, short hair in black curls, a map of veins along her neck stretched taut like guitar strings, glittering brown eyes half open, smooth hard jaws with skin stretched to an open mouth hungry for the microphone a few inches away—she is pulling back as if taking a deep breath . . . and my narration ends there. I always wonder what it is she is going to sing. Without the song she sings, the photograph is incomplete; it always leaves me hungry.

I take a long drink, and lugging my remaining beer, I skip the three or four barstools between us to sit next to the old white woman. Early into New Year's Day, we are the only patrons in the bar—everyone else has a home to go to. This is an exceptionally bad time to be alone. We do not speak for a while.

The bartender and owner of Eagle's Bar looks over to see if we need drinks and then turns his attention to the muted TV tuned to some New Year's celebration in New York. A former college football quarterback who is ageing like the cliché, he's also a jazz aficionado who delights in reciting names of musicians he's met (he can't have—he seems to be in his thirties). He doesn't like me, because when I get tired of staring at the dead imitations of the dead, I remind him that the photographs are photocopies of the original and that the live recordings he pipes through his expensive Boss system have lost some of their original groove in the machinery of mass production. It is a symbiotic dysfunctional relationship—I am the asshole drinker and he is the asshole bartender.

A home away from home.

You need a white mother are her first words to me, so I try to choose mine carefully. The surprise makes me smile. I cannot think of anything clever.

"What would make you say such a thing?" I finally ask, feigning annoyance. Certainly an insult would have been better, but there is something about her that reminds me of grandmothers. Old people and children radiate infectious warmth in the same strange way, I have found. Is it the vulnerability that cannot be hidden? And there are things learned at the pain of death—we do not insult our elders (though to be quite fair some people shoot them: for land, for their money, because they are old, for a host of reasons), and a few choice words that normally would have ended this conversation are of no use. In addition to her British accent authenticating a relationship that neither she nor I have any control over, I have revealed my hand by moving to sit next to her. I become aware that she knows all these things. I cannot leave until I have heard what she has to say.

"I have watched you for a long time watching our old friend Billie. What you need is a white mother."

I know exactly what she is doing—she is offering her credentials.

"Why do you say that?"

"Only a white mother can guide you through your journeys." She laughs. This is not the same laughter I have come to know from afar—a heckle followed by a wheeze. She laughs, well, like she is with a friend. "The father, your white father, was a colonizing bastard, but you see, he was a husband, a son, and father. I can help you understand him," she says. "He was a real human being, flesh, blood, dick, and all."

She is drunk . . . or crazy . . . but fuck it, it is New Year's, I am alone, lonely, homesick, drunk, and hungry for conversation—the touch of words. My first girlfriend used to say there is a difference between being alone and lonely. Well, I am both. So I play along.

"Interesting," I say, trying to be sarcastic as I take a sip of my beer. "So—mother of mine, you want us to plot against daddy?" I ask her with venom. "I can't possibly be your son," I add and reach for my wallet, flip it open, and point to an old photograph of my father and mother.

"See, these are my parents. I am as black as them." My eyes rest on the photograph on the other side of the wallet. It's Sukena. My own personal Billie Holiday, personal reminder of hell, savior, totem—exile has turned her into whatever I am in the mood to find. It has been ten years. I order two beers for myself. The old lady doesn't order another drink; she sits poised, waiting for me to ready myself for what she has to say.

"I am offering only . . ." She reaches for the words. " . . . intimate spaces. A family will work. No plots and counterplots."

She reaches out for her drink and then changes her mind. "You can be the mother and I the son if you like. It really doesn't matter," she adds with calculated carelessness.

I am thinking probably my father could play the role of her son better than me. His wife, my mother, died in a car accident a year after I was born. I do not remember her, though I recognize her in this vague feeling of growing up without balance, as if I had a phantom leg that worked. A few years before my departure, he finally told me that he'd been planning to divorce her. But her death turned him into a widower, and this came with duties that he could not pass on to anyone else. So he dutifully tended her grave, planting rose after rose until there was no more space left in the graveyard. What went through his mind? Did his betrayal of her weigh on his conscience more because she died before their divorce? Sometimes I feel that he brought me up in the same way he looked after her grave—doing something that was expected of him, doing his duty. How often has he reminded me that he did his duty by me? That he created a citizen of the world?

The paradox of exile—years and years at home, and I never really thought about these questions. I was too busy living and fighting. Here the downtime is like being in jail. Every wound, big or small, eventually gets excavated and reexamined by time.

It was from him that I learned of our past. With a schoolteacher's zeal, maps, historical documents, and a magnifying glass on a Ping-Pong table that he had converted into a general's desk, he would point, pontificate, drill, query, and pull my ear until I understood our history. His version of it, at least. He has a favorite maxim—"Love is knowledge, knowledge is love."

Yet in spite of it all I don't think he ever quite believed that the colonizers did what they did to us—concentration camps, poisoned water holes, cut-off hands, lips, and ears, and the rest of us thrown into their plantations and mines.

Tracing a colonial map along the mighty River Elan, he would pause over a poisoned well and ask himself, "But how could they do this to another human being?"

Yet just a few moments before, he had told me how we were not human beings to them. At other times he would tell me how we had lost our land. Often he took me there. The way he held the soil that had been his father's and let it course through his fingers, I knew he took me there to remind himself that it was all true, that it had all happened. Yes, I very well understood this trail of broken treaties. I had been walking it since I was born. In fact, I had walked it right into exile.

Unlike my father, I have never doubted what I know to be true—that the same hands that embrace one's child will squeeze the life out of a neighbor's child when war comes, that the same colonizer who built a church to save the native did not hesitate to burn it down when it housed rebels, and that my country's leaders, black like me, speaking my language in tongues and praying to the same god, had sanctioned my torture by night and driven their children to school in the morning. Perhaps I am better than my father in that I know all these things to be true. Or maybe I'm worse off, more jaded and more tragic. If in my realism I lose faith in my neighbor, how could I have faith in myself?

But I did learn a lot from my father. I can see him now, telling me how right from the beginning of colonization, there had been skirmishes between whites and blacks. "It is not true that we did not fight back," he was quick to remind me. Movements were formed and banned, leaders jailed, killed, or exiled, and whole villages of people put in concentration camps.

"Pretty much the same as it is now for your generation, only your leaders are black," he would say. The ebb and flow of resistance and repression continued until . . .

"Happy New Year!" the bartender yells to a passing friend through the large glass windows. She waves back with a gloved hand. My thoughts interrupted, I turn my attention back to the old white woman.

"Listen, I don't think even my father qualifies to be your son," I say to her.

"Oh! But he does. He didn't believe what he saw with his own eyes, and even though you think you're different, neither do you."

Damn it! Had I been speaking out loud?

She reaches into her red handbag, which I notice for the first time dangling by its strap on the barstool. She pulls out a red lipstick, pouts her lips, and unhurriedly applies the color. I catch a flash of her as a young woman, sexy, confident, and self-assured, years before history caught up with her.

"Look, I know more than you think I do . . . I know after your husband finished raping his slave, he rested for a bit and then turned on you. In town he was cheap and a drunk, and in the fields he was a murderer. At home he was much worse because he could not kill, so he learnt to torture his wife and children without leaving scars. Whatever little game you are playing here, know that I see you," I say.

"And, yes. I am also judging you," I add, more for effect, because it sounds good.

I notice I am clutching my glass tightly, and I take a deep breath. Or maybe she is the one losing it, because she turns her back and beckons the bartender for another drink. The bartender returns with a vodka and tonic too soon. We both could have used a break from the conversation. She motions for me to continue talking.

Instead I walk over to the jukebox and play Kool and the Gang's "Celebration." What the hell, it's New Year's, after all, and the song reminds me of home.

The bartender, annoyed by the sudden intrusion of sound, turns the music down. I knew he would do that; in his book, music other than jazz is only OK for young college kids. I ask for another drink. Perhaps she can tell I'm stalling, because she is watching my transactions with a look of amusement. Finally I sit down and continue where I left off.

"My grandmother had my father when she returned from your homes where she worked as a maid, nurse, cook, gardener, or whatever it was you made her do for you. But you, whom did you have? You had no place to return, no sanctuary. Everyone you would have known would have—" For the first time, she interrupts me by signaling me to stop. I am doing well, I have hit something that wounds her, I have drawn blood, so I yield. But oddly enough she does not jump right into the conversation. She hesitates, reaches into her bag once again, and removes some Wrigley's gum. She offers me a stick and carefully unwraps one for herself. I can tell she used to smoke by the way her little movements fill nervous space.

"Perhaps it was worse for me. But if my husband raped your grandmother—did your grandfather let her back into his bed? Back into his homestead? He is a man, after all. Men speak the same language," she says, emphasizing each word in the last two sentences. I want to hit her, but I would be jailed for life. No judge will ever accept the opening of wounds, even those as deep as history, as a reason for attacking a drunk old white woman in a bar on New Year's.

"Had it been my grandfather, I think he would have understood. We are talking about metaphorical grandfathers and mothers, aren't we?" I ask but do not wait for her to answer. "He would have beaten her up, and the kids too, and kicked the cat and the dog, but he would have had no choice but to take it, until he was tired of it and decided to fight back—he had no choice. Nor did our mothers, nor any of us . . . well, some of us."

We must look quite odd. The whole world is celebrating and here we are, a young black man sitting next to an old white woman in a bar called Eagle's. I wonder if the bartender can distinguish our accents, mine weighed down by Kyukato yet trained to sound like hers, and hers, a proper British English inflected with a midwestern drawl. Or to him, a typical American, maybe we are simply both foreigners to be watched.

"You are right but also wrong. Yes, I passed your grandmother on my stairs as she climbed up to my bedroom . . . She saw my life on the lily-white sheets. She might have thought that I did not see her, that I left the bloodied sheets and underwear there because I did not see her. Maybe that is what she would have told you. I don't know. I don't think so. Right there was my SOS written in my blood. There is no way she could have mistaken it . . . as a woman."

I don't know why we are talking like this. Granted, we have had a few drinks. Perhaps we are not strangers—two people, one a product of her country's misadventures and the other a victim of the myths that come with those misadventures, cannot be complete strangers. Maybe for the one year we have been seeing each other without talking, we have been communicating. Or maybe we just have needed to talk so badly, so urgently, that we had to dispense with the protocol, the small talk. Who cares about the weather? This is Wisconsin winter—it's always fucking snowing here.

"Celebration" has come to an end. The bartender walks over to the jukebox, puts in some coins, and starts flipping through the albums. "Why are we speaking in metaphors? Let's catch up—we do have a lot to talk about," she says in irritation. She has a good point there, I concede to myself. So I brace myself for what I am about to reveal to a stranger.

"I can't speak for my mother. She died when I was very small." I wait for her to say how sorry she is that she dragged my mother into this, or for her death, but she says nothing. "But you want to know what I think? I think she would have hated you. She had her own problems, you know . . . without yours. And you, you would have held on to your white skin. It still would have shielded you from some things . . . like, you never went hungry. But I can only speak for the living; at least they stand a chance to defend themselves." The conversation suddenly feels out of hand and uncomfortable, threatening. But given where I was a few minutes before—in front of Billie Holiday—I'm happy talking with her. The bartender's first selection has kicked in. I can't tell which of Miles's songs it is, but I know his voice, a trumpet sound that reminds me of bouncing smooth pebbles off the surface of the pond that was close to my home.

"Listen, why don't you tell me your story. Surely, surely we won't get anywhere like this," I say, going for broke, as Sukena would say. It feels good to use her words. Ten years and her stock phrases still spill out of me.

"Take me home, young man, and I will teach you a thing or two," she says in mock flirtation. She jumps off the barstool and offers me her hand. I accept, and pretend to climb down off my barstool even though I am taller than her. We both laugh for the first time, and I feel her warm but vodka-laden breath on my face.

I ask the bartender if I can buy something to take home. He refuses. I promise him a book on Charlie Parker, a biography. We haggle over the price. Eventually the old woman and I stagger out of Eagle's Bar with a bottle of whiskey in my winter coat pocket. But not before the bartender says it's good to see the two of us talking—as if he had reconciled two feuding friends. And maybe, in a way, this is true and he has come to see his one-year project come to fruition.

Outside the bar everything is covered in snow. It's beautiful. The snow makes everything brighter. It's cold enough to make me feel winter on uncovered skin, but not oppressively so. A mild wind is disturbing the snow off the lampposts, rooftops, and magazine stands to make a second showing of the snowfall—an encore. A white police officer driving up the street slowly comes to a crawl when he spots us. The old lady slips her hand under my arm and laughs, looking in his direction. The officer shakes his head from side to side and steps on the gas; the car swerves dangerously before it finds traction and drives off.

We walk in silence, occasionally slipping into each other on the ice that has formed beneath the snow. Sometimes she slips away from me and I feel an urgent tug of her arm on my elbow. By the time we get to her home, we are no longer familiar strangers. Once the veneer of mutual suspicion has been removed, we find we already know a lot about each other. From the outside, her house doesn't look like much, but it's cozy inside. Not at all what I would have expected had I had more time to think about it. It doesn't have that stale smell that is peculiar to old people's houses. I notice that the lamps have shades made out of stained glass—the kind one would find on church windows. Her wall has all sorts of art on it, all original, she says, with figures contorting in pain or pleasure. It's hard to tell.

As I'm about to take a seat in the dining room, I notice she has a photograph of a Samasi warrior. After I walked across the border disguised as a Samasi, the same white tourists who waved as they passed me shortly after my friends dropped me off close to the border snapped photographs of me when I made it to Kiliko town. Behind me, a failed coup, so much death, and there were tourists who had escaped the coup happy to at last have a souvenir. Not now—I don't want to remember—I should have died that night, I tell myself. So I stare closely at the Samasi warrior, wondering if it is me. Nope—that would have been something, though.

The old white woman puts on some Masekela, and his voice booms, "There is a train . . ." before she turns the volume down. Now that's strange. The only people I know who listen to Masekela are the African exile types. I open the bottle of Jack and place it between us. She takes a swig and passes it to me. I do the same and we settle in for a long silence. It feels like we are speaking even in the silence. Or maybe we're just making space for room to speak, because she suddenly makes a sweeping impatient gesture and begins telling me about her husband.

"You're right. He couldn't leave his work at the office." I know what he did even before she says it.

"I loved him at first," she says. I feel like she is trying to convince herself. "The bastard was a colonial district officer. I don't know why I followed him. Perhaps you can tell me later. Even after all these years I still do not know. For what I went through, love alone cannot be the reason."

I wonder along with her. She doesn't strike me as the type to fall in love and follow her husband around the world, nor, for that matter, does she seem the Florence Nightingale type.

It should have been the other way round—her husband following her. But years pass and people change for the better or worse; some become weaker and others stronger. Into what have I mutated?

Afraid of what's coming, I walk over to her stereo and turn the music up slightly, just so I can have a cushion, something to soften the harshness of whatever is coming. I sit back down, take a swig of the whiskey, and pass the bottle to her. Our hands brush, and she smiles politely. Placing the bottle between us, she leans back. She moves forward again only when she starts speaking.

"He was in charge of security in his area. When what we called the little troubles and what you called the uprisings came, he was in charge of collecting information. But his love for what was to become his life's work started even before he came to your country." She says *life's work* with a twist of her mouth. "He was a large man, about your height but very large, with very blue eyes, too. It was his eyes . . ." She caught herself midsentence, then continued. "When we were dating, he once told me that he liked to hunt and kill deer. He enjoyed seeing the color of their eyes change from brightness to a dull stare. Nothing should have come as a surprise after that. He was trained to collect information by an expert on African affairs—Dr. Joseph Howard. You might have heard of him, or read some of his history books. Dr. Howard spoke six or seven different African languages and was an expert on 'the African mind.' In his books, he never revealed how he got his information, but he taught my husband everything."

She pauses, taking another swig from the bottle. I know the types she is talking about; they are still walking around as if they own the continent. *Only in Africa,* it is written on trucks and buses. How does it feel to be studied, poked with needles and theories, and talked about as if invisible? I imagine Dr. Howard torturing an old man for anthropological studies.

"Then the little troubles began, the blacks started slapping back, and everything changed," she says. I am struck by the way we have come to share language. *The little troubles*—outside how we met, our tragedies, our histories, our stories, those words would have had no meaning.

I understand her so well. I understand the words underneath those words. I too am here because of present little troubles, related to her little troubles. It was the increasing frequency of my little troubles that brought me here. And there are so many all over the world whose lives ebb and flow with little troubles.

"He enjoyed, no, wait . . . he loved his work. I was the chaser, after the main course and dessert. Work slowed down, I became the dessert. We had a garden boy, an old man really . . . his name was David." I am about to take offense at an old man being called a boy, and then I remember that we, Kwateeans, use the same terms: *boy, girl,* or sometimes just an anonymous rude *you* for those who till our gardens, cook, and look after our children.

"I can't remember his African name. I was sitting outside with my husband and I was looking at David—he was just there, so I was looking at him. I didn't hear him leap from his chair. *Why are you looking at David? You want to fuck him? You want to fuck him.* I woke up later in bed, swollen all over. It excited him to think of me and David fucking. Or David fucking the two of us. Or three of us just fucking. David lost his job. Had it been a few months later, my husband would have shot him just for his desire."

I need a break. I ask her where her bathroom is. I go in there and wash my face in the sink. My heart is pounding violently. It is quite simple: I am afraid of what this old woman is going to tell me. But even as I think that, I also know I am going to listen, so I calm myself and walk back to the table and sit down. She continues as if there had been no interruption.

"Dark sunglasses most of the time . . . Once we had a picnic party—All the women in white dresses, white pearls around their necks, white tennis shoes and hats and dark sunglasses. We laughed and sipped our wine." She lifts her little finger up gingerly, pretending she is delicately holding the stem of a wine glass. "We talked about our husbands and the little troubles that our maids and servants were giving us. We were a sea of whiteness but underneath . . . only tears. I do not know what the men were talking about, but as they got louder our laughter grew louder too. It became a madhouse. We were all mad. We needed a whole lot of shrinks." She lets out a laugh that in exile I have come to know well. It ends abruptly, a burst of steam that dissipates just as suddenly.

"It kept getting worse. An epidemic had broken out among our husbands, and the cure was our bodies . . . My neighbor stopped visiting me. I knew why. Underneath the glasses and white dresses . . ." Her voice wavers, as if it is going to break. "And who knew what the black men would do to us when . . ." she trails off.

I can't let her finish. I jump to my feet. I've been nice enough and played along. But this is too much. It was they who came to our country, and they, woman and man alike, got what they deserved. I have no empathy. I need it all for myself. I have to do something, before I lose it. I've come too far. I'm almost healed. I'm going home in a year. Wounds have been slowly closing to form scars. What I and others sacrificed for is finally coming to pass. Elections will take place this year. The Dictator will be voted out of office, and my exile will be over, because the party I joined at its inception is going to win the elections. But now, more than opening her wounds for me to see, this old woman is also opening mine, and she doesn't seem to care. I just need to survive another year and I can return and these things will be behind me. People like her are always taking. She is still taking, always taking . . .

"Jesus Christ! Can't you see you are still taking? You are a taker and have always been a taker," I shout, interrupting my own thoughts with speech. "Can't you see what you are doing?"

"What I am doing?" she asks very calmly. "Didn't I tell you that you don't know everything?"

"Stories are what my grandmother told me at bedtime. This is torture. You deserved your husband!" I realize too late what I have shouted. She says nothing, letting the silence gnaw me into guilt. I reach for the bottle, take a swig, and wait.

"Please, sit down." It is half plea, half command.

I sit.

"Look, things are not as simple as you are making them out to be. It is not just you and your husband. Can't you see that it was not all about you?" I am feeling calmer now.

"Explain yourself." She leans back into her chair and folds her arms across her chest. I go on.

"Well, for starters, we had our own lives too ... My grand-parents worried about their children; they talked about their history and prayed to their god. They did not stop living be-cause you came—that is what you hated most about them. Also, let's face it; you guys were not as scientific as you try to make it sound—lots of massacres, accidents, and lies. Your Stanleys and Livingstones were liars and cheats." I pause to catch my breath.

"There is something I must show you," she says abruptly. As if whatever she wants to show me will lay all my doubts to rest.

She walks upstairs. I hear drawers being pulled open. Whatever it is, she's not fumbling for it. It could be a gun. And then silence. I take a generous swig from the bottle and still she has not come down. Crazy stuff is running through my mind. Perhaps she is stripping upstairs. There are all sorts of stories about old white women who come to the beaches of Kwatee for sex with young black men—and the men in search of the dollar or a good time, a green card, drugs, you name it, oblige. But she doesn't strike me as the type—*How do I know the type?* I ask myself. Another swig for courage and I go up the stairs. The first thing I see through the door she left ajar is open drawers. I push the bedroom door wide open, and as it creaks all the way to the wall, I hear grunts, which I soon recognize to be snores. She has passed out on the bed. I try to lift her up, but she is surprisingly heavy, so I roll her to the edge, pull the blankets underneath her, roll her back to the center, and cover her.

My heart is beating heavily, and for a moment I cannot tell where I am. I regain my senses and walk outside—it's almost light out. I am beside myself with curiosity, but I tell myself she was drunk. What was it that she wanted to show? Will I ever find out? I know this is going to be an interesting year.

January 4th

FURTHER REFLECTIONS AND SURPRISE

"Hey, fuck-face, where is my white mother?" I drunkenly ask the bartender at Eagle's.

"How the fuck should I know—maybe you killed her," he answers back. I am in a prickly mood, which explains his answer. He hasn't seen her since that night. But just as I am about to lose or find myself in Billie Holiday, she walks in. She doesn't say hello, though I see a slight smile on her face. Well, two can play that game. I am not biting, this time around. And so we sit around the bar for two or three minutes not saying a word. Then an idea—I walk to the jukebox and play Lightnin' Hopkins's "Bring Me Back That Wig I Bought You." She lets out a chuckle as soon as the song is over. She plays Tracy Chapman's "Sorry." Before the song is over, she beckons to the bartender—buys a bottle of Jack and heads for the door. I follow her, and we walk together in silence. I have to find out what it was she wanted to show me.

We get to her home. She opens the bottle and brings out two glasses but drinks from the bottle. "You will need this," she says, as she passes me the bottle. As if we had paused a DVD movie, we are back where we were on New Year's. "I have something to show you," she says. I brace myself.

She is not gone for long. She walks back into the dining room carrying something round like a soccer ball, covered in expensive-looking rainbow-colored batik cloth. She places it on the table. Like a magician, she ceremoniously unfurls it.

Something clatters onto the dining table, its jarring sound mixing in with her chuckles. When it finally settles and I lock my shaking eyes on it, I find a human skull. I let out a quick sharp scream.

"What is this? What the fuck is this?" I stand up abruptly, knocking against the table, and the skull and bottle dance crazy hula hoops. "What the fuck?" I notice that my right hand, instinctively stretched out to save the dancing bottle, is trembling. I break into a thin light sweat and with my knees feeling foreign I find my seat but then stand up again.

"This is the price of freedom!" she says lightly, now laughing in pure delight. I can't reconcile her with the old woman I have come to know. For a moment she flashes back into a young woman, wild red hair, round full breasts pressing against a black bra visible through her thin white shirt.

Did I just check out an old white woman? I can't help it; I start laughing too. I reach for the bottle and take such a long swig that she reaches across the table and gently takes it away from me. She takes an equally long swig. She picks the skull up, gives it a kiss, cradles it in the crook of her elbow, and sashays around the dining room. "Well, son, this here is my husband," she says in an imitation American Southern drawl.

In this madness, I remember my father's history lesson as Ogum and I listened in fascination: The ebb and flow, resistance and repression had gone on for years. Then Kwateeans made one bold move that changed everything. They kidnapped the head of British National Security, a former district commissioner who had proved to be very able in native pacification campaigns. They held him for a few days, and when there was no sign that the white government would cease its campaign, they killed him and buried him in an unmarked grave. The colonial government went on a rampage and killed hundreds of Kwateeans as it searched for the "black terrorists" (my father would say *terrorists* with a wink).

This in turn sparked a nationwide movement that gave birth to the People's Freedom Party, the political wing of the People's Freedom Army that eventually forced the white government into a stalemate. And from the stalemate came a stillborn independence and the betrayal of the nation by the People's Freedom Party. My father's version was much longer than I care to remember at this instant, but the general point was that the kidnapping and killing of the national security head was the watershed moment for the first independence. And here he is right before me—the head of national security.

"Is this Oliver Shaw? The one and only Oliver Shaw?" I ask as if meeting him in person for the first time and simultaneously announcing his entrance into a boxing ring.

"Yes, this is him." She runs her hand over the smooth skull. "The one and only," she adds.

"What happened to him?"

She holds up her free hand to slow things down. "He was drunk. I tied him to his favorite chair and sat up all night waiting for him to wake up." She says this like she had been waiting for a loved one to wake up from an illness. "Then I killed him."

"How?"

"Seven o'clock in the morning. I opened up the curtain and told him to look at the rising sun. It was red and beautiful. 'Look at it well.' He didn't ask why. He was a soldier only doing his duty. 'Do you love what you do?' He said yes. *Can I have a glass of water and a cigarette?* His blue eyes were darting from side to side like . . . *I always offer them a glass of water and cigarette.* —'And the ones who do not smoke?' He grunted. *Nothing.* I took a tobacco and paper from his shirt pocket and rolled him one—just like he taught me—lit it and held it to his lips—his first thank you to me. I took his gun off his belt, placed it on his forehead, and shot him." Then she adds, "That is also how I quit smoking."

I sit down. As I reach for the bottle I see for the first time the neat hole through the forehead. It looks so neat, no jagged edges, as if it's been filed.

"How did you get away with it?"

"Lions and hyenas—whichever . . ."

"What about his skull?"

"Our soldiers used to cut off heads belonging to troublesome chiefs . . . boil them until the flesh came off. It was to keep the victory alive; to cradle the skull of your enemy is to savor the victory forever."

"Yes, I know. That is what they did to our hero, the freedom fighter Shakara . . ."

"Is that what they say we did to him?" she asks.

"You were never suspected? How did you get away with it?" I ignore her question and ask my earlier one.

"After a few days, I put on my pearl necklace, white dress, and shoes and went to the police and reported my husband missing."

"You didn't choke?" I'm leaning into the dinner table. With her leaning forward as well, I imagine we make an arc across the table. I want to know more. I nod impatiently for her to continue.

"No, I did not . . . Remember our white dresses and hats? I stayed on in Kwatee. I was there when the Union Jack was lowered. Did you know that it was done in the dark so as not to shame the Prince?" She asked. My father never tired of telling me this.

"I left when your new president, Samuel Johnston—that was his full name before he became African again—called to say that I would still get my widow's pension. I could continue farming. Even though he couldn't say this in public, he felt my husband, while cruel, still embodied greatness." She stands up, stretches her belly, and pretends to be snapping at suspenders, continuing to imitate our first president. "Madam, while I respectfully disagree with your husband's racism, we do indeed share a common belief in law and order. Without respect for property, we cannot build a prosperous nation."

"Do you judge my act as revolutionary?" she asks somberly. She does not wait for me to answer. "What does it matter? I am part of history even though history doesn't know it," she remarks bitterly.

"What about all those hundreds, hundreds of Africans who died as a result of your husband's death? What about them?" Enough with her theatrics, I decide—she was still a colonist. "Your freedom, your silent freedom can only be selfish," I add, to which she keeps quiet as she reaches for the bottle. I push it her way.

"I don't know. They would have died anyway . . . perhaps . . . but then again perhaps not. But they got what they wanted, didn't they? A symbol to rally around? I don't know . . . I really did not wish for the life I lived . . . that I have lived." She reaches for the bottle again—I jab it with my finger into her hand, which is shaking; no one can remember all these things and remain sane.

"And the skull?" I want to know the rest of her story.

"No one stopped me at the airport. Once again I was dressed in white." We both escaped in disguise—me dressed as a Samasi warrior and her as a white woman.

"Which version of that history did you teach?"

"The only known version. Who would believe me anyway?" she says, as though considering the option. "I told you, I'm a martyr in more ways than one," she adds dismissively.

"There's DNA testing," I offer.

"What makes you think I want people to know? My history . . . this is a private party for a single gal. Let the dead remain buried." Underneath the lighthearted tone, I can tell she is serious.

"No matter what, people deserve to know how their history was made," I counter, even though I know it's pointless. A secret this big would never be let out by any Kwateean government; it would remain buried. There was a lot that got buried, both during the struggle and after independence—all the secret deals that were made, that had made a mess out of things, the assassinations, illegal arms, land grabs, Swiss bank accounts, and power-sharing deals. This would be just one of them—a concession by someone for the truth.

"But where do I fit in all this?" I ask.

"I told you. You are my son—or, if not, midwife," she says seriously.

"No. That cannot be. I have a father and mother. I am not an orphan, not even of history."

"You can only reject me. I am your midwife, and I died giving birth to you."

"Independence would have happened anyway. No. I cannot accept your offer."

"It's not yours to accept . . ."

I stare at the bottle. "Look," I say. "We make good drinking friends . . . The rest . . . in the course of time we shall figure it out," I offer. At the end of it all, she's just another lonely old lady and I . . . I'm not sure what I am except that in a year I will wear the punishing moniker of returnee. I am going back, and that is all there is to it.

There is silence for a while. Past exhaustion, I look at the time; it's 7:00 a.m. I take a swig from the bottle and pass it to her.

"Come and visit me again, but only if you come bearing gifts," she says, sending a wink toward the bottle, which I am still holding out to her. She writes down her number and house address on a piece of paper, one arm resting on the skull.

"You kept it?" I'm surprised when I see the name on the piece of paper.

"Being called my name is like rubbing a genie bottle—the thing that pops out reminds me of my victory. These independences are elusive. Do you think we are going to lose again?"

"No, Mrs. Shaw." At the sound of her name she smiles. I am calling her by her war name. "I don't think we will lose again." I feel happy and light. I stand and put on my jacket.

"Mine is Kalumba Wa Dubiaku," I say, and when I hear no answer I look and find her passed out on the table—this is fast becoming a habit. It's not the most comfortable position to sleep in. I lift her up and stagger with her to the couch, surprised all over again at how heavy she is. I leave her there, in makeup, boots, and everything—a feisty grandmother sleeping off too much booze . . . so much history in that little frame. *As for you, terrible Mr. Shaw, you were not felled by our sleeping grand-mother,* I think, in the direction of the skull. The terrible Mr. Shaw is now a decapitated white skull on an old lady's table.

I wonder what to do with this knowledge. What does this mean? Not even my father, who refused to teach the government-sanctioned history, could possibly believe this. Even I am having trouble believing that it's anything but a dream. And yet it's true. I saw it with my own eyes. I'm now a believer of sorts, a believer whose god is out of focus. Outside it has started snowing again. A few days into the new year, people are going to work. My world is upside down. I stagger home and go to sleep.

January 6th

SHAKARA

What a fucking hangover. Yesterday. A whole day gone in front of the idiot box in the sickroom that my one-bedroom apartment has become.

Here is the kicker to Mrs. Shaw's story. In the early 1900s the greatest Samasi chief, Shakara, welcomed the British to his kingdom. As he asked them, why fight the waves of the future? And so the British loaded him with money and weapons with the idea of using him against the neighboring kingdoms. They trained and equipped his army.

On July 4th, 1905, the story goes, on the day Shakara was to invade his neighbors at the behest of the British, he turned around and unleashed his army against the unsuspecting British administrators and army officers. He ordered the bodies delivered to his neighbors as a peace offering and declaration of independence. What followed was to prompt later historians to refer to Kwatee Republic as the first site of a British gulag (but only if one forgets the Native Americans, the Scottish, the Irish, and god knows who else). The British sent in troops with orders to pacify the rebelling natives by any means. The usual recipe followed—the survivors saw their villages turned into concentration camps. They were forced to dig deep trenches around their villages and spikes were put in the trenches so that there was only one way in or out. Still Shakara, equipped with British weaponry, remained strong, and soon it became clear to the British that a stalemate was the only possible outcome—and stalemates spell victory for the weaker player.

The British used the only thing they could against Shakara—his sense of honor. They told Shakara that if he came to their fort they would sign a peace treaty that would guarantee the existence of Kwatee as long as trade between the nations could continue. They gave their word that he would be safe. This has since been a matter of contention—should he have agreed? Was he being naïve? I mean, nations sign treaties all the time and enemies meet in order to allow for dialogue—but treachery has to be defeated first. They waylaid him on his way to the fort, and that was the last that was seen of him. Some say that he was buried alive in an unmarked grave. But Kwateeans who worked at the fort say he was beheaded, his head boiled and his skull sent to Britain.

No Kwatee Republic government has seriously tried to find his grave, and the British records have been sealed—no one is invested in this beautiful history being unearthed. A dictator does not want resistance history known, and the British have no interest in their sins being unearthed—they want their history to remain as white as snow.

I have always felt very close to Shakara. Sometimes to find peace you have to trust your enemy with your life. Sometimes betrayal is inevitable. Soon his death will bear fruit.

Is this where Mrs. Shaw got the idea of taking her husband's head with her? It does give new meaning to "off with his head."

January 20th

HOPE

I am surprised at how little can happen in a day. Whole days spent in front of an idiot box. I have been in this country for ten years, yet I do not have much to show for it. I want to understand for myself what these ten years mean. I have wasted them—a decade of my life. If I live to be seventy, in truth I will have lived for sixty years. Menial jobs, drinking, and useless degrees equal ten years. Is that how I measure my life? No money, wife, or children, not even a good educa- tion—is that how I am supposed to measure my life? What about sanity? Me, torture, amnesia, Ogum's father and exile and the List—always the fucking LIST. Who drew up the List? Who gave up Ogum's father?

But at least I am back in school finishing my PhD—history and African literary criticism. It sounds good, important even. The title I gave my dissertation defense committee is "The Literature of Exile: Psycho-analyzing the Self in the (Ex-) in/of Exile." It is a waste of time for all concerned: for the professors because they will pass it without understanding it, and for me because I really should be back home. I feel that what I should be writing is what is going to be in this journal, though at this point, the exact content is unknown to me. Yet I need that piece of paper that shows I am a Doctor of Phi- losophy. I tell myself that I need it to get a job back home. But now that I am trying to understand what it is I'm doing, I am certain it's so I can show the diploma to my father.

I will be home soon! What an exciting time we are in! We are about to win. Jesus! SIDCF, SIDCF, SIDCF—How I used to love saying the name of our organization over and over again. Five hundred years of unbroken domination starting with slavery to our present-day Dictator is finally about to be broken. And I want to be in that new nation. I deserve to be there because I am a survivor of its second war for indepen- dence. I am not all hopeless—even in my worst moments, I always send 10 percent of my salary to the organization. It is the glue that holds me together.

I want to be part of my nation's new education initia- tive. I will teach literature and history at Kwatee National University.

Mrs. Shaw surprised me—I would never have thought that she supported the SIDCF. Why didn't I tell her that I was in exile because of my involvement in it?

January 21st

DREAMS . . .

I want to keep a journal of hope. I am tired of letting blood out of my veins. I want to reclaim what is left of me. What is it of myself that I lost in exile?

This is the journal I offer myself. I will look at it from time to time and remember those terrible days. It is a journal that will become the past.

This is the journal that I will show my children to tell them of those terrible times that our nation went through. This is the journal I hope to show my children when I am no longer ashamed of what I became in exile.

This is the journal I envision as a bullet that fires from a pen, which uses ink for gunpowder—my liberation song.

I do not think it is fair of me to put so much hope in one act, yet I must. This is the journal I have named *breaker of chains.*

This is the journal that says—I hope I hope, and I believe I believe, I believe I believe . . .

February 1st

IN THE FUCKING PIT OF MY MIND AGAIN . . . OR PTSD?

They had found me. So soon! I could not believe they had found me. I had been stupid. I had relaxed; what had I been thinking? That they would forget or forgive? That they don't keep late hours? The fucking bastards, so close to defeat, are desperate! These are the last days and they will kill and destroy all that stands between the Dictator and the bottom of the ocean.

I was leaving my apartment in Madison. I do not know what happened. The stink of rotting eggs. Next thing, I was in an empty bathtub. I didn't know where I was. Naked, blindfolded, handcuffed to the faucet. The water started running—cold at first but warming up. Very hot. I started yelling for help. Scalding hot. Somebody grabbed the back of my head and pushed my forehead into the water until my lungs felt like they were going to explode and my face was going to peel off. The pressure was released, but before I could take in some air, my head was thrust in again. The back of my skull banged against the faucet handle. Blood filled my dreads. I was lifted to my feet, slammed against the wall, and before my arms could tear out of their sockets, I was submerged in the water. They kept banging my head against the side of the bathtub. The blood felt warm, thick, as it soaked through my dreadlocks, through the blindfold, and into my eyes. Darkness. A loud voice.

"Give us a list of names. We want a fucking list!"

"What list?"

Calmness . . . Silence except my heavy breathing and the sound of water as I turned and twisted my body in the water. The water drained out. After it was all gone, the knob turned again, and it started filling in with cold water. I heard someone fumbling for matches. I heard a match strike. Kerosene. They were going to set me on fire. I was going to die before I got back home. Tobacco burning.

"My friend, do you want a cigarette?"

"I don't smoke."

A cigarette in my mouth.

"You think cigarettes will kill you? You die today," the voice said, laughed till it broke into a smoker's cough.

I puffed and started coughing. A sharp sting, several more sharp stings all over my upper body, the smell of burning flesh. The coldness was rising and rising, and I felt my skin beginning to shrivel and my lungs constricting. I heard a sound. They were adding ice to the water. The kerosene smell, it must have been a cigarette lighter.

"Give us the list," the calm voice said.

"I don't have a list."

"Then make one."

"I can't. Can't you see I can't?"

A thin gun barrel pressed against my temple.

"Why did you let him die?"

"Who?"

"You know who!"

"There was nothing I could do. I would have died too. They would have killed me."

"You killed him. You are a murderer. Don't be self-righteous. Give us the names!" the voice yelled.

"I did not kill anybody."

"But you kill for freedom," the voice reasoned.

"I do not let people die."

"Do you want to die? You leave us no choice."

"No."

"Then why don't you tell us what we want to know? This can all end. You can be home by tomorrow evening. Airfare and everything, Kwatee Airlines. Look, we can tell you have been making a nice life for yourself since we last met . . . Do you want to give it all up?"

Moment of silence. I thought of Sukena. I heard a click. I braced myself, and just when I thought a bullet would come crashing into my skull, the phone started ringing. It wouldn't stop ringing. My cell phone. I hoped they wouldn't answer it—my friends will be in danger. They must be monitoring my calls. Not another dead body. Will they let me answer it?

"Answer the fucking phone, fuck-face, answer it. If they hang up, it's your balls!"

A blow to my head. My lips opening up once again and a salty warm light taste in my mouth. I hate the taste of my own blood. I can't take it anymore. GIVE THEM WHAT THEY WANT!

I lifted my hands, and the handcuffs came off. I removed the blindfold and opened my eyes. I was in my bathroom. I was trembling in cold and pain. I opened the door and was blinded by midafternoon sun. For a moment I was in a hollowed-out baobab tree trying to hold my stomach in place, blood draining through my fingers.

Then I start making out the walls in my apartment. Where did they go?

My cell phone is still ringing. I follow the sound and answer, only to find Mrs. Shaw on the other end. She wants to know when I am coming over for dinner. I suggest tomorrow or the day after. I don't wait to say good-bye.

Everything in my bathroom is broken. I know it's all me. I look for a mirror. There is one in my bedroom. My appearance is far worse than the last time I was here. I have cigarette burns all over. The skin on my arms is split open. The skin on my forehead is all burned. I go to the fridge and remove a frozen steak and try to level the bumps and bruises. After a while I give up. I get dressed and walk to Eagle's Bar to stare at Billie Holiday. I simply cannot find my song. Why do I keep doing this? I really, really wish I could stop what I am doing to myself. This thing: Is this what I have become?

February 3rd

MELISSA

Strangest thing! I wake up in my bed to find a naked woman poring over my burns and scars. I cannot see her face, only a mass of curly black hair. She is peering so closely that I can feel her nipples grazing my legs. As she makes her way up, I can feel her breasts tracing her movements up my thighs, penis, stomach, and chest. With her fingers she traces the scar running across my stomach up to the point where it begins to fade at the beginning of my rib cage. It feels soothing.

"You have to let me paint them," she says without looking up.

"Paint what?"

"The scars."

"I don't want to be painted," I answer.

"I am talking about your scars, not you. You probably won't even recognize them after I am done."

She looks up and straddles me so that she is sitting on top of my stomach. She grazes a few of my burns but does not say anything when I wince. She is beautiful, naked, and a stranger—yet this seems like the most natural morning in the world, as if for the past ten years I have been waking up in bed naked with a beautiful woman who wants to paint my scars.

"Do you burn and cut yourself in any particular pattern?"

"No. Some of the scars are mine, but most of them are not."

I know the question that will follow, but suddenly with her (though I think the circumstances might have contributed) I desire to hide nothing. This life of mine has been hard . . . to say the least.

The fucking scars. It is the scars that made me give up pick-up soccer. The panic of whether I was going to be on the skins side. Once I almost got into a fight with another player who couldn't understand why I couldn't take my shirt off. The day was saved by a fellow player, doctor and all, from Haiti who offered to switch sides. He had his own scars, from bullets, knives, jagged beer bottles, bites—must have been one hell of a ride—but he didn't seem to care. I was jealous that he was so comfortable with his scars. He, even though we never could become friends, understood.

"Whose are they?"

"The scars?"

"What else?"

"Torture . . . I don't remember most of it. I suffer from memory loss. Selective amnesia . . . It sounds as if it is much better to forget than to remember, but it's very violent not to remember something violent happening to you."

"So you torture yourself to remember?"

"Yes. I don't remember if I confessed or not. There was a list that the government drew up. A soldier came to see me with it afterwards. I have always wondered why. Perhaps I gave up those on the List."

"Hypnosis?"

"Tempted? Yes, but not for me. Whatever is buried down there is down there for a reason. I think my subconscious has placed a lot of landmines around it. I am afraid that I would find what I think I should find in order to survive but not the truth of it. What I need is to remember when I am awake. Besides, I always imagine even seeing a shrink as making a date with a torturer. I cannot surrender myself to someone else like that . . . Too much power," I try to explain. This, whatever it is, is mine and mine alone. What I need to do is to remember for myself, wide-awake. I cannot surrender my mind to another human being.

"If you will not accept help from people who have been trained to deal with these sorts of things and yet you don't remember, it is dangerous to wonder about it. You might as well let it go. What happened with the List?"

"Well, after the soldier left, my friend Ogum and I contacted as many as we could. We thought everyone was safe. Then there was a coup attempt, and that changed everything. The government used it as an excuse to weaken the opposition. Ogum's father was amongst those who did not make it. I watched him get shot. Him, others . . . the soldiers too. I was hiding. I saw it all." I am close to tears, but over the years I have learned to mask my pain so well that she does not notice any shift in tone.

There is something about it that was unreal, talking about it in the United States, in the middle of winter, ten years after the fact, with a hangover and in bed with a naked woman. In ten years this is the most I have spoken about it. Does she understand? Perhaps she can feel the pain in the silence of all else that I have not told her. We keep quiet for a long time; for over an hour without exchanging a single word, she straddling me, tracking the scars with the tips of her fingers like a blind person, trying to commit them to her painter's memory, I think. There is something very familiar about this—empty spaces that do not demand to be filled.

For the first time in a long time I think about Sukena. She and Ogum are getting married. I imagine them fucking, search for bitterness, and find it has abated. I decide I will write to them soon.

Melissa and I start kissing. I do not mind our bad breath, a mixture of late-night pizza and alcohol. But I am too fucked up and cannot keep it up. Haven't had much use of my dick lately except for pissing—been drinking too much.

The embarrassment as she rolls off me and my fucked-up wet dick makes a *plop* sound as it falls on my thigh.

"Does this thing ever work?" she asks, laughing. But to her credit she says nothing more—we stay in bed, half her brown face wrinkled and crisscrossed from having slept on an unmade bed.

"Melissa Rafael, listen, I think we might have covered this last night, but where are you from?" I cannot remember anything from the night before except her name.

"I'm surprised you remember my name. I'm from Puerto Rico," she answers. "I came to the mainland to go to art school. I don't remember much of last night either."

"My name is Joseph Kalumba Wa Dubiaku. I believe we met at Eagle's Bar."

Jesus Christ, I think, even in drunken stupors exiles, the wounded, and the infirm can smell the gangrene on each other even though masked in perfumes and colognes of well-being. We walk with a limp even when we think we don't. First Mrs. Shaw and now Melissa Rafael—we could scent each other across continents.

She has to leave, so we plan to meet tomorrow evening. After she leaves I remember I am supposed to be going to Mrs. Shaw's for dinner. I figure I will call and ask her if she minds an extra person over for dinner.

February 3rd

E-MAIL TO OGUM, SUBJECT HEADING: ALL APOLOGIES . . .

Brother,

I hope you will accept my apologies for not having written in well over a year(s). I am not the only guilty one here—you haven't written in years yourself. Even though I have moved quite a bit, I've kept the same e-mail, as you are aware. As you might have guessed, I sank into what I can only call the pit of my mind. My mind caved in, a black hole from which nothing could escape and everything that came in was without taste or form.

The past for people like me is never far behind and sometimes it is an anchor in a sea of sorrow. And being away from home only makes it worse. Like a ghost, the past is always present, and yet without physical form, how can one fight it? Perhaps had I been able to stay home, over time you would have forgiven me for those things that I couldn't have helped and those I could have. Perhaps, I could have gone back to the stream where I witnessed your father's death and over time I would have become used to it, the massacres. Perhaps I could have laid some flowers there as I have seen people do here in sites where an accident has taken place and they have lost a loved one.

Perhaps I could have passed by the building where I was tortured and remembered some of the things that happened to me in there. I saw in the papers here that if we win, our new government will open up the torture cells for tourists and national healing as they did in Azania.

But here, on my bad days, even a running tap of water can plunge me into a deep depression. I have been defenseless because I do not live here. We are heir to a time where we can say we are citizens of the world but even then a citizen of the world has to have a home and has to be able to go back to it.

You once wrote to me and said that by sending money to the movement, I was making a lot of things possible. I am not sure how much money I have sent to the movement over the years. For me it was like paying tithe or penance. But it never bought me sleep. This is not to say it has been all bad. I mean I have survived, made one or two friends and even on many occasions been happy—I suppose it has been a lot like life. But damn! Ogum, I could have used some less complicated and more pleasant crossroads.

I know you did not write to me to hear about my problems. You wrote to ask for my forgiveness and I was quite reluctant to give it. I felt a deep sense of betrayal and blamed you more than I blamed Sukena. I was quite willing to forgive Sukena but not you. "He is my brother. How could he do this to me?" I kept asking myself. Is it because in spite of all my talk, I felt that Sukena belonged to me and you had stolen her from me? And if I truly loved Sukena, why should her betrayal sting less than yours? I still haven't settled these questions but please do know you have my forgiveness even though I recognize surely it cannot be mine to give.

I have been dead for many years now. Widows are allowed to remarry—what about those who love exiles? Shouldn't they be allowed to find happiness too? At any rate there is nothing for me to forgive except for a bruised warrior ego.

I have decided to return shortly after the elections. I have returned to school to finish up, though if we succeed in building a strong society that is less corrupt, it should take a while before I find a job! I will let you know of my plans as they progress but I expect to be coming back at the beginning of next year. Call everything I am doing here to make this possible, my one year plan.

Please share this letter with Sukena and my father. I wrote it with them in mind as well. In your letter you also said that Baba is worried and wants to hear from me. I will write him a long letter. I promise. There are many things that could not be said ten years ago between all of us. Can we say them now? Tell Baba that soon I will be watching the evening sky with him and we will be able to talk for many hours.

Do you forgive me?

Your brother,

Kalumba

February 4th

OGUM AND SUKENA

Anger is funny—once it has a name it goes away. For years I have been angry at Ogum and Sukena. I knew even before they told me that they hooked up a few weeks after I left.

They could have at least waited for my dead body to get cold. A few miserable weeks.

Also, why the pretense that he writes to me all the time? The last thing they wanted after they hooked up was to have regular contact. Now that I might be returning, they want to resume communication.

But this anger, I am putting it behind me. Having met Melissa, I now know that anger had the name of loneliness. And having heard from Ogum, I know my anger also had the name of a pain ignored. What I hated all these years was the thought that they had gone on about their lives—without the least bit of guilt. Now, don't I feel foolish. I also know now that my anger had another name—being forgotten, yet missing my friends, my family, and my country. This is a time of hope.

February 5th

Melissa Meets Mrs. Shaw

Melissa came to my place so that we could walk to Mrs. Shaw's together. She wore earrings that seemed to coil and loop forever. I asked if in winter they get cold, and she laughed and said yes. She had on a long black skirt and brown leather boots. She lifted up her skirt to reveal some really ugly winter long underwear, then added that she wanted to look good because she felt like she was going to meet my parents. I thought to myself, *If only she knew.*

I also had tried to look good for her. Soon after finishing Ogum's letter, which I might or might not mail out, I washed my dreads. I hadn't washed my hair for a long time, about two months, and I watched dead skin and oil congregate around my feet in the shower. My wounds stung from the soap, but I did not mind much. The burns have closed—though I still had to drip dry.

I had to wait a long time for the hair to dry. I put on a pair of new jeans, leather shoes, and a black sweater, taking care to have a cotton T-shirt underneath it.

The jeans now have a personal history. In the small store where I bought them, I was asked a total of seven times by different salespeople if I needed help, until I started to think that even though I didn't, perhaps they knew better than me. But I was in a good mood and did not want to sully it with insults. It is tough being black in this country. I miss the luxury of being an ethnic majority. I have counted the different kinds of racism—overt, class, institutional, historical, paternalistic, violent, subtle, with a goal, without a goal, conscious, unconscious. To be black is to be in a constant war—one has to weigh battles and fights worth the trouble and those that detract. But no matter, I had a good evening ahead of me, an evening so rare that had the salespeople been dressed in Ku Klux Klan outfits I would still have bought the jeans, happily too.

It still has not been dastardly cold, so the walk was pleasant and unhurried. It feels like we have been taking these kind of walks for a long time, yet this is only the second time I am seeing Melissa. The snow has, however, been piled up along sidewalks and roads, and it has lost the uniformity and beauty that comes with the first fall. It is now quite ugly and uneven, treacherous looking. We didn't talk much on our way except when we stopped at a store to buy some wine and debated on what kind to take. Eventually we decided on plenty and bought a huge jug—my kinda gal.

I knew something was wrong when Mrs. Shaw opened the door looking very much like a grandmother, but I couldn't quite place what it was. She had on a heavy-looking dress with yellow polka dots on it and a fading blue shawl wrapped around her shoulders. Her hair was wound loosely into a bun with grey whispery whiskers jutting out all over her head. It looked like she was chewing on something, and when she said hello I saw it was her gums, the way old people constantly move their gums as if looking for their teeth. I began to think that in our last meeting I was probably drunker than I thought.

Nevertheless, she had made a delicious pork roast, which we ate with biscuits and homemade gravy. She did not drink any of the wine we brought over. She drank several cups of hot chocolate, and since she was not partaking in the wine, neither I nor Melissa could indulge in it liberally, but no matter, by the end of dinner that was the least of my worries. She was definitely not the Mrs. Shaw I had met earlier: either she was in character then or now.

"What do your parents do?" she asked Melissa.

"My father is in a jail. He is a political prisoner but was tried like a common criminal . . . a Puerto Rican and a Nuyorican. My mother teaches at a high school in New York," she answered.

"And they let her teach?" Mrs. Shaw asked Melissa, sounding combative.

"It is one of those alternative schools," Melissa answered.

"I suppose we all must fight for something," Mrs. Shaw said, as if she didn't care one way or another. "My dear, would you like something else to eat?" At this point, Melissa looked at me to ask what was going on, but I didn't know.

So the dinner dragged on. Just when I thought it couldn't get worse, Mrs. Shaw asked Melissa, "Remind me again, which percent are you? Which fifty percent are you?"

What the hell is going on? I wondered. *Where is my Mrs. Shaw?*

"Oh, you mean the 1998 referendum? I am the fifty that no one hears about—independence," Melissa answered.

What to make of it? Very odd behavior. After dinner I took the dishes to the kitchen and started washing them. As I put the pork away, on the fridge I saw a poem written with refrigerator magnets. As soon I finished it, I knew it was a coded message for me.

In life,
sometimes we wear masks to live.
How can I show my face to a stranger
if behind it lies an empty skull?

Who and what do we kill in order to live?
If you want to see the skull behind your mask
Then you must learn to walk in here alone . . .

"It's a lovely poem, isn't it?" she asked, as if she had just found it there.

"Did you write it?" I asked. At this point Melissa came into the kitchen to bring back the bottle of wine, so I am not sure if Mrs. Shaw's answer would have been different.

"No, don't be silly. I don't write poetry. It could be anyone who has passed here through the years. It has been there for as long I can remember. It was there when you were here," Mrs. Shaw said as Melissa leaned over her to look at the poem. Melissa didn't say anything, though I thought she betrayed a look of irritation at the poem. After she left, Mrs. Shaw said, "Now that is a good young woman. Very sturdy hips," and she followed Melissa to the dining room. Disturbed, I numbly finished off the dishes, and soon Melissa and I left.

"I liked her. Could be anyone's grandma, you know? She looked a bit lonely if you ask me," Melissa said as we made our way back.

"She has a skull for a husband," I said somewhat bitterly. I had to tell her the whole skull story. She listened in amazement, laughing in disbelief when I finished.

"History based on a profound lie that does not matter— what a contradiction," she summed up. "What do you fight and die for?" And answering her question for me, she said that we should go see her father in prison. "Since we are doing the meet the family thing," she added.

"You haven't met my family yet. I am going next year if you want to visit," I offered, to which she replied that Mrs. Shaw is close to me, scars and all, even though I do not know it. That response irritated me, and I didn't say anything for a few blocks.

"I belong to the other half," she said to me.

"What other half?" I asked.

"The other half you don't hear about in the news or read about or hear people discussing," she said. "The other half that voted for an independent Puerto Rico at the referendum . . . The freedom half," she explained proudly.

I had to remind her she'd already told Mrs. Shaw.

We got home. When she was in the bathroom I realized that I was in love. Just like that, no frills and thrills. In the tenth year of my exile, ten months before my return, I had fallen in love. Not the kind of love that was in my past, that buoyed me even as it destroyed me, the kind of love that I'd once, and possibly still, had for Sukena. This was different. It was a lazy love, the kind that went to dinner and got drunk sometimes or often, that slept in, and that enjoyed being with Melissa and me. It did not demand a revolution out of me— all it asked was that I be there. Now that, I can do! It hit me suddenly but with no surprise. Perhaps I had fallen in love with her the first time I saw her at Eagle's Bar and had for-gotten in my drunkenness, this love was familiar. "We need another mirror in here," she yelled. "And soap. Hell, we need a new apartment," she said as she walked out, long underwear in hand.

Nothing spectacular in bed . . . I have to seriously con-sider laying off the booze or, more plausible, get on the Viagra wagon of happy old men. But last night no choice so thank god for oral sex—went down on her for what felt like a long time and I thought she would rip my dreads out. "At least one of us is satisfied," she said mischievously as I emerged all tired from between her thighs.

The last time I had enjoyed sex, truly enjoyed sex, was two or three nights before I had left . . . ten years ago with Sukena. We didn't know then that disaster was around the corner, but it was one of those evenings when sex feels special for no rea-son. We were both in the mood—wanted to see how much pleasure we could give each other. Sukena is the only woman I have known who takes pleasure in small doses, orgasms like it is medicine. But still, that night, she was willing to overdose.

Ten years ago ... have to start living. Good fucking sex—here I come!

FATHERS AND BAD POEMS, ETC.

No doubt inspired by Mrs. Shaw's refrigerator poetry, I have spent the past few days playing around with a poem I am including in the e-mail to Ogum for Baba. I am stalling— It would be easier to simply tell him that things have been fucked up, but I think he will understand the seriousness of it in this form. I will see how it goes, but in the meantime, I am happy to write to him in Kyukato—whenever things got serious we spoke in our language, so perhaps even more than the words and meaning, it is the gesture that will count. I am returning. I need to find a home when I return.

NEITHER HERE NOR THERE / OR PARALLELS

I

Walking down State Street, looking up
or down, a parallel universe. Here or over there
I am on Mandela Street. No matter what I tell myself,
this world of world giving birth I cannot touch.
I am on a full stomach here. In that other world
I am not hungry—this stomach of mine belongs to us.
While I am here I name that other world sunrise
to try and surprise it in evening, but between
the divide of day and night, this world and that world,
the sun sets or rises ready to orphan. I am
the proverb and riddle that tugs at the same body.
When I am here I am here. I do not sleep; my eyes
are always open. I have no name, I have two names
or four. Who am I? Whose am I? And when I cry
my tears cut deep like acid, reveal bone. Farther ahead,
I see others like me—Wiwa or our Shakara. One

will be hanged and the other was buried alive—thought
is always treason. Into what do people like me die?
Into what worlds?

II

Always outside my window—my shadow flustered
like a ghost waiting for me. But at times my shadow
keeps getting lost under trees, in tunnels and restaurants.
But when I left home to come here, I found my shadow
dancing under the tree where I was hanged. When I close
my eyes I find my world changing form, twisting like
a snake in search of a second skin. And I tell myself I will
make a home out of a house, level the earth and then drive
my demons to sea. But my heart lives in the shadow—I
always return to things I cannot name. In our world, there
are epitaphs waiting for our names. One day I will meet
them—one day I will meet myself.

III

Baba, home is longing not to be at two places at the same time.
This morning when I woke up to bullets and mourning,
the graves are shallow and the paper I am writing
on is as deep as a gold mine. This morning, I woke up
pretending there is no pain, and blood is mud painted colors
of well-being. This morning we are one hundred years old,
Shakara was being buried alive as Guevara watched, and when
they hanged Kimathi years later, Waiyaki was there—both
were there when Puerto Rican nationalists were hanged.
Baba, let us plant fruits instead of planting shadows.
Baba, I am writing these words to tell you that I am coming
home to see if I will find myself there, old, tall and straight,
the baobab tree you planted.

After the poem I end up thinking about Ogum's father.
Ogum simply couldn't stand him when we were growing up,
hated him. I think I understand it now. You hate that which

forces you to grow outside your home. His childhood he spent always being teased, always the one to conform, always the outsider, and to top it all off, with a preacher for a father, unapologetically Lulato. Maybe that was why he spent so much time at home with me and my father. Beyond tending my mother's grave and telling stories about the old, my baba was not up to much. Strange, I used to envy Ogum; his father was a man of action, unlike mine. Didn't take shit, spoke his mind, and died for the truth. Maybe everyone wants everyone's parents but their own.

Is this why he is so angry with me? That I know he did not love his father? Still no consolation for my demons—I cannot say that for sure. His heart broke that night—I saw it later when eventually my own grief let me see other people.

I should have died that night—I have to stop saying that to myself. I am alive, aren't I? For years I have felt I should have. Now I am not so sure, ten years later—I am not so sure.

When the prodigal son returns from exile, what does he find? Do I really want to find out?

February 28th

TELL TALES OF . . .

My grandmother told me a lot of stories: One day a hungry hyena was invited to a feast of bulls and cows, human kneecaps and other joints. Hyenas love kneecaps more than flesh because they can chew one kneecap for days. This feast of flesh first and endless chewing into kneecaps meant that the hyena would eat into perpetuity. He came across a fork in the road and on sniffing which path to follow discovered that both led to feasts. On listening closely he could hear the sound of mouths lapping and teeth gnashing into kneecaps. Now, he thought to himself, *This is quite a conundrum. If I attend the one on my right, I miss the one on my left. And if I attend the one on my left, I miss the one on my right. This is my failing— there is only one of me. But I have four legs, a front paw and a hind paw on each path. I will walk both paths.* And so he did, only the distance between the two paths became wider and wider until he split into two and died.

Exile!!!!

March 1st

REPLIES TO E-MAILS SENT

I received an e-mail from my father in response to my poem. I am not sure he knows how to deal with me but that's okay, it has been many years. It feels very warm to hear from him even though he does not say much—not his old voluble self, no history lesson, no talk about my civic duties as a citizen of the world. He has changed, but how? To me he is that man from ten years ago who saw less and less of me as I grew up, as I became political and paid my dues to whatever it is that we owe life. He gave me a wide berth: your mistakes, your successes, your life, he would say. I have seen the freaks that are churned out by controlling parents—evangelicals' kids becoming devils as adults, doctors' children becoming murderers. Maybe all we want from our parents is for them to share the burden of our living. My father could have shared the burden of my mistakes and my exile, Baba Ogum the burden of Ogum's internal exile, and Sukena's parents the burden of her dreams. Maybe it's easier said than done.

E-MAIL FROM BABA, SUBJECT HEADING: SON, WE ARE ALWAYS SOMEWHERE

Dear Kalumba,

I am pleased to see that you have decided to finally resume communicating with us. And even more, I am happy when told that you are planning on returning home. Home is home and I would not be happy to hear that you fear returning. Even at its worst, if you find a narrow opening that allows you to return, then you should, so that you can help to rebuild the country. I will write again but let me say you would remain my child even when the country rejected you.

All is well,

Your one and only Father.

March 10th

HARD LABOR

Dearest Diary, I know I haven't been writing much. My life has fallen into a predictable pattern. Melissa comes each evening. We cook, eat, smoke pot, and make love. I suppose that is something new, but let's face it, sex is most remarkable when you are not having problems getting it up. After numerous false starts, I am just glad to be taking it for granted.

I wake up early and work on my dissertation. I have been thinking of getting a job because I need to save up some start-up money when I return. I do not make enough as a teaching assistant. Out of my 1,100-dollar-a-month paycheck, I spend 400 on rent, 60 on electricity, 100 on the phone, 160 on food, 150 on beer, 100 for SIDCF, 50 on movies, plays, or music shows. That leaves me with about 80, which I save up to pay the 350-dollar university activity fee. I could cut back on some things which might afford me a plane ticket, but I'd still arrive back home with nothing except a piece of paper that says *Doctor* on it. I am also worried about the pot, and I have decided to cut it out altogether in case I decide to look for a second job. Perhaps it would be easier to apply for research grants and use that money to make my escape.

I have found that I dread working as a laborer once again. Six years of hard labor is enough—washed dishes, loaded trucks, painted houses, waited tables, delivered mail, etc., but what else could I do after dropping out? I knew my father would be disappointed, but I was done with living for him, or in the spirit of honesty, for myself.

I couldn't stand the teachers who hadn't lived for a day, who didn't know the stink of nationalism or the coldness of torture yet stood in front of class and psychoanalyzed exile, did a Marxist critique of Africa and a deconstructionist reading of postindependence nationalism—fuck 'em! I often wondered what it would be like to be a surgeon who taught the theory of surgery without ever assisting at one. I left in a huff and puff, but here I am at it once again. Perhaps I was wrong, or this is all I know how to do. But no matter . . . I know the smell of teargas and much worse, and those things that I remember, I cannot forget, and those I can't remember should remain unremembered.

Life as a laborer—what a time that was. A new hire from Haiti loading trucks in Atlanta's heat says he used to be a doctor. Funniest thing we had heard in a long time, and we laughed for an equally long time—a tragedy, of course, but funny in that we had all been something. Poor doctor did not speak very good English and therefore couldn't take a medical conversion exam. In this merciless crowd, a sneeze, a cough, and a fart were all referred to the doctor. But I stopped laughing as hard when one day, I wouldn't be skins in a football game—the doctor just took off his shirt and took my place. My scars bring me shame; his did not do the same to him. What am I guilty of?

Strange that we never went to each other's homes, never spoke about the things that brought us here. We smoked cigarettes, shared an occasional joint, drank a lot of beer together but never spoke about these things that caused so much pain. We were what we were—what would have been the point? We were alive, weren't we?

Also a Palestinian engineer who used to tell us his mother would take him and his sister to the West Bank and point to land that used to be theirs, pointed to stones that walled her in when she was a child. I saw myself as a kid. In exile, as a Muslim engineer he was unemployable—what if he made bombs at work? So here he was hauling boxes with the doctor. And a Vietnamese old man who hardly ever said a word, always with a broom, sweeping all the time. The hub was laced with white workers who mostly kept to themselves.

So there we were—me, the doctor from Haiti, a lawyer from Jamaica, a computer scientist from Ghana whose credentials were not recognized and who was retaking some exam, an unemployable Palestinian, and several historians from an assortment of Third World countries—a medley of exiles loading trucks in the motherboard, as the computer scientist called the US.

Why did we come here? We know why we left, but why did we come here? Versions of Sukena's parents, only with a better education and access to credit cards? And to differentiate ourselves, we always recalled the lives we lived when we had gardeners, housemaids, and servants. Poetic justice—now at least we understood how they felt. Not that our experience here would make much of a difference: one day we will all be returning to reclaim our stations in life that come with house servants. Like slave foremen, we will probably be meaner to them than the bosses who did not taste the demeaning labor of exile.

The guy from Haiti always came to work dressed in a suit. "Got to look your best," he would say, and underneath the suit, a labyrinth of scars. Perhaps he was right. What you are inside is bad enough; why look like it?

March 11th

Why Do We Come Here?

I woke up with the question of why we come here ringing in my head. We left because we would have been disappeared. But why didn't I, for example, go to Zimbabwe or Cuba? I could have taught literature there at a high school. Why the United States? Why the belly of this fucking whale that will not spit me out? The doctor from Haiti, but for his conscience, could have thrived alongside Papa Doc. Papa Doc was a dictator so vicious that even in my country we were scared of him, I liked to joke.

Why do we come here? I know why I left. The answer is simple. But I do not know why I came here and now I am returning. Or perhaps I choose not to know. But I do know that the movement does not complain about the dollars I and others like me send—they are able to do more with a US dollar than a Zimbabwean dollar. The movement sent me here for the dollars—but why did I come here? Perhaps I was following the glossy advertisements of a super-sized America that covered the walls of Sukena's home.

March 12th

MISSING MRS. SHAW

I have been thinking about Mrs. Shaw a lot. I will go see her again in a few days—I am excited. The prospect makes me feel like I would when I was little and we would go with my father to visit my grandmother. I haven't seen her again at Eagle's, though with Melissa on pot and at home, I have had no cause to be up and about the town. I still haven't seen Melissa's paintings, though from what I gather she lives off her work. I'm not very interested in paintings as a general rule, though I am curious to see hers. Last night she mentioned that we should go visit her father in jail sometime in April. Icarus Prison—the name itself a reminder, but of what? There is no escape? That is the reason they are in prison?

I'm very eager to meet him. From what Melissa has told me about him, he is quite a character, very talkative, political as hell, and, she said with a laugh, *easily agitated*.

March 14th

MINTING MONEY

The sweetness, the sweet smell of the almighty dollar—Jesus be praised. I gave a talk on exile and the movement. I was invited by the English Department at Yale for a cool 1,100 dollars. I joined the movement while at Nairobi University, and I often think of those days of naïveté. Since then I have not been in the picture, save for my 10 percent. From what I have gathered, career politicians have bought shares in the move-ment. A message was sent out a few years ago that argued that we had to grow up as a movement and accept that if we are to play a role in national politics we have to play ball with the big boys. I did not agree with this move, for too many movements have been bought out—it happened with the independence movements. Surely we ought to know better.

But of course I didn't say all these things at my talk—in-stead I spoke of the positive things. How the movement has influenced the youth culture, how it is poised to take over, and how it understands history. I felt like ambassadors I've watched squirm on public television as they try to explain away genocide. Luckily there were no tough questions during the Q&A; everyone wants hope—*willing seller, willing buyer,* I say. Maybe I'm being overdramatic; I need to remind myself things are really getting better in Kwatee.

What was interesting about the Q&A—even though I hadn't talked about it, I was asked about forgiveness and how a French philosopher whose name I cannot remember said that forgiveness could not be asked for but had to be given. Could I comment on that? Would the movement extend for-giveness even before the Dictator and his cohorts requested it? This was an interesting question, and I took time to think about it. I thought about Mrs. Shaw's skull, my own torturers, and the past ten years.

"Of course you have to forgive your enemy even when they don't ask for forgiveness. I have read of people forgiving their torturers and tormentors even when the perpetrators haven't asked for it. That is how the victim heals. But the situation is more difficult when the enemy still wields more power than you, mostly acquired through theft and murder. I would suggest that forgiveness begins with the return of stolen goods, which in our instance means freedom, and the material basis of that freedom," I said. I am not sure, but I think either Mrs. Shaw or I had said the same thing at our first meeting. Or did my father say it? Or Ogum's father?

"But can there be forgiveness without redress? An absolute forgiveness just because it is the nature of forgiveness to forgive?" the same man asked again. *Just what the hell is going on here? Get your head out of your ass!* I thought to myself, then replied "No" and left it at that. I couldn't understand the difficulty of *return what you have stolen before we speak of forgiveness.* Perhaps I was being simplistic, but if you have stolen land from somebody, shouldn't your giving it back be a condition for forgiveness?

Other questions were along the same vein. For example, Would I say I had been hosted well in the United States? And what are the conditions that a guest is supposed to meet? I thought about my years as a laborer, and I had to say that I earned my living just like anyone else, had been underemployed and exploited with others like me, alongside some of my hosts who happened to be from poor and black backgrounds. I thought about black people who had been shot in Los Angeles and New York and how the United States supported the government that had sent me to exile. What conditions should a guest meet? "I'm not so sure I am a guest. We have been living in each other's houses for so long, it doesn't make sense for me to think of myself as a guest. Rather, I had come to collect what was owed me, only my 'host' was not so obliging—so I continue to labor and to plot." This last part drew a huge applause. So I repeated it again. And the questions rolled on and my answers rolled out.

And my last words to leave my listeners with something to take home and mull over? "Look," I said. "How many of you know the name of the leader of our movement?" Only a few people raised their hands. "You see, no one knows his name, because we do not cultivate cults of leadership. We have a movement that has leaders without leadership. Betrayal will not be easy," I said, to wild applause and murmurs of recognition.

A professor of mine had recommended me to a professor at Yale who in turn invited me. After about ten hours of preparation, two hours presenting, and a dinner with faculty members and students at that school, I was 1,100 dollars richer. At the moment of receiving my check, I suddenly knew what I needed to do. I would become a professional speaker. I would specialize on the immigrant and exile topics. I would try to give the same talk once a month. I would learn the same speech by heart. That will be 11,000 dollars, give or take, by the time I am leaving. That should be enough to set me up. Exile will buy my ticket back.

March 28th

My Dream Catcher

Shit! Yesterday was my birthday. Hitting forty now looks inevitable. Mrs. Shaw has something I want—old age.

Melissa brought me a painting for my birthday. I have to say I do not understand it. It has swirling colors that swim around bowls that keep emptying out more colors, at times dominated by red and at other times dominated by black, into other bowls. It's dizzying, but even though I do not understand it, I feel attracted to it. It has a cycle of giving and taking that at times seems both violent and communal, something like a chain gang or plantation workers or people mourning, only these are bowls.

Womb she called it. The scar that runs through my stomach inspired it. It was as if a bayonet had reached into my insides and ripped out my womb and now exile was doing it over and over again. I shuddered at the thought, but I will hang the painting anyway. Nightmares will be afraid to come near the horror—a perfect dream catcher.

We had dinner, pork ribs and rice, she smoked some pot, we made love, and then we went out to Eagle's Bar, where after a few birthday shots I was ready to come home. I am changing rapidly. We spoke about going to see her father.

Melissa never really talks about her mother, but I assume she will be there as well. She doesn't talk about her mother, probably because the dad, well insulated in jail could do no wrong, while the mother, as the reigning law, had plenty of opportunity. But then again, I don't talk much about mine either, mostly because she died when I was young and there isn't much to say except to talk about her absence. It is very real, almost like a person, this absence. But often I would rather not talk about it. It is quite strange how Melissa and I fit together, demanding nothing from each other, living in near silence. I am sure this will have to change, though I don't understand what there is to gain in sharing each other's pain. Love inhabits all sorts of spaces, even silent ones, I think.

Yet it's not that we don't talk—we talk about a lot of stuff. She was amused by my idea of becoming an expert on exile. I tell her everything about my day and memories from my past. And she does the same. But it does not feel like talking. It seems like talking should lead to tears and blood. But this is working for us. At least it is for me, having spent the better part of my life drawing blood and tears from myself and others. This is different. It is nice to feel light with someone else. But there is a certain amount of desperation to it as well. It is as if we are protecting each other from ourselves and from each other.

Suddenly the terrifying thought—what if Melissa left me? What if tomorrow morning she said that she was leaving and did not want to ever see me again?

April 1st

Is Spring Really Here?

9-11 was just a few months ago, and Madison was in mourning—but we have recovered better than most. Or perhaps we have tried too hard to forget. Spring is here. Mrs. Shaw says that in spring, people come to life; like roses they blossom as they shed their winter clothes and emerge in short skirts and tops that reveal legs and cleavage, and men who have been going to the gym all winter, well—legs and cleavage.

But this is Mrs. Shaw, and something about spring reminds her of the fall. Gumming her teeth, she adds something about the trees and how their changing color is as a result of the leaves asphyxiating. They cannot breathe in the winter as the air gets colder and colder and the sun disappears. So beauty is death. And me, of course it goes back to how pissed off I would be if somebody found my dying beautiful.

State Street attests to the truth of her words—the whole city seems to be in ecstasy. In midafternoon people are sitting outside cafés, restaurants, and bars, others leaning over the balconies of their apartments. A spontaneous carnival of loud music, different kinds of music, from hip-hop to salsa, obscenely loud music with bass lines that thud out your breath, street musicians with guitar cases open for tips, a drummer who uses cans and plastic containers, an old man dressed in orange who plays a shrill flute, people dressed to match the rainbow—it is a good time, especially past the only African restaurant in town, which kindly billows out smoke from roast meat into the street.

This is Wisconsin, and what does it care about spring? Rain by 6:00 in the evening. A cool rain with thick heavy drops that tear into the face. This is my favorite time. It is the closest I feel to being home. A storm is water. That I am returning at the end of the year, that by this time next year I will be home, that my future is now mine to win or lose—this makes today's rain all the more delicious. I walked through the rain to Mrs. Shaw's house and asked if she wanted to go for a walk. So there we were, the old woman and the young man, hopping and skipping down State Street straight into Eagle's Bar—and proceeded to get stupidly drunk as the storm raged outside. I sat there until a poem that had been inside of me rushed out.

9-11—AT EAGLE'S BAR

Blinds—a thousand half-slits. Sliced sunlight
makes parallel stripes on painted feet, as face half-
blinded by sleep rests on palms cupped to cheek.
The sun keeps falling and the parallel stripes,

laced with smoke, keep climbing up painted feet,
climbing up higher the dark green bar walls till,
as darkness outside finishes its embrace of the day
to bring night, lit bar lights drown them—daylight
has been hell. Now, it's a little past 2:00 a.m.—the jukebox comes to a halt—a last glance at an unfinished pool-
game and an unfinished love affair—feet, hesitant lone
steps herd to the door—it's been so quiet— The night
feels so certain—safe—without mirrors, without shadows
—no aeroplanes—no moon or stars in the sky—then
on the tracks, a terrible last train moving West to East

April 4th

REMEMBRANCES

"Kalumba, I am dying. I have Alzheimer's," Mrs. Shaw finally said. She had invited me over for dinner, and remembering the message on her fridge, I went alone. She had roasted
some goat in her oven, to remind us of home, she said. She
remained very quiet throughout dinner, and all my attempts
to engage her in conversation were met with silence. I was
thinking that in a very short time, we had become very dysfunctional, like a real family, and was beginning to smile at the
thought when she said she was dying.

At first I laughed heartily but realized she was—damn it,
I can't resist the pun—dead serious. "What do you mean,
Mrs. Shaw?"

How could my feisty liquor-guzzling lipstick-wearing red
cowboy boots–clad mother/grandmother be dying?

"Without my memory I am nothing. You must promise to
take care of it when the time comes."

"Take care of what?"

"It . . . this, my shell, whatever it is that remains when
memory is gone," she said, gesturing toward her chest.

"You mean your body? I am leaving for home soon." I
thought later just how naturally I said home to include her as

well. Unconsciously I think of her as a fellow exile too. And who is to say she isn't?

"Yes, my body, and I don't care where you are going to be. I want you to kill it. If I can't remember myself, what good am I to myself? Promise you will destroy it!" She kept referring to herself as if speaking about a tree.

"Mrs. Shaw, I will not do it. I am not a killer. Besides, you look well," I offered. "Can't you see the headline? *Troubled Black Man From Black Africa Kills Old White British Woman.* I would be fried on the spot," I added, trying to lighten the conversation and to buy myself some time to think.

She did not laugh.

"You find a way. You are not to leave me a shell. Do you understand me?" she commanded. "Do you want to know what's going to happen to me?" she asked, then continued when I said nothing.

"I will forget everything: taking my medicine, cooking, people I knew, things I did. I will not know who I am. I will have to be helped to the toilet by strangers. They will hate me for holding on to life. I will forget everything. Like why there is a skull in my drawer. If I can't remember my revenge, what good is that life? So you must find a way. Being like putty in the hands of strangers is like falling into the enemy camp. I would rather be shot by my own blood. Promise me."

Mrs. Shaw spoke firmly, urgently, but her eyes holding mine reminded me of the look Baba Ogum had just before he got shot—hope, fear, resignation, dignity, and then peace. Hers now were all dignity.

I promised her I would find a way that would leave me in the clear and, in her own words, leave history safe. She was worried about what I would do with the skull. I repeated to her that I didn't think in the eyes of history the killing of her husband mattered. Another incident would have happened to provoke the same anger, same freedom, and same history. We would still have Eagle's, or others like us would. But what did she want me to do with the skull? She did not yet know, she said, but she thought there was one last joke left in her—she would figure something out. This old lady never quits.

"There is another thing you should know." Her tone became serious, even apologetic. It turns out that she had called the African American mail carrier "boy." The old colonist in her was coming out as her true self got lost in amnesia. He wasn't amused. He had started leaving her mail by her door instead of ringing the bell like he did before. I told her I would have done the same thing in his shoes.

"But we are family," she said, as if at last she had won our argument.

"So is he," I retorted.

But the guilt, the fucking guilt—was it my father who used to say we are all guilty of something? Even from life itself? His luxury in having not done much, and we who had made choices, we watched others die or get killed? What about our guilt? Is that all that remains?

"It is almost as if it is wired in another part of me," she continued. "I will not forget the first lessons of racism, the fear since I was a day old that was put in me, to fear all that is not me, all that is not white, and to trust and love all that is white. Racism is a language I will never forget. The devil gets me in the end." She was close to tears. The loose skin on her hands twitched uncontrollably.

I did not know what to tell her. I was feeling guilty because I was fascinated by the idea—that in the end, racism and hate could become the bookends to such a remarkable life. And if love were the first language that we learnt, then wouldn't it become our bookend?

"Listen, but that is not who you are," I assured her. "You are leaving who you are behind, in the world that you have changed and in the lives you have touched. Mrs. Shaw, if you can't remember, how can you be held responsible?" I was thinking of my own situation.

"Where did you learn that crap?" she asked harshly, then more gently added, "But I appreciate it, though. I just wanted to give you fair warning in case you take offense when you come to visit me one day and I ask you to fetch me a glass of lemonade and call you 'Juma boy.'"

"Mrs. Shaw, I might as well ask now. Why didn't you just leave him? Your husband, I mean?"

"I had to go through him. It had to be through him. I might have left him and been safe, but I would never have been free. It had to be done," she said. "And I loved him," she added softly. "I must have loved him."

I wondered who she was trying to convince, herself or me?

"And not that I care one way or the other, but what are you going to do with all your stuff? Give it to your English relatives? Your house, car?" I asked, more curious than anything. I really do not care; my gigs as an expert on exile were bringing in an extra 1,000 dollars or so a month. And for less work than my TA-ship. For my return, that is more than I need. I could not take her money even if she offered . . . well, perhaps.

"Give it back to Africa. But not to the politicians. I cannot trust a politician, even a revolutionary. Not even the movement . . . an endowed chair for exiled African professors. The one condition is that they must be political exiles. Doesn't matter whether it's the reactionaries kicking out the revolutionaries or revolutionaries kicking out the reactionaries," she answered.

"You are my first professor of choice," she added. She is not joking when she says she has one last joke left in her.

"No, thanks. When I am gone I am not returning," I said.

"Returning depends on which way you are facing. Well, just in case. You really never know."

"Just in case," I admitted to myself as much as to her. When I was not thinking about returning, I needed everything to be perfect: my relationship with Sukena, friendships, etc., even the SIDCF. Now that I am returning, questions I had long buried are coming to the surface. Or rather, truths I have long known are becoming real.

There was nothing more to do. I stood up, and Mrs. Shaw walked me to the door. I reached out and hugged her. I felt like she had disappeared in my arms.

"About Melissa, I felt terrible. When she was here I was in a panic. You don't know what it's like to doubt what you know and don't know . . . what you knew and never knew. I wasn't sure if I had met her before or not . . . your wife or friend, my daughter. Good days and bad days—It was a really bad day," she said as we let go of each other. "Remember, this will only be a shell. I will be long gone," she whispered.

I stepped out her door, down the three or four steps. I wanted to look back and say something comforting. Baba Ogum and his sermons: *Always look back. Even if you might turn into a pillar of salt.* So I did, and still at the door, she looked crooked, gnomish, hairy, and strangely white because of the full glare of the lights behind her. I laughed and waved and she waved back.

How will history judge her? Is it even aware of her? If the history we know is not the history that happened, which one counts more? A whole nation has been built on a lie that we live as if true. Would we have been a better nation if the truth about our independence was known? How much of the truth that will slowly erode from her brain matters? Can history be so trivial as to depend on one single act? I often wonder about that.

For now, there is just me and her. I understand I am closer to her than to most people on this planet of ours. And it is not just the crossroads of our history, our being exiles. There is something more primordial here, something from before the British ever set foot in Kwatee—A grandmother recognizing her grandson? Two human beings in a friendship? Solidarity just by being human? Perhaps something fundamental does a better job than the primordial. There are so many things in each other's company we take for granted. And now we can add remembering and forgetting to that list. Some die to forget and others to remember. Whether for life or death, I need to remember what happened to me. I need to know what exactly happened to me in that torture chamber, what I said and did not say. I need to look back, and to really look back I need to return. Well, then, all in due course.

April 14th

ICARUS—THE BIG APPLE

To get to Icarus, where Melissa's father is serving life imprisonment for bomb making, trumped-up charges, we took a plane to the Big Apple, and then from JFK we took a taxi. The airport looked the same as it had years earlier, except there were armed soldiers every ten feet. Everyone looked tense, and those meeting their loved ones seemed more relieved than happy when they spotted them across secured arrival gates.

I can recognize fear. I grew up with it. I have seen all it all my life: in buses, bars, schools, churches, funerals, and weddings. Or perhaps it was just my nerves. I knew going to a prison to meet Melissa's father would bring back memories, but I think without a doubt this is not the same JFK. Except for the shrill of politicians drilling a wounded population for war, the America outside Madison and other college towns has become a lot quieter, as if everyone is walking around in doubt. The politicians know this fear and anger have to find an outlet—a war is coming!

Even though we were arriving into JFK and it was a domestic flight, me and Melissa were pulled to the side and frisked by airport security to the point of it becoming pornographic: fingers run through hair, bags emptied out, contents questioned. It was only when they brought big German Shepherd dogs to sniff us out and we started laughing that they realized they were being ridiculous and they let us through.

We drove in the taxi for what felt like a long time. We came to a long deserted bridge. There was water all around us, and it was almost pleasant. The sun was out, and in the taxi I could pretend that winter was completely gone. Shortly after the bridge was behind us, everything started turning ugly. Barbed-wire fences that prevented the noise of New York from reaching the prison went up around us. The road was thin, only one lane, and every now and then we had to let pass a truck returning from carrying supplies to the island.

Finally we reached the gate. On it was a sign: "Icarus Island. Home of New York's Boldest." The ambiguity of who is bold fascinated me for a while—the daring criminal or the daring cop? We showed our identification cards. Our names were recorded, and we were directed to a visitor's parking lot. Buildings had no colors—a monotone of brown bricks and white roofs.

Melissa was quiet most of the way, but I could tell she was nervous. "I hate this place," she said. I nodded in agreement, thinking that this could very well have been my fate. Even the flowers planted around the office where visitors are processed looked lonely and imprisoned. They looked as if they were counted every day so as not to exceed the amount calculated to spell prison for the prisoners and home for the warders. There are ten jails on this island, home to 10,000 people, a plaque on the wall said. It is like visiting an industrial park only here it is human beings that are processed according to crimes committed.

After the first checkpoint we went through another five or so until we came to the James B. Thomas Center. Here is the irony announced by a gold-colored plaque—the first jail to be built on this island, it was named after the first African American warden. Now it houses political prisoners—criminals to Americans, prisoners of conscience to the rest of us. I had to wonder what the black wardens and the black political prisoners thought of the dubious honor.

We went through several rooms that kept getting smaller and smaller until we came into a huge room surrounded by thick, see-through glass that I took to be bulletproof. We must have been frisked about fifteen times by the time we made it through. I could see why Melissa hated coming here. It becomes a prison for the visitor as well. Fifteen or more pairs of strange hands at some point come into contact with your body. I was feeling dirty by this time.

Through the glass I saw a guard and a prisoner arguing about something. The prisoner raised his handcuffed hands and started walking away in the direction they had come from. The guard beckoned him and very slowly removed the handcuffs. Neither the prisoner nor the visitor can wait in dignity. It is important for the system that the visitor understands he or she is not being hosted by the loved one; rather, they are both at the mercy of the guards. The man was buzzed into the room, and he started walking toward us. I noticed that many guards surrounded the room, and it felt as if we were in some sport—we the players and they the spectators. Is tragedy a sport?

Melissa's father was not very tall or short. He was thin and wore spectacles, and his gray hair was whispery—he was balding. He had a full beard on a broad face. His skin was paler in comparison to Melissa's, which was a full brown. He was in blue prison overalls and sandals. I had to wonder how it felt knowing that he would probably die in here. Melissa met him a few feet before he reached the table, and they hugged silently, swaying from side to side. He tried to lift her up but failed. They started laughing as if in some sort of childish conspiracy. Melissa had asked him what that was all about with the guard.

"He is new. He has to be broken in, you know, otherwise he will walk all over you. He wanted me to wear my handcuffs to come out here. And I told him, look, even within a prison I have some rights. I will walk back and then it will be between you and Amnesty International." He laughed and added, "That is the one thing guards are scared of—Amnesty International." To me he said, "My name is Rafael . . . but everyone calls me Rafael." We laughed.

I told him my name, and we shook hands.

"My daughter told me she had found herself a politico, and I told her to be careful; I know where they end up. Warning: by coming here they will open a file on you." He spoke fast and jovially. I could feel it was going to be easy being around him.

"My guess is, they will call it the internationalization of terrorism. It has always been that way," I said. Melissa's father laughed. I was surprised that they did not have guards around, writing down everything that was said. Probably the tables were bugged.

"Melissa, is your mother not coming today?"

"I don't know. I haven't spoken to her for a while." She did not sound apologetic.

"That is no good. She is your mother. In here I am useless. Are you trying to orphan yourself?" To me he sounded more concerned than angry, but Melissa shot back and said that it was she who would decide whether she was an orphan or not.

"Why must she blame you for everything? I am just tired of hearing it," she added.

"But I am to blame. I am in here," he said, matter-of-factly.

"For love, for freedom," she tried to help.

"Yes, but I am in here. Therefore I am to blame."

"I came here to tell you something very important. Kalumba is going back home in January. I am going back with him," Melissa announced, and then waited to let her words do their work.

Her father was in deep thought for a few minutes. So was I. I was stunned. I had casually mentioned that she was welcome to go back with me, but I had no idea she was thinking about it enough to reach such a decision. And I cannot stand the idea of uprooting another human being. What if we traveled all that way and I went Mr. Shaw on her? Even if things never got that bad, marriages fail. And then what for her? I never insisted that Sukena come with me. Now that I know what being away from home means, I cannot ask this of Melissa. Yet I love her.

"I was not aware of this," I said, opting for the old maxim—when in doubt tell the truth.

"It's not for you to decide. I mean, you can decide if you want me to or not, but the burden is on me," she said. But she also gently tapped my hand with her fingers.

"I don't understand. I can understand love and all that romantic stuff, but you haven't even spoken about love. What about your painting?" her father asked. "As your father, I must say you have known him for only two months." He said this looking at me. I did not sense any hostility; he was just saying the things he would have said had I not been there, things that also needed to be said.

"I have a big opening here in New York in October. After that I will be able to paint anywhere."

"Come and see me then as well, will . . ."

"It is the principle behind my decision that counts. I want to see freedom. If I am going to end up like you, then at least I want to know what freedom looks like before I die for it."

Her father looked away. "Freedom . . . it is so abstract. You will only get your heart broken . . ."

"You are not talking to a lovesick little child here . . ." She was getting angry.

"Let me finish . . . Ever since you told me about him, I have been following their politics. The SIDCF will not bring freedom to that country. Kalumba, you must know that. Tell her!" he commanded. He was no longer the amicable thin fellow who had shuffled his prison-issue sandals to meet us.

"Your father is right," I said, trying to think of what else to add. This was a conversation I did not want to have myself, much less with her father.

"Listen to me, both of you. I refuse to be a conversation between two men. Tell me what you think I should know, but I will not be bound by an agreement between the two of you."

She was very angry, and to myself I conceded she had a good point. We cannot sit her down and make decisions for her just because we love her. Who are we to decide from what she needs protection? I am in political exile, her father in detention. No one stopped us.

"Besides, *you* have been in jail half your life and *you*—" She meant me "—have no memory. What can you tell me?" she demanded, jabbing an angry finger at each one of us. I had avoided speaking about the massacres in depth for ten years, but here in Icarus Prison, it seemed appropriate.

"Before I left home," I started, "a soldier about to be involved in a coup came to my father's house. He had a list of names, of people to be jailed or assassinated. I was on that list. My best friend's father was on the list too. If the coup failed, the people on the list were bound to be rounded up and shot. Even without the coup, the government was going to get us. So I ran. The coup failed. Where I hid, an army truck unloaded some soldiers and movement leaders all handcuffed, rounded them into a group, and shot them. There must have been over a hundred of them." I paused, waiting for them to say something. I could feel my body tensing up.

"They piled up the bodies to burn—they were very neat about it—and it was then that I saw one of the bodies begin to move. I could not yell out a warning for him to stop moving. Between the fire about to be lit and the soldiers around us, he was dead anyway. Our eyes met, and I tried to tell him to be quiet and play dead and he just might survive. It was too late. One of the soldiers saw him move from the corner of his eye and shot him. Shot him like he was an afterthought. They burned the bodies. That man was my best friend's father," I said, trying to distance myself from my words, trying to watch them from afar as a stranger would.

"I told Ogum. It was hard, but I did. He took the information to the leadership, and it was hushed up—I have never found out why. Since then, I have wondered what happens to such a movement once in power. "

I didn't even know I had been questioning the movement this deeply, and at that moment I worried about where this road of exile and return would leave me.

Why did Ogum not speak out? That would have brought the whole system down. I suspect it was the leadership—probably the Dictator used something to blackmail the leadership. I know Ogum blames me for his father's death, but isn't he too betraying the memory of his father? For so long I carried the guilt of his death with me; I should have died there too. Neither Melissa nor her father betrayed any pity for me. I suppose it made sense. I was only a witness, and sympathy should be with the dead, but then again, I hadn't told them about the pain. Besides, this was about Melissa—I can only give a warning which even I cannot articulate.

"Kalumba, thank you for talking so honestly . . . It is hard," her father said.

"Well, sir, you are in jail for life and I am an exile. Who else would make a better listener than you?" We all laughed. At some point I will have to think about how and when we laugh. What is it that makes us laugh at certain times, in certain places?

He said to Melissa, "If you think I am trying to stop you because you will not be coming to see me anymore . . . that is not it. What I am going to threaten you with? Cutting you from my estate? But do not idealize their struggle. It is as fucked up as ours is. That is all I am saying. Who do you think gave me up? That was before the days of triangulated cell phones. I was betrayed, Melissa—as their movement will be betrayed. So if you go, go with your eyes open," he said. I thought he felt he had said more than he intended, because he would not look in my direction.

But suddenly he looked up at Melissa. He reached out and held her face between his hands. "Do not even think it." His voice almost gave out. "When you are betrayed by someone you love, something in you knows. Your mother would do no such thing," he added.

Melissa let out a long sigh. I saw tears well up briefly and then disappear. She smiled at her father a smile that I will never forget. She smiled so broadly that her eyes seemed to close. Her lower lip, even though not badly chapped, broke, and little droplets of blood welled up. I had never seen a smile like that on anyone. It contained something deeper than gratitude and love, it radiated life itself—with those words, Rafael had restored something Melissa had lost. I too choked up. He let her face go and held her hands in his.

"Betrayal is not guaranteed. There are many within the movement that see what is happening." I had to say that. Mostly because I hoped so and also because I knew people like Sukena were around. My generation has witnessed so many betrayals that we are the least likely to be fooled. Each generation has to believe it has the capacity not to repeat the mistakes of the one before it—though my father's generation had said the same thing. The cynic knows this and uses it as an excuse not to act, but the revolutionary also believes it and uses it as an excuse *to* act.

"You know, in this country they kill us with silence. You know how they put Indians in reservations; well, think of this prison as a reservation. First we are criminalized. Like myself. I was accused of making bombs even though I am a writer. Not to say that writers do not have technical minds, but Jesus Christ, me a bomb maker? And that is what I was jailed for. Criminalized. Then of course the silence. You want to know the truth of this country, Kalumba? It is built on silence. Look at me: who sings my song? I have been in jail so long that Mandela was released and declared me a prisoner of conscience. How about that?" Then he nudged me with his elbow and added, "Eh?" Which prompted more laughter from all us.

"Kalumba? Ask him why he refused clemency. That is why Mother is not here," Melissa said bitterly.

"I never asked her to wait." He sounded defensive.

"Don't get self-righteous all of a sudden, Papa. You almost had Kalumba believing. Why didn't you accept the clemency?"

"You think I should have?"

"Don't put it on me. Kalumba wants to know. He chose exile. I paint for a voice. Why didn't you accept a pardon?" At this she put her hand on his balding spot majestically.

I nodded my head. I wanted to know.

"Melissa, I don't think he chose exile. It was forced . . ."

"She is right. I did choose exile. There were others who refused to leave. They said it was not up to them to choose. They said it was their right to be at home minding their children, their farms, their loved ones. They were where they were supposed to be. It was not for them to choose. They are dead. I think they were right. I chose. I surrendered something. I gave up choice. I gave up something I cannot articulate," I explained, more for myself to hear than for them.

"You are alive and you continue fighting. You know, Aristotle once said there is a difference between being courageous and being foolhardy. You survived," her father said. He had made a different choice—to stay in jail. Yet he understood that I was not entirely wrong in leaving. I only wish I had done more in exile.

"Why did you refuse clemency?" Melissa asked him again, for my sake.

"I have done nothing wrong. I have harmed no one. All I have done is speak for freedom. How can I be pardoned for that? How can I be pardoned for asking for what is mine? It is not in me to do that," he said. His chest was heaving, I thought because of the heaviness of his words. The words that he spoke lived in him.

"But, Father, others like you accepted the clemency, and now they are out there fighting. Some are even back in jail. But the thing is, they gave themselves one more chance to fight," Melissa said.

"Your mother is a high school teacher. She is doing what she loves. I do not blame her. I do not question her. It is not my job to question. I have no right. It would be wrong of me. Those that accepted clemency, I cannot speak for them. I cannot judge them. They are out there trying to break the silence that keeps others like me in here. I am sorry, Melissa and Kalumba, but I can only speak for myself. Do not ask me to judge," he said.

"How do you answer the question for yourself, then?" I asked in a whisper.

"Well, some give a false confession and once outside they continue fighting. Others refuse to give the false confession. Who is right? Not much of an answer, but take from it what you will," he said. My dilemma with the List remains just that—a dilemma: did I confess or did I not? Perhaps not remembering is a chance for me to start again. Either way I can only continue fighting.

"You know what? You are alive and so am I, and so is she. Let us try to make that count for something," he said. "It's almost that time," he added.

I could see what was happening. It was important that he be the one to remind the guards about the time. You cannot concede your need to them, even the need to hold your daughter a little longer, because they will exploit it to weaken you.

"Come next visiting day. I know it's expensive and not even necessary but come again. I felt alive seeing you here today. Melissa, promise!" he implored.

Their relationship kept changing: at times the father acts like the daughter and vice versa. It reminded me of Mrs. Shaw. I have been neglecting her—have to correct that now.

She nodded. "I love you, Papa," she said. He took her love, laughed, and raised his fists. I thought of my father, who never showed much emotion. He beckoned the guard and winked at us. He walked toward the door.

"I love your daughter. I am a ghost but I love your daughter," I yelled at him. A strange thing to say but it felt right.

He didn't yell anything back. He continued walking toward the door.

Ever since I decided to go home, the most beautiful and, I suppose, bizarre things have been happening to me. Mrs. Shaw, Melissa, Rafael, and for the first time in a long time, I have felt my heart beat. I am thawing.

Am I being rewarded for the decision to return home? It is almost as if I am living the last nine years in this one. I believe so!

We walked from smaller room to bigger room until, thoroughly frisked, we made it to the outside. We got into the taxi and headed back to New York. Out flight wasn't until tomorrow. A cheap motel in Jersey City, the trains, and we had a night in New York. It was time for a beer.

I am in love.

April 15th

HARLEM!

"Let's go to Harlem," Melissa says. A few trains, getting lost, and a few hours later we are in Harlem. The last time I was here was ten years ago. I recognize nothing except the feeling of getting lost. It is strange being black among black people after a long stint of being surrounded by whiteness. I feel lost but very warm. I feel safe. We find a bar somewhere and walk in, order our drinks, and take them to a corner booth. The bar reminds me of Eagle's. It has the same photographs, only these look much older. The photograph of Billie Holiday is browning at the edges, like it is being consumed by intense heat; it even looks bubbly.

"Listen, I want us to do something. This once, here in New York, here in Harlem, ask me any fucked-up question that you like," Melissa says suddenly.

"Tell me why you want to come with me." I feel timid.

"That is not a question. I answered it already. I mean—ask me anything you would like to know," she says.

"Why do you paint?" I ask.

She starts laughing. "Seriously?" she asks.

"Yes," I say. "I wrote a poem to my father a few months ago. I want to know why you paint," I add.

"I paint to stay alive. Each painting is a reprieve note. You know how in death row the prisoner is about to be gassed and at the last minute, a reprieve is granted. Each painting is a reprieve. It justifies my existence." She is running her fingertips across my hand.

"I hope you are not idealizing death. I can tell you it's not pretty," I say.

"Now you are being patronizing. You meet my father for a few minutes and you begin to sound like him. Damn, the coalition, how quickly it . . ." She withdraws her hand and places it on her lap.

"Explain your answer to me, then," I say, attempting to make peace.

"You know why the soldier picks up the gun or the bomb maker makes a bomb? I mean, they both could choose other weapons of destruction but they choose those ones. I love paint. Does it make sense to say I love my form? I love paint, its heaviness, how it feels. I love painting because I love paint."

"And the end result? Do you the love the painting?"

"No. It is the splatter of brains on a wall. I do not care much for the end result. I look at the painting, and I see the painter at work in love with the paint." She is getting into it; her eyes are glowing and redness has rushed to her face. I grunt to say I don't quite understand.

"Let me try again. I love my paintings. I love to see them on a wall. I love to see them provoke discussions. I love them, and I love paintings by others. But I love the smell of paint more. How can you love life without loving blood?" She pauses. "Now it's my turn. Tell me about your mother," she commands.

"I really don't know that much about her," I protest.

"If you have lived this long you must know enough," she says. I am not sure what she means by that.

"Well, I have black-and-white photographs. The one I remember vividly, in it, she has short hair. She looks very young, about eighteen, and she has very big eyes. You can see she enjoys the attention of the camera. My father says she was shy but I don't think so. There are photographs of her pregnant with me and after I was born and even when I was very little. I don't remember her, though. She always wanted to be a nurse. For a while, after independence, she was working for the first black doctor in our area. One day coming back from work she was in a car accident. She died." I am straining to remember. Did I as a child hate myself for not remembering her?

"Did your dad ever remarry?"

"No, he slept around and tended her grave. He was fucking my neighbor's wife . . . She always brought him fruits. I don't think they were ever happy—he and my mother, I mean. He was going to divorce her, but she died in a car accident. The guilt . . . all he did was tend her grave and sleep around. I suppose one fed the other. But he is a good father. I will ask him to remember her for me. You know, I don't know him that well, either. I suppose it's an age thing." It is good to sit there with Melissa and look back.

How was my father as a young man? When he was my age, what did he dream? So many details that go into making a life and I know very little of them to say I know my father. We have lost a lot of time. There are things that he could not have told me then, that he would tell me now, that he would have been telling me as I grew up. Exile stunts relationships. There are many things that I would know just from being at home.

"Do you regret your involvement?"

"I am not sure. I never had a choice. It's like you and your paint. What choice is there?" I sound bitter, not about her paint but that sometimes we find ourselves in situations not of our choosing. I chose exile over dying. Outside Icarus Prison, it does not feel like much of a choice.

"Get fat and die," she says in an attempt to lighten the mood. We talk for a long time: loss of virginity, best and worst sex, music, favorite foods, and all the little details that make up a person. We had started by falling in love. Well, I guess now we are walking backwards, filling in the empty spaces.

We left later in the night as a jazz band was setting up. We took the train to Jersey City to our cheap motel room. We did not make love, even with the thrill of being in a cheap motel. It was a long flight back, and by the time we got home, we were tired of being around each other. She went to her apartment. I showered, wrote some, then went to sleep. Keeping the journal of whatever this thing is has become very important to me—things are no longer real unless I record them. It feels that way, anyway.

April 16th

POEM FOR MELISSA

SKETCHES FOR MELISSA

I

I cannot regret meeting you or loving
you etc. It is the fear of knowing
that when we meet again, I will still
guide you to open that door, I, used
to the salty lick of open wounds,
that you tried to close like glass windows
against a hurricane that I regret . . .

II

Love and agriculture, tools for irrigation,
curve pathways light enough for waters
to nourish, but not deep enough to flood
that which we cultivate—delicacy
of infancy—seeds hesitant, in the explosive
glare of the sun, to sprout yet frightened
by the darkness under the cover of soil—it's
with you that our shadows have feelings
touching even when our bodies stood
and sat and danced apart

III

At the lake, an oasis in small coal mine cities,
a wooden bench, a bottle of wine and words

that find themselves only when we touched,
trees and brushes siblings of a landscape
where nakedness smells like animals in a barn
and passion stripped of dead leaves
and letters to become a raw need
that finds . . .
Absence is not a metaphor—it's a hole that . . .

I wish I had more lines for this poem. It will make a good gift.

April 20th
Wrote a long e-mail to both Sukena and Ogum about Mrs. Shaw and the skull. They probably think I am baked out of my skull so I don't much expect a reply.

5 Kalumba's Diary Continued

June 1st

LESSONS FROM MAY

Dear Diary,

I have been too busy living to feed you often, but here is May in flesh and bones.

In preparing for my doctorate exam, I learnt a lot.

I learnt how the Enlightenment discovered rationality and the sublime for the white man and none for the woman or the blacks and Indians,

And how it was the blacks, Indians and women who built the European homes, skin for rooftops, brain to light the lamps, and womb for seeds to grow,

I learnt how the Renaissance utopia reads like a conservative document, the best of the world a temperate king, a benevolent elite looking after their flock of peasants,

And how Romanticism lived uneasily but still side by side with slavery, how the Romantics hated the poor and the passions of man that breathed fire in revolutionary France,

I learnt how the French Revolution hated the Haitian revolution, and how Napoleon assassinated L'Ouverture,

And how a revolutionary Marx was not a Marxist, and how Marxists fed racism and blacks to the working-class revolution, bypassing lynching and Jim Crow,

I learnt how the Berlin Conference divided up Africa into pieces of bread—let them eat cake and the body of Christ, she said,

And how when warring elephants make love the grass suffers, and when the grass suffers people starve,

I learnt that people can fight in wars that are not theirs, fight while black for white democracies, fight for white freedom for black enslavement,

And how the African fought the missionary, the explorer, administrator, and soldier and how Africans were buried alive,

I learnt of negritude, how we came full circle and claimed irrationality for the African and rationality for the European,

And how Marxism became African socialism and African communalism and how it was stirred in African pots till it turned into a blinding mist,

I learnt how African independence became Western democracy rising out of slums and shantytowns, land and factories held by black hands to feed white stomachs,

And of genocide in Africa, in the Americas, in Europe, in Australia, West Indies, in all corners and centers of the Earth,

I learnt that when the volcano erupts, the hot lava that cascades down the mountainside is held in bank by black bones.

And how the River Elan floods to mourn those who died in the middle passages of the Atlantic Ocean and the boat people of Haiti,

I learnt of science for bombs, culture for racism, education for watering down the questions, media for disinformation,

And how we have come full circle, turned theories on their heads so that women became with the mind, and the male, he of brute strength, became the brain,

I learnt how those that speak freedom descend from Hannibal and Caesar and how they want to fit the whole world in their back pockets,

I learnt how love was lost, how we never had love and how
when the revolutions came it was the heartless,
   those without souls,
   the blind,
   those without conscience,
   the gluttons
   it was they who betrayed tomorrow for yesterday,
   . . . And we let them.

─────────

When I heard through my window police sirens on the
morning of my exam, I woke Melissa up and said, "Honey, I
am ready for my exam."

"What time is it?" she asked grumpily.

"Time to wake up."

"You will do well. You have been studying hard," she said.

"Yes," I said. "But I have learnt nothing. We have learned
nothing!"

And I went and took the exam and passed. Now for the dissertation itself—a few months of writing what I already knew.

May 1st

FUNNY STORY

For the life of me I don't know why I remembered this—
maybe because of all the fighter jets flying around because of
the May 1st worker day celebrations in Madison.

One of the guys we worked with in Atlanta, he was from
Nicaragua. One day he comes in walking haltingly. Naturally
we ask him what the problem is. As it turns out, on May 1st
early in the morning he was making love to his wife. Everything was going well—*you should have seen me, Neruda would
have been proud,* he says—when ten or so F-16's, flying low,
pass by his house.

He remembers his days as a Sandinista being hunted down
by US fighter jets—the *pendejo puta* contras, he says. "The war
never leaves you." He pushes his wife off the bed as he jumps off

to take cover underneath. Only he still has a massive hard-on. The first thing that hits the floor is his dick. And instead of keeping him hoisted and balanced a few inches above the air (*like a fucking see-saw*, someone adds, to our laughter), it caves into his body and he feels like it's being snapped into two.

"Man, can a dick break?" someone asks. There are about five or six of us listening, and instinctively we all hold our dicks and balls, as if to check that they are still there, and hobble around yelling in pain. Nothing like the threat of emasculation to tap into our common humanity! Well, that was the end of his pleasurable day off. He did not know whether this constituted an emergency, so he waited for the next day and went to one of those free clinics. There was nothing they could do for him except to tell him to relax and avoid getting stiff.

"How can I resist that?" He reaches into his wallet and removes a photograph of his wife.

"She is all that and a bag of chips," we all chime in.

" . . . barbecue flavor," someone adds.

We get confused. "What are you talking about?"

"She is all that and a bag of chips . . . barbecue flavor. You gotta mention the flavor."

He continues with the story. When he gets home from the doctor's, his dick develops a mind of its own, remembering the unfinished business. So he spends the whole day trying to douse it down with cold water.

His wife, meanwhile, shows no sympathy and keeps teasing him. So he comes to work in the afternoon—loading trucks will keep his mind off things.

June 2nd

MEMORY LANE

Today Melissa and I went to see Mrs. Shaw—it had been a while. She was not lucid—on a good day she is almost the Mrs. Shaw I met, and on bad days, without her memory she is unrecognizable. I saw that she had her photo album on the dining table, and Melissa suggested we go through it. Probably the photo album was her attempt to remember some of herself. Is it possible that she has forgotten how she looked as a young woman? What would it mean not to see yourself as a young person? I always imagined her to be a femme fatale but to the contrary—poor and fat, very chubby. In one black and white photo, her small brick house is the background in what Melissa and I assume to be rural England. Her hair is in a bun; white socks that run to the hem of her school uniform; one hand held to her eyes to shield them from the sun.

In another photograph, there she is with a young Mr. Shaw standing outside what appears to be a factory, where we assume they both worked before the enterprise of colonialism looked more enterprising. This is not the same Mr. Shaw that was feared across Kwatee. Here he is holding a Stetson hat in one hand, very baggy pants inside weathered boots—he just looks to be in a state of general unease. Mrs. Shaw is laughing at something—probably him?

There are other photos of her, as a toddler, what we assume to be her in primary school with friends, in high school, and one of her and Mr. Shaw about to leave for Kwatee. There is a ship behind them; they look very happy holding hands and waving good-bye.

Mrs. Shaw wanders in from somewhere. She stares at a photo of herself—she cannot remember herself as a young woman—traces the photograph with shaking hands, asking for its secrets—she stares at herself—she cannot remember herself. *Mrs. Shaw, this is you,* I want to tell her, *Mrs. Shaw, this is you*, but what is the point? It was her.

June 10th

Home Is Where Your Heart Is . . . M

Home Is Where Your Heart Is—it says on the doormat as you wipe the dust off your shoes on the funny-looking furry heart. Is it true, though? And what if your body is here and your heart over there? Or maybe there is nothing metaphorical about this cliché—you are where your heart is anyway. Reminds me of those apartments along the highway that advertise by saying *If you lived here, you would be home.* For me, home is where I am not—simple and to the point. When I go home I will miss this place. It is inevitable.

June 15th

Meeting the Native American Me

They are after me again. Behind me I hear dogs growl and howl and voices shouting *there he is* and gunshots. Tree branches snapping in my face as I leap and bound my way to safety. Ahead of me, up on a hill are rows and rows of wigwams. I am confused. On my hands, I feel two bracelets, and I look to find chains. The earth is swirling. I start crawling toward the wigwams. From where I am, I can see Indian warriors with war paint, guns, and bows and arrows, but they cannot see me. The faster I crawl the farther they move away and the closer I hear my hunters.

I crawl and suddenly the earth opens in front me. It forms into a deep gorge. There are spikes in it. This is how they tried to starve the Mau Mau to death. Trying to jump means death. I realize I have to stop and fight. I turn around to face them. The dogs and the hunters begin to recede farther and farther away until they vanish and I find myself in a tepee. There is Melissa, and our daughter. They are dressed in Indian clothes. I begin to say something but wake up somewhere between a dream and a nightmare, both scared and warm. Melissa is sleeping. I am glad not to have woken her up. I lie in bed trying to understand where this dream came from until I stumble onto myself seven years ago in Boston, Massachusetts.

Seven years ago someone kicked at my feet and I woke up to find myself lying on a beach in Cape Cod. I looked up to find a tall black man, two long braids down to his waist, staring down on me. He had the shiniest black skin I have ever seen. Not oily like mine, I mean it's shiny in pigmentation. "Are you okay?" he asked me.

"Yes, just a rough night, that is all," I said. I felt beat but okay, in spite of a rough night. My then girlfriend, Mary, had a friend whose father owned a beach house by the Atlantic.

Cape Cod is one of the most beautiful places I have ever been. People have taken time to make it look good. The grass is greener, cropped and cut in such a way that it looks ironed. Shrubs are measured and round like boxing gloves. The houses are huge colonial types, nothing over three stories high but massive things that rumble close to the earth. But the beach's beauty is wild. The ocean has not been tamed. That is how I ended up on the beach drunk and high as a kite. Behind me the kind of beauty that we think we own and in front of me the kind of beauty that we will never own.

Everyone was back in the house passed out. I couldn't sleep, so I rolled another joint, took a bottle of Chivas Regal with me, and went out to the beach. It was a beautiful night. I hadn't seen this kind of beauty since I left home—not in similarity but in principle. The moon was shining on the ocean, fields and fields of shimmering light that were nevertheless interrupted by gentle waves. It was as if the moon and the ocean were rocking each other back and forth. Then the wind, which at first only ruffled my shirt, started getting louder and louder. Then it got mad and violently pushed the ocean to where I was. I couldn't move.

The water reached my waist, but just as soon as I started to panic, it began to recede, kept receding as the wind grew louder. The wind started kicking up sand and whirling and whirling until when I turned around I couldn't make out the house. It grew louder until I thought my eardrums would burst. The sand began to feel like little shards of glass beating up on my body. Wet as I was, the cold was almost unbearable. It went on like this for a while and then suddenly just at the moment when I felt myself being lifted off the ground everything went quiet. I was quite shaken, and even though I reasoned that I was probably caught up in a whirlwind or something like it, I never told anyone about this incident. It felt mad.

But I was not one to be dissuaded from enjoying what remained of the night. I removed my joint from my shirt pocket and lit up. I thought I should join Mary but decided against it. She was passed out on a couch. The beach would be my bed. Armed as I was with the joint and the bottle, it was only a matter of time before I passed out. A few hours later, I woke to someone prodding my feet and sun streaming into my eyes. I was so hung over that I could not even slip into a PTSD episode.

"Who are you?" I asked.

But instead of replying he asked what I was doing passed out on the beach. "Don't you know you can drown when the tide comes in? Quite a number of people die like that."

It made sense. I hadn't thought about it. But then again, how I could I have in my state, I reasoned to myself. And what would it matter?

"Well, there are a lot of black people in that ocean," I said instead.

"There are a lot of people," he replied.

"What are you doing here?" I asked.

"I live here," he said simply.

"Cape Cod?" I asked, though what I really meant is how it came about that a black man owns a home here. We all live in Roxbury. Roxbury, poor and depressed, is our Bantustan, I had become fond of saying.

"I am a doctor," he said, by way of explanation. "Come with me. I will make you a cup of coffee. Bring the empty bottle with you; no point in littering."

His place looked very much like the others. Except inside it was decorated differently, not like Mary's, cushioned and comfortable. Naturally, my eyes locked on Billie Holiday—the same photograph that a few years later I found at Eagle's Bar. But more than that, there was artwork from different cultures, some I recognize as African, others as Indian and European. I didn't find the extravagance of rich homes back home. My uncle who is very wealthy has a huge house full of junk. There are huge plastic ducks, ceramic tables, marble tables, thinking men, screaming men, tasteless nude sculptures of men and women, a plastic boxing Helena, etc., in his sitting room. In this house, everything was spare to the point of being sterile. But everything seemed to be there because he wanted it. My uncle's place, on the other hand, everything is there because it validates some sort of deep hidden complex—for god's sake, the man has candy machines from Europe, as if the bubble gum tastes better from a European dispenser.

He made some black strong coffee, which he took with no sugar. My stomach was in a fragile state so I had a glass of orange juice. He had been out for a morning walk. I agreed that it was a beautiful morning. The sun was out, but it was not yet very hot or humid.

"You see, all this beauty, it was ours to share. The whole state . . . the whole damn country, we owned it without it being ours—different nations with different cultures but held together by the land," he said. "Judging from your accent, you must know something about that."

I nodded my head in agreement, thinking that had we met last night, I would have been a better conversationalist and, being high, cared more. And who still says *my people* unless they want something inconvenient forgotten? Glossed over, as we say in my field?

"Did you notice the street names named after our heroes? Geronimo Street?"

Another fucking nationalist except for one thing—he was black like me.

"But sir, you are African American. I saw quite a number of black people yesterday evening as we drove in," I said. I was confused.

"I bet you did: mostly maids and houseboys, pool cleaners, grocery store clerks, limousine drivers. I have been to parties and been asked for champagne refills. You are mistaken, though. I am not African American per se. I am a descendent of the Seminole-Negroes," he said rather proudly.

His great-great-grandfather was an escaped slave who had found his way into Seminole territory. A people resisting and on the run, runaway slaves who made it to their settlements and sought their help were considered part of them. The Seminoles refused to hand over the escaped slaves—how could a human being own another human being? Many wars were fought and many lives lost, but they would never surrender this one principle. Nobody, of course, talks about this, how the government made laws prohibiting the red people from helping the black people. But we are one. Anyway, his great-great-grandfather was welcomed with open arms. He married a Seminole woman, fought in their battles, celebrated their triumphs, and cried at their losses. It was remarkable. He became one of them, and his children became Seminoles.

Strange how things never change, even across continents. When I was growing up, every evening walking home from school, I saw villagers from Kamuingi village being dropped off in huge trucks. Having worked all day in the tea plantations, they looked haggard and sunken. Every now and then I would spot Sukena's mother and father, but I never dared say hello. It was better to speak to them in the sanctuary of their home.

"And now?" I ask him.

"Well, we are still here, though not necessarily in Cape Cod. The majority of us are in the reservations, backward, drunk, and illiterate. There are a small number of us all over the place, in the Senate, the House, you name it. Don't get me wrong. I understand my history, but look, if I can make it, anyone can. I am a doctor because I worked hard to become one," he said with a finality that suggested no need for further conversation. There was no bitterness in his voice. He was saying these things as immutable facts and lessons from life that he had picked up along the way.

I remember not wanting to get into it. Besides, in my condition I had no right to judge him. I had heard the same argument from my uncle who, together with my father, had been born in a poor family. My uncle, to strengthen his argument, was illiterate as well, and he would say at every opportunity, "Look, I can't even count my money in English, yet I made it. If I made it, anyone ought to be able to." And no matter how many times I tried saying that a poor person getting rich was a matter of chance and no one likes being poor, he would add that it's a question of who wants the chance more. And what if there was only one chance for a million people? His answer would remain the same. History, for him, counted for nothing. Only the present counted, each day erased the night, each day was a new beginning for those who wanted it. And I sensed that my host here was steering me in that same direction.

"Do you ever go back to the reservations?"

"Yes, I do, to remind myself where I came from and also to show my people what they can become, to offer myself as an example. Not modest, I agree, but it has to be done. And you, do you ever return?" he asked with genuine concern.

"No, I haven't been back," I said to my fellow exile.

"No matter what you think of me, you should always return home." He was trying to offer advice, but it fell short, not because he wasn't genuine but simply because history has demanded something more out of me, a deeper sacrifice that he could not allow himself to see. It would remind him of his people sitting in jail with Rafael.

"I can't. I would be killed within a day," I told him. Sometimes you have to wear these things for honor—here I was using my exile to establish my credentials, or maybe I was using it as armor. He looked a bit taken aback. I think in some way I might have reminded him that history is still here and sometimes herds us in a direction that goes against our will.

"But I would return at the first opportunity. I left love and everything behind," I said, having established my credentials.

"The world is harsh. No reason to destroy yourself, though. Don't you think?" He was right, of course. I really have no logical excuse for the things I do. I just find myself doing them. But is it so simple? The world is harsh, no reason to take it on yourself, to remake yourself in the image of a fucked-up world—easy enough to say, until the demons of history, electrodes in hand, come calling.

But I shook my head in agreement. I felt as if I was having a conversation with my father. Do all older people think the same? They see the youth, and if they don't recognize themselves, they only see shortcuts to make themselves into someone else?

"I intend to survive," I said.

"The point is not to survive. It is to live." Again the simplicity.

"Do you call this living?" I made a sweeping gesture that went around the kitchen, into the sitting room, and into Cape Cod itself. "You know what I was hearing last night? Ghosts. Ghosts in the wind, of all those that jumped into that ocean rather than die slaves, ghosts of others who with hands and feet bound were pushed overboard so the traders could escape from their pursuers, and yet others who died fighting. The ghosts of those who never made it to shore and of those that did, but died dreaming of returning. I might be a drunk, but I haven't built a million-dollar house on the bones of my ancestors. I don't swim in oceans where millions were drowned. I do not mistake the cry of a ghost for a cooling wind. So don't tell me the point is to live when all that surrounds you is death. I think I would like to go now. I have broken a lot of protocol in one morning," I said. I was not bitter. I was just tired.

"What protocol?" he asked. "You are in need of help," he added.

"I have been rude," I said. Yet what else could I have said?

"No, you said what you needed to say. So let me tell you something in my million-dollar house: be careful that history does not become an anchor. Be very careful that history does not become an anchor."

I did not say anything. I merely pointed out that the bread in the toaster was done. He continued.

"Let me tell you something else in my million-dollar house. My name is James Joseph." He said it a little too fiercely.

I had to start laughing. That was the funniest name I had ever heard. "That is what my parents named me," he said defensively.

"No, no, that is not it. Joseph Kalumba Wa Dubiaku . . . that is my name," I said between gasps.

"And you are from Africa? You were named Joseph in Africa?" he asked incredulously. He started laughing as well. We laughed so hard that we woke up the whole household: his African American wife, their son, and their Mexican maid.

Of all the strangest things, this one tops them all. An African American–Seminole Indian in Cape Cod named James Joseph meets a passed-out African named Joseph and they end up having breakfast in his million-dollar mansion. Strangest . . . until I met Mrs. Shaw a few years later. I was sure my friends would not wake up soon, and I ended up staying the whole morning, swapping stories. Two Josephs from different continents had a lot to talk about.

We became friends, but it wasn't the kind of friendship that can be sustained. So we never called each other after we parted. Still, thinking about it this morning as I lie next to Melissa, I am sure that if I called him six years after we met and told him I needed some money to return, he would give it to me with no questions asked. Would I consider him a good or bad guy? What does it matter? I can say he is a good friend.

I end up thinking about Mary and Boston. Whatever is she doing now? She wanted to be a special education teacher and was studying at Harvard at the time when I met her. I loved going to the Beer Can Bar, where little Joe Cook, eighty-something years old, sang the blues. On Saturdays, he played for a college crowd, and I and my friends would go in search of a quick lay. Not that we got lucky often enough (or even occasionally, for that matter) to warrant the constant hope, but we went anyway. It's what men did—went in search of women.

But on Sundays Joe Cook and other blues musicians from the area would have a jam session. That was the time when I saw his blues guitar play until something in him snapped and he started crying, all broken up, but he played as if held together by the guitar strings. That was the first time I felt the touch of history in the blues. They touched something in me that I didn't even know was there in me, something old and ancient, and I started crying too. Or maybe it was we who were already troubled enough to be in a bar on a Sunday evening.

I met Mary on a Sunday. She was dancing by herself so I joined her. It was more like swaying, so we swayed together, she contorting into various bohemian forms and I shuffling my drunken feet. Had more drinks, danced some more, and eventually we ended up at her place. She loved bluegrass music. Whatever happened to her? We dated for a while, about six or ten months, and then I moved.

I should have used the story of Joseph for my earlier lectures on exile, the guest, and the host. We are both hosts, yet history wants to treat us like guests. Exile—it is an American condition, as American as apple pie. Sometimes history provides perfect moments. What Joseph described of the Seminoles is true hospitality. The host and the guest become brothers, and the host is prepared to defend his brother with his life. It is that simple, and history provided the answer. But the philosophers continue to pontificate as if their intellectual theories alone can create what history already provides. Yet, still, in a moment of honesty, my need to return made my exile hostile—I would not have used his story, for it would have disturbed the sleep of the American philanthropists paying my fee.

Thinking of Joseph, I am aware that it was not that good things were not happening to me ever since I came here. Joseph was a good thing, the people I did hard labor with were good things, and even Mary was a good thing. I was just too self-involved, always listening to my pain. It could have been a very worthwhile ten years.

Melissa stirs awake. Even though we have been together for only a few months, it is rather obvious to me that I want to marry her. Perhaps I will be coming back to the US after my return. I have now started thinking about that possibility. After I return, it can no longer be exile and I can go anywhere I please. I will simply be moving with the woman I love because I can. Decisions do not have to be made now. Certain that whichever way life goes we end up together, there is no urgency in our love. We finally get up. We have breakfast, then she goes to her apartment to do some more painting. Often she jokingly says that she comes to my place for a nightly vacation and returns to her work refreshed.

July 1st

Waking Up

I woke up, always waking up, I wake up, she is beside, always beside me, contorted, different shape each morning, this morning her breath on my face, her knees threatening my balls, I wake, we are always here. Love is this—I want to be here.

October 9th

Melissa's Exhibition. . . .

Melissa's exhibition went well. Practically all her paintings sold. The day after the show, there was a photograph of her, myself, and Mrs. Shaw in the *New York Times* Art Section. She was wearing a black dress and high heels, with her hair braided to her shoulders and smiling and me, looking uncomfortable in a black suit, dreads neatly pulled back into a ponytail, and between us Mrs. Shaw in a white evening gown. The caption read, *Melissa Rafael has finally arrived,* and below the photograph, *Melissa, her grandmother Mrs. Shaw and her partner, Kwatee exile Joseph Kalumba Wa Dubiaku.*

How many times do I have to tell people I no longer go by Joseph? I have always been uncomfortable with that name, hardly ever used it even while in Kwatee, and after meeting James Joseph, I consciously stopped using it. And from where is Melissa arriving and where is she landing?

The art critic who introduced her called her a Puerto Rican painter *stabbing at the conscience of the mainland, a sister and a comrade.* And she went on to talk about Melissa's art as offering *a deconstructionist reading of the mainland from the periphery of without*—Jesus fucking Christ, don't they ever stop?

I laughed inwardly. I remembered a discussion I had with Melissa. She said that no painter or writer can be deconstructionist in the production of art. "I mean, I have to have a beginning and an ending stroke no matter where I begin in telling my story. The canvas itself is form. Can it contain me? Who cares? Who ever said it can or it should? Perhaps I can be in how I say it but not in what I say; you know, even meaningless is meaning. I hate this kind of talk. People like me always have things to say. We create, we are always saying something, especially if the background is colonialism and the foreground continuing imperialism . . . even when all we do is love," she said. And remembering some of my experiences, I added that I am suspicious of someone who uses words like *interrogate* in their discussions.

"I will be brief, because standing next to my paintings I know I am in a competition I can't win. As most of you know, I have been shaped by being Puerto Rican, by what my grandmother"—and she waved at Mrs. Shaw—"calls the other fifty percent. I would like to dedicate this opening to my father, Rafael, who could not be here today, because he is locked up in the mainland for fighting for an independent Puerto Rico. Thank you very much." The clapping was polite but firm, and with that the show opened.

It had taken a lot of debate over whether we should invite Mrs. Shaw or not. Melissa thought we should, and I thought we shouldn't. Melissa argued that if memory was the beginning and the end of human life, then we might as well live on plain porridge and water. *Why should she eat good-tasting food if tomorrow she will not remember what she ate? If she was going to enjoy the art show then she should come regardless of whether she remembered it or not.*

I did not quite agree. Mrs. Shaw has been getting progressively worse. Sometimes she tells the same story several times. Like once with this black and white photograph of her in Kwatee. She kept forgetting she had told us the story. Each time she looked down at the photograph she was looking at it afresh and she would begin telling it again. Each time, she told the story exactly the same way—she even paused at the same places and laughed at the same places. I thought it would be torturous for her to keep waking up and finding herself in a taxi, in a plane, in New York, and in an art gallery without knowing what she was doing there. But eventually Melissa won. What mattered was that in the duration of seeing she was going to enjoy herself. Her experience was worth something even though it would soon be forgotten.

I think we were both partially right. First Mrs. Shaw couldn't remember whether she had agreed to come or not. At first she said no; we asked again and she said yes. We went with her final answer. She couldn't remember getting on the plane, and it terrified her when she woke up from a nap several hundred feet above sea level. Once we made it to our hotel, she was like a little girl. She became very excited and went over the room in great detail—the bathtub, number of towels, water faucets, how the beds were made, and of course the minibar.

It was good that she had taken a break from her home— hence the excitement. Her house was beginning to have that old people's home smell, probably because the curtains are always closed and the windows never opened. And at the gallery, with strangers she knew to be strangers around her, she was having a ball with the attention. Especially when she told them that she had lived in Africa. And since no one stayed around her long before having to move on to the next paint-ing, forgetting and repeating the same story did not matter.

I don't know much about art, and I hope Melissa finds this refreshing. During the opening, I roamed from painting to painting trying to locate Melissa in them, or my scars, or Puerto Rico. I finally stopped by a painting of what resem-bled a sculpting of a black stick figure in a woolen dress. It was lying flat with its head raised. On its head was a wooden Victorian clock in a coffin box that had been roughly beaten into the shape of a rectangle. The tongue of the stick figure was forked into two, one short and pointing to 12:00 and a long one that wound its way to 6:00. Its title was simply *En-glish*. I spent a long time staring at it, wishing I could afford it and surprise Melissa when one week later she would walk into my apartment and see it. But at 1,500 dollars it alone could buy my ticket back home. I had already spent too much money traveling with Melissa to New York as it was.

There were other paintings I found interesting: One titled *Double Consciousness* was of a woman cut neatly into two equal halves, one half polished to a black shine till she sparkled and the other a multitude of colors. Another titled *Mainland— Freedom* was of a rose growing through the eye of a skull. The skull was in tall harsh brown grass and lay untidily. The rose grew straight from it, with machine guns for thorns, and tiny grenades as little dewdrops on its leaves. The petals were a bright red, a heavy red so that they appeared to have been painted with swirling thick blood.

I found Mrs. Shaw by a painting of a small boy holding up a bullet for his father to see. The boy looked very happy and proud, while the father was smiling and proudly reach-ing for it. At the boy's feet there was an unopened wrapped package and torn wrapping paper lying in dry sand. In the background a mud hut and beyond it a dry riverbed. It was morning, and both father and son were squinting from the sun. "What a clever title," Mrs. Shaw said. The painting was titled *Christmas*.

"I have one major regret," Mrs. Shaw said soon after, as she traced her fingers on the painting even though there was a sign that clearly said Do Not Touch. "I was never with someone who loved me yet was better than me. That I could look up to either because of his decency or a talent that he possessed that I did not have and yet who loved me back as his equal. She is better than you and yet she loves you," Mrs. Shaw said, pointing to a woman I had not met who waved back at us.

"But Mrs. Shaw . . . that is not Melissa," I said gently. She laughed mischievously—lately she's been full of little tricks. I noticed someone coming in. She was tall, in high heels and a bright-colored red and blue kimono such that it seemed to shimmer around her full figure whenever she took a step toward me and Mrs. Shaw. She looked as if she was in her late forties but was obviously much older given her deep wrinkles. But instead of betraying her they seemed to accentuate her face—same thing with her long black, graying hair. Melissa looked busy, she explained, and that is why she had to come to us first. I felt attracted to her—not in a sexual way, though I have to admit that Melissa's mother is a fox, just a familiar tug toward her. Of course she expected that I would recognize her or at least know who she was when I saw her. And I did. Either Melissa has been talking to her about us or Rafael has. She looked at the painting of the boy with the bullet, and I saw her wince—as a parent she could recognize the pain in the painting as opposed to its beauty. Melissa came over. They hugged stiffly and then stepped away from us, talking heatedly for three or four minutes. Hugged again, this time not so stiffly, and Melissa's mother waved good-bye to us, smiling broadly.

Melissa walked to chitchat with more people. It was hard to tell if anyone else wondered if that was her mother, or perhaps everyone knew—and dysfunctional relationships are part of the art world. It made me think of my own relationship with my father, ten years ago. Perhaps if I had stayed we would be like Melissa and her mother. Certainly Ogum and his father had been heading in that direction. The evening flew by quickly. Melissa was a whirlwind of activity for the rest of the night. By the end of it all, she had sold practically all the paintings. After the official party was over, most of us went over to the art critic's house for a party.

Mrs. Shaw insisted on coming—proceeded to get very drunk. I tempered my drinking, remembering we were going to see Melissa's father the following day. I wanted to be lucid. Mrs. Shaw, on the other hand, went nuts. Perhaps she senses this is her last hurrah? She danced, yelled, until she finally had to go to sleep. The critic put her in her bed and the party continued.

I, for the most part, spent the evening answering questions on exile, and it felt like I was at a dinner after one of my talks. So I gave the same answers. I was invited to give a talk at New York University later in the month. For 3,500 dollars, I accepted. I was now assured of making it home and setting myself up. Close to three a.m., it was time to leave. It was walking distance to our hotel, but we had to take a taxi because of Mrs. Shaw, who giggled all the way. We had to share the same room because we were afraid of Mrs. Shaw wandering off by herself in the middle of the night. But we need not have worried. We had to wake her up in the morning and explain why she was there with a raging hangover. And as soon she knew why she was there and all that had transpired the night before, she was in high spirits again and we could hear her whistling some tune as she showered.

October 10th

Meeting Melissa's Mother

While Mrs. Shaw was in the bathroom, Melissa was filling me in about her own evening. She was very excited, more excited than I have ever seen her. "Kalumba, I have indeed arrived," she exclaimed as she flipped through the morning *New York Times*. "And it feels like shit!" she added, laughing.

142

"Of course I am joking. I am happy, but I don't feel any different. It just means I can paint from wherever I want. I have made no compromises. It took a long time, but I am here." She was wearing a white hotel bathrobe, looking outside the window. "Jesus, what an ugly city." Myself, I did not say much. I think I was a little jealous. And why shouldn't I be? It has been a long time for me, too, and what do I have? But I was also happy, and I told her as much. I did not ask her about her mother, knowing she would tell me if she wanted. Mrs. Shaw didn't ask either, though I suspected she simply forgot.

We started kissing and caressing and stopped when the whistling from the shower stopped. It was time to go see Rafael, but first she had a surprise.

The surprise, it turns out, was breakfast at Melissa's mother's in Harlem. She had made a huge breakfast: bacon, scrambled eggs, toast, and tea with squeezed orange juice. It was terrible. I never thought it possible to overcook eggs, burn bacon, and squeeze bitter orange juice. We struggled through the breakfast, though Mrs. Shaw kept smacking her lips with satisfaction—made me wonder whether sense of taste can also be lost. Melissa also bravely struggled through the food. She's usually critical of her mother; it was most unusual of her to be so quiet. Her mother tore into the food, saying how rare it is for her to cook for guests, that it was a treat.

Afterward we sat out on her porch. I could see Melissa's heart sink when her mother produced several photo albums—parents, photo albums, and guests, very universal. The happier times, her mother and Rafael as a youngish couple, yet untouched by Puerto Rican nationalism, grandparents, Melissa holding up a tooth soon to be lost to the tooth fairy, her first day of school tearful and defiant, until we got to the arrests, trials, and newspaper clippings, and after that there were no more photographs. Perhaps that is where Melissa's paintings begin, recording memory when her parents stopped. We chitchatted amicably—nothing heavy, the way in-laws meet, not hiding that which is visible but certainly not digging into the closet for skeletons with or, in my case and Mrs. Shaw's, without skulls. Melissa's mother told us how she had met Rafael—at a political rally, of course—about Melissa as a child, etc. Mrs. Shaw told anecdotes about being English in the United States, and I told the story of Oruka, a primary school bully whom I almost killed with sleeping pills. Melissa spoke about her first painting when she was about ten years old—an eclipse. We told stories, and for the three hours or so, we were a family gathered to enjoy each other's company. Then we left with promises of coming to visit soon—felt normal in a very dysfunctional way.

It was the closest I have felt to being home. It felt really good just sitting there and entertaining each other with stories. I could not help feeling sad at the prospect that Melissa was going to add more distance to these kinds of moments by returning to Kwatee with me. But when it comes down to it, it is really just a question of money for airfare. It is possible to move easily between the continents, unlike in the old days of great treks and ships.

As we were driving to see Rafael, Melissa said thanks, and Mrs. Shaw asked for what, to which she replied for eating her mother's cooking without complaining. Mrs. Shaw and I laughed, at Melissa and her mother, and Melissa laughed too, at herself I suppose.

Some people are not visibly strong, in political strength, I mean—they are not in exile or in detention or martyred. They teach history at the local high school, or they make sure that their children grow up to be unselfish painters, or to recognize love when it hits them, or to stand up after the inevitable fall, and are there to welcome their children when they return. There are all sorts of strengths and loves: Love in a time of peace and love in a time of war. Love in a time of peace does not know what it has; beautiful, it doesn't feel itself, it just is. But for me, Melissa, her mother, Rafael, Joseph James, Ogum, and Sukena, etc., all us have loved in a time of war. It is a strong beautiful ugly frightening love, it nurtures and it kills. But when it survives, as I am sure it will between Melissa and her mother, it will be beautiful and fierce. Same hope for all of us, the wretched . . .

ICARUS REVISITED

We were thoroughly frisked once again. Not even Mrs. Shaw was spared the pat downs, and not surprisingly she complained with every touch. I also imagine it must have gotten increasingly difficult for her, since the guards look all the same.

Again Rafael exchanged a few words with the guard before he was allowed to come into the visitor's hall. I realized I was more nervous this time, partly because I was not sure how this meeting would go with Mrs. Shaw here, and partly because I now think of him as quite possibly my future father-in-law. And also because I'm returning home soon and feel pretty sure I won't be seeing him again for a long time.

The guards were staring at us. Not surprisingly. A black man with dreadlocks who spoke with an accent, an old white woman, a beautiful young Puerto Rican woman, and a crazy bomb maker who had turned down a presidential pardon because it did not come with a presidential apology. We all laughed when I told them why I thought the guards were staring. But Melissa's father added that they probably were under instruction to watch us. There were some who saw us as we were—a threat. An African political exile, a former professor of radical history, a radical daughter of a political prisoner, and the prisoner himself.

Melissa had brought Polaroid photographs from her show. As he looked at them, I could sense Rafael becoming sadder and sadder. "At moments like this I feel the full weight of being in prison. What they have taken from us is family"; he finally managed to put his thoughts into words. I can relate to that. In his words, I am able to find my exile. The moments with my family and my country had been taken away from me. And no matter that I was still alive and no matter if I had thrived in exile, there is a life, a life that is rightfully mine that exile denied me. Bitterness at the hopelessness is the thing that eats the insides of prisoners and exiles. Melissa's father could only share his daughter's triumph through Polaroid photos, photos of the experience and photos of paintings. And I, in another world hundreds of miles away, at this exact moment, I was supposed to be having dinner with Sukena and our children. If we lived several lives at the same time, parallel lives, maybe one of them would be the one we were supposed to live—me and Sukena and our children, Rafael in a free Puerto Rico or someplace like it helping his daughter grow—fruitful lives not wasted on getting to the starting line, wasted in struggles. But there are no parallel lives, so I weep on, struggling to get others to the starting line.

It was not a painful parting when we had to leave. Melissa will be coming back from Kwatee from time to time. Her relationship with her father is mostly through phone conversations and letters anyway. We said our good-byes and repeated the process of returning to the outside world. We were all very tired. The more tired Mrs. Shaw is, the worse her memory becomes. But she survived New York, visiting Melissa's parents and returning home without much incident. Melissa and I did not even get undressed before getting into bed. I had some really horrible dreams about rotting teeth that had become so brittle that I could remove them with my hands.

October 29th

LOVE

Love, what a strange concept really. Two strangers meet accidentally, fall in love, and decide to spend the rest of their lives together, kids and everything. Coincidence into destiny— that is what love does. A chance meeting that becomes life itself. After meeting Melissa, I am very sure I do not want a life without her. I feel all the braver for it, more committed to life, its beauty and truth—whatever that means—than when

I was a full-time revolutionary. I would kill a dictator for love before killing him for justice. Strange, very strange to see this written down, yet it makes perfect sense in my head.

November 10th

FADING MRS. SHAW

I called Mrs. Shaw to see how she is doing. She doesn't recognize my voice even though she pretends that she does. Everyone is a stranger to her. It is excruciating going to see her. As she predicted, all that remains of her is a young white British woman in an African colony, in a rather ragged old woman's body.

She is condescending—sometimes afraid of me or Melissa. Sometimes she is flirtatious, I suppose as she would have been in her twenties around African men—I am not sure what to think of this. At other times she is depressed as she waits for her husband to return from work. But we keep going to see her, to update an elaborate system of notes that keep her alive. Notes are everywhere, anything that we think she will look at. The alarm goes off at six o'clock a.m.—old people wake up very early, it turns out. The note says, "It is morning, time to eat some breakfast."

Downstairs there are three alarm clocks set for the next three meals and a snack. For her medication, Melissa and I take turns calling her to remind her. We do this at least four times a day. On each medication bottle there are instructions on how many to take. There are notes that say what to do in case there is a fire or another emergency.

Her whole memory is taped to the fridge, water faucets, bathroom, clocks, walls, stairs, etc. She is lucid enough to know that she doesn't want a nurse—of her instincts that remain, the strongest feed her racial anxieties and a strong sense of independence. She is still alive, but I have begun missing her deeply.

6 Victory Night!

Soon after the elections, fear was gone. Almost as if it had taken on a body of flesh, the space fear had occupied could be felt and seen. People spoke more loudly, drank more, made love more, and ate more. There were more greetings that broke into spontaneous embraces. There were fewer fights in the streets. Even the gangsters took a break, and people could walk home late at night from the celebrations. Disputes between neighbors were put on hold. Children cried less and played more. Once the fear was gone and freedom began to take its place, the whole country glowed. It seemed that the whole country was preparing for a massive wedding. Expensive dishes were prepared, and a stranger could walk into any house and be fed. It was a beautiful time. Everything bordered on a joyous excess.

Ogum, who spent a lot of time walking the streets in amazement, finally understood why this moment was worth all the sacrifices he had made. To see the whole country breathing and celebrating in unison, to feel a collective sigh of relief being released into the night, to see millions and millions of people without shackles, unbound and free, made the sacrifices worth it. He could not have regrets. These were moments of excess, moments experienced in the first independence. He also understood why those before him had kept fighting. They had tasted freedom too, and once tasted, they could never let it go. Not completely. Underneath the veil of fear, it was this first taste that had kept them fighting.

Kalumba was going to be here soon, he would find the new country an infant, and he would cradle it in his arms and together with the movement they would help it grow. There had been rumors that the Dictator would at the last minute stage a coup, order mass assassinations, do anything to keep the fear from being rolled back. But those rumors had not come to pass; the deal he had made with the movement allowed him to enter into history as one of the few African leaders to hand power over peacefully. After years and years in power, he wanted the world to believe that his conscience had finally caught up with him, or that he had simply been warming the seat, waiting for the newly independent nation to grow up. And now that he had nurtured the country into maturity, it was ready for freedom. But the people did not care how the Dictator intended to fade into history. The night of the second independence rolled in, and it was going to be ushered in, in style, and Kalumba would find the newborn alive and strong.

For the many that could not make it to the Kwatee National Stadium, celebration centers had been set up all over the country. In each district, there were multiple sites where huge outdoor theater screens would broadcast the handover of power. But most of the country, it seemed, was trying to make it to the stadium. Roads were jam-packed with buses, lorries, cars, bicycles, and donkey carts. Were it not for the people laughing and singing, the chaotic scenes would have been reminiscent of refugees returning home after a long and hard war.

When the line to the stadium stopped moving, the traffic police started asking people to veer off into the nearest small city or village for celebrations. It was hard to believe, but the capital city, like a small theater or clubhouse, had simply filled up. Even the tributary small cities on the way to the capital

149

were filling up, and thousands of people found they had to set up shop where they were. Little transistor radios and battery-powered small TVs, so small that from a few feet away the screens resembled shining postage stamps, were produced as if from nowhere. SIDCF cadets dressed in T-shirts that had the emblem of the double-fisted black power salute sprouted every few hundred meters. Food and drink to have been consumed in the stadium were put out on makeshift tables to be shared by all. With well over forty different ethnicities on the roads to the capital, this was going to be a colorful feast.

By the stadium the situation was even more chaotic. People had to be plowed off the road to let the VIPs pass, but they just closed back in behind the expensive cars, like displaced water. Ogum, Sukena, and Kalumba's father were lucky to have arrived much earlier in one of the VIP cars; otherwise, they would not have made it to the stadium. And even then, they still found the whole place packed with people who had been camping there for several days. This was a moment that happened only once, the people would say, but there would be somebody to remind them that it was in fact happening for the second time, only to be shushed. Even Kalumba's father, usually reserved, was visibly excited, and he kept whistling in amazement and saying, "Even the first one was not this big."

At the stadium the VIP section had been roped off. Ogum, Sukena, and Baba Kalumba sat down and were served samosas and cold Fantas by waiters and waitresses in smart white uniforms. Ogum asked for a cold beer. The handover would be at twelve o'clock midnight, but it was one of the hottest and most humid nights of the year, and everything was sticky and sweaty. Ogum had worn light clothes, but even in his movement T-shirt, he was boiling hot. It was even worse for Sukena, who, thinking that the evening might get cool, had to deal with a cumbersome jacket. As they mingled with other party members, themes of forgiveness, reconciliation, new beginnings, second chances, redemption, economic growth, and safeguarding democracy dominated the discussions. Even though the movement members looked haggard and had swollen eyes from all the campaigning and nights without sleep, they were euphoric. It is one thing to usher in a New Year and another thing to usher in a new era for millions of people.

Ogum left a group of fellow activists and stood surrounded by strangers, where he could be alone for a while. He wanted to steal a few moments of this freedom for himself. He wanted a piece of this night to remember just for himself, without somebody else's words being inscribed on it. But he soon found his mind wandering, trying to find Kalumba. "He should have been here. This is his moment as well." In that moment, he decided to let the issue of the List go. This was a time for reconciliation, and if Kalumba was guilty then Ogum was going to forgive him and if he was not guilty then there was nothing to forgive. He took a deep breath, filling his lungs with the sweat-filled heavy air of freedom.

His mind wandered to Sukena, whom he eyed, speaking animatedly to a group of activists. The two of them were getting married in a few months' time. They would have been married sooner were it not for the negotiations between the two families. They probably shouldn't have decided to take the traditional route, but they wanted to. They wanted to make the statement that two traditions can marry. And that required patience, as each detail—where the wedding would take place, where they would live, or who would pay bride price—was being negotiated. Once they decided on this route, they found that they had very little control. Bride price was not important for either of them, but it was for the extended family on both sides. It had as yet to be settled. In addition there were tensions and mistrust that had nothing to do with them but with history. But at least, perhaps due to the changing political scene in which all was becoming possible, there had been no vehement objections to their getting married.

The beer got to him, and he had to go to the bathroom reserved for the VIPs. On his way back he heard someone call his name. It was the ambassador, who wanted to introduce him to his wife, leaning affectionately on the ambassador's shoulder. He had never seen her before. She said hello with a heavy Ghanaian accent. Remembering the ambassador's office, the paintings and the Fela Kuti music, he wondered if she was yet another addition to his Africanist sensibilities. But just as soon, he thought of himself and Sukena and all they had endured for loving across cultures, how she was Kyukato cultural property, and he conceded that the ambassador's love for his African wife could be genuine. He smiled as he shook her hand.

The ambassador was leaving soon, and he mentioned that he had told his replacement about Ogum. Ogum thought back to their first meeting. It had not been a joke. The ambassador was here to watch his hard work just like Ogum. But whereas Ogum would be celebrating his work toward freedom, the ambassador would be trying to find a way of destroying it. He was here looking for fault lines like Ogum. He recalled their conversation about who was compromised. Forgiveness was the code word. Ogum said good-bye and returned to his seat. He asked for a samosa and another cold beer to try to liven himself up. The joy in the stadium and outside was too contagious for the ambassador to ruin his evening. Sukena and Kalumba's father soon returned, and they chatted away, waiting for the festivities to begin, watching the VIPs file in.

There were all sorts of VIPs, including some from the ruling party, with fat stomachs and sinewy faces, trying to look dignified in their loss. Whenever they spotted someone from the movement they over-shook their hands as they expressed brotherhood, making Sukena remark, "Look at the snakes squirm. Thieves, murderers, criminals who should be in jail. But here they are in the full glow of the second independence." They were already jostling for power.

There were presidents from other African countries who, even though recently elected, had already started banning newspapers and framing members of their own party with political crimes. There were ambassadors from Western countries who for the most part sat in their own corner looking like a hungry pack of dogs. Then there were army generals from various nations who brought their favorite weapon, contractors, instead of their wives. And there were some who were there for no other reason than that they were wealthy or had contributed money to the movement. Anyone who would collect something in the future was here to make sure that the nation was on its way to full recovery. But no matter, this was a time of celebration, Ogum kept reminding himself. Revolutionary times reveal the best and worst in people. He would rather dwell on the best.

On the field, all sorts of festivities had been taking place all evening. Bands played their most popular songs and then gave the double-fisted salute at the end of their performances. Students from the primary and high schools performed previously banned political plays and African dances. University students attempted to perform a play, which they had tellingly titled *Once Bitten Twice Shy,* and were booed off the stage. A Samasi dance troupe took the stage, driving the crowd crazy and inspiring the foreign dignitaries to ululate.

Then, as the army band began playing the Kwatee national anthem, the top members of the movement began arriving. Each VIP was driven in a spotless black Mercedes to a red carpet in the middle of the stadium. Later, Kalumba's father was to describe the Mercedes Benzes as without blemish— sacrificial lambs, but for whom? Fireworks raced into the sky and exploded as each VIP stood in the middle of the field for a split second and then walked to another VIP section specifically reserved for them behind the president's dais.

An announcer well known for his deep rumbling voice that broadcast football matches declared, *Here comes Mr. So and So. He received his education from_____. In the movement, he was responsible for _____. He is well known as a former political prisoner who spent _____ years in the former you know what's jail.* And they kept filing in until one section of the stadium was dotted with shiny black Mercedes Benzes. The crowd, perhaps understanding the prosperity displayed before them as a promise of their own prosperity to come, cheered the VIPs on.

And then the *former you know what,* as the announcer referred to him, was driven into the stadium in a stretch limo. It was so long that the people first gasped before erupting into jeers. But he held himself in dignity and, flanked by the secret service, walked up to the VIP section. Ogum, even though in the different VIP section, had never seen him at such a close range before. The man was balding. In the past he had straightened his hair to cover that up, but now he opted to be bald, like Tupac Shakur or Michael Jordan, as he liked to joke. He was old, well past eighty, and when he turned to look around and their eyes met for a second, Ogum felt the old fear.

But the soon-to-be-former president smiled at him, a kind, gentle smile, a grandfatherly smile that bordered on being senile, and Ogum was all the more scared. The man who had held a whole country in fear, who had declared himself president for life, whose face was in every office, voice booming through every TV and radio, whose photo appeared on every bank note, shilling, and penny, who was responsible for the death, jailing, and exiling of many, was just another old man whose senility was now showing. Ogum smiled back and gave him the double-fisted salute. The president laughed and returned it, at which a number of the VIPs in both sections cheered. The former dictator was celebrating. His sins would not follow him out of office—tomorrow or the day after, he was going to be asked to settle a regional conflict. His destiny was with history.

The president-elect arrived in a beat-up jeep. The army band pounded on the drums and blew a hurricane through the trumpets. Fireworks were set off, sounding like huge bombs. People clapped, yelled, laughed, stomped their feet, and wailed. Never before had Ogum seen anything like this. The president-elect waved to the crowd, giving the double-fisted salute. Without much fanfare on his part, without even using the red carpet, he walked with military efficiency to the VIP section and sat in his assigned seat.

Whereas the former president insisted on his throne-like chair, the new president was in a normal office chair, the kind his soon-to-be ministers were sitting in. He was a man of the people. Tall, gaunt, with a head full of white hair that he combed into an Afro, his charisma was unmistakable. He was a leader who did not have to show it. And therefore he did not. He was Comrade the Leader.

Then the speeches started. The first speech was given by a veteran of the first war for independence.

"I am old. I have earned the right to speak as I like," he declared. Everyone clapped and egged him on. "Well, we fought the first time and we ended up with nothing. After the celebrations ended, we still ate boiled maize and beans as our *furu* fishes disappeared up Queen Liza's bottoms."

Here the crowd cheered and laughed.

"The Homeguards took over the country. They imprisoned the men and freed our women into miniskirts, made in the USA. I am an old man, and I like good legs just like a young man. But not when everything is upside down. Shall we let that happen again?" he asked rhetorically, and the crowd answered a loud *no* back to him. "There was a friend of mine, a preacher, he gave haiku sermons. I listened to him before *you know who* made him disappear. Reading from the Bible, he said,

No one puts new wine into old wineskins, or else the new wine will burst the skins, and it will be spilled, and the skins will be destroyed. But new wine must be put into fresh wineskins, and both are preserved. No man having drunk old wine immediately desires new, for he says, 'The old is better.' A people marching for freedom are the wine and the government that they erect into power is the wineskin. Fight for the new; accept the new!

"He was a man of few words. So before I sit down let me tell you a story . . ." He paused and waited for the crowd to catch on to the joke. The people yelled to him to be like the preacher. He waved back to much applause as he left the podium. As Ogum and Sukena happily yelled him off the stage, Ogum could not help thinking, with a feeling of pride, that Kwatee would never let his father be forgotten. Even after the second independence, his sermons would continue to inspire—words that contain truth do not die with the martyred.

As more speakers took to the podium, the denunciations of the past became more and more violent. Some called for an immediate public flogging of the Dictator. Others suggested that the hand that carried his symbolic fly whisk be cut off, while others suggested that he be hanged. Some even called for a firework to be stuck up his ass, to much laughter. And it went on and on. The Dictator sat trying not to look afraid, but anyone observing him closely could see that he kept looking at Comrade with growing alarm.

When it seemed that the crowd would break into the VIP section and break the Dictator into little pieces, Comrade walked to the microphone. The crowd went silent.

"It is not my turn to speak yet," he apologized, "but I have to, in order to ask for your cooperation. We have been patient and have fought for a long time; surely we can hold on a few more moments. We have to show the rest of the world, even if they fought against it, that we have matured into a democracy," he said, pointing in the direction of the European diplomats. "We have to show our African brothers and sisters that democracy, in which law, and not revenge, is supreme, is possible." The crowd calmed down but not before giving him a huge hip-hip-hurrah.

And so when Comrade called for the former dictator to speak, he did not have the authority of a former president; he resembled the old man who was the first to speak. He was here because the movement allowed him to be. His power, which had thrived on fear, had been demystified. Ogum understood that there was nothing spontaneous about the whole show: The movement had orchestrated this humiliation. He had been undressed in public. Even though the program indicated that he had been allotted thirty minutes, with midnight almost near, he had to cut short his speech. So he mumbled a few words to the effect that he was *proud to have in a small but profound way contributed to democracy.* He had always been planning for democracy but had been waiting for the right moment—at which someone from the crowd yelled that the right moment was now. It was a few minutes before midnight. He beckoned Comrade and swore him in.

As they finished exchanging vows, midnight struck. The whole stadium went dark. Lights came back on after a few seconds to find the national flag being brought down and in its place a white flag, with two double fists rising up in the air. Fireworks roared high into the sky before exploding into black-fisted sparks that showered down on the people. Some people fainted while others spoke in tongues. And amid the joyous wailing the new president stood up and began speaking.

"Ladies and gentlemen, or, to be truer to this historic moment—my fellow comrades!" He paused and waited for applause. "Comrades! As many of you know, like the preacher Grandfather reminded us of, I am not a man of many words. In fact, as you all know, I do not stand on ceremony. Therefore, I will be brief so that we can get a good night's rest before the work of rebuilding our country begins tomorrow.

"It must in fact begin today, now. We have been dying for close to six hundred years. Slavery, colonialism, neocolonialism, all have been systems designed to expropriate our labor, our sweat and blood, siphon off our wealth for our local elite and their masters abroad. We defeated the slave driver, we defeated the colonizer, and now we have defeated his dogs. Let the world hear, if it has ears. Africa is no longer for sale. The African is no longer for sale. African sweat will no longer be packaged for the consumption of the elite. We shall fight to the last of us if need be.

"But comrades, I know you understand my liberation words, my words of war, a soldier's words. I want you to also hear my words of peace. We have learned to die like men and women worthy of life. Let us learn how to live like men and women worthy of life. Forgive where you can, but do not forget. Forgive, forgive, and forgive. We know how to die. Now let us learn to live."

And on that note he stopped, as if at a loss of words, then started to speak again, but as the crowd collectively lurched toward the microphone, he abruptly stepped away and, shaking his head from side to side, walked over to the old man who was the former dictator and extended his hand to him. Then they hugged. And the whole stadium hugged and cried. And the whole country followed his example, and people hugged those closest to them. The country would never be the same. *There was no way, after tasting this promise, that the people would ever allow it to slide back to the days of dictatorships,* Ogum thought.

Later, when much calmer, Ogum would remember how he and Sukena had held each other close as the words *forgive, forgive, forgive* hypnotically played in his mind over and over again. Comrade had repeated the word three times, the same amount of times Peter had denied Jesus. But is it possible, could it have been possible under different circumstances for Jesus to deny Peter three times? And if so, wouldn't Jesus have been right?

The Benzes came to life. The VIPs started filing out in the order that they had come. The former dictator and the president walked together, but instead of the president jumping into his jeep, he helped the former dictator into the stretch limo and was himself swallowed up in it and disappeared.

Sukena, Ogum, and Baba Kalumba started making their way back. It would take a long time to get back home, but they were not in a hurry. They thought of stopping at a hotel near the stadium, but all of the hotels were booked. They joined the traffic jam to wait for morning. But the adrenaline was still flowing. Horns were blaring and car stereos for miles and miles around were tuned to the same radio station playing songs that almost everyone seemed to know, to which everyone was singing along. An occasional firework tore into the sky, and loud cheers followed it.

"Well, it is certainly a night to remember," Sukena said, to invite conversation.

"It reminded me of the first independence," Kalumba's father said.

"How? Were they that similar?" Sukena followed up.

"Same dog, same old tricks, different audience! Boys and girls, brace yourselves," Baba Kalumba said, laughing, in a tone that he might have used with his students.

"No, seriously," Sukena insisted. She understood Baba Kalumba's caution but at the same time was deeply infected with the optimism with which the whole nation had greeted the lowering of the flag.

"It was the same, even the speeches. The British flag was lowered in the dark too." His tone had become a bit more serious.

"But it was supposed to be a surprise for the people. It was supposed to mark a new dawn," Ogum said desperately.

"Metaphors and symbols can be accidental—the lowering of the flag in the dark now has only one meaning. Who knows what these guys have been doing in the dark?" Kalumba's father asked. He could remember the first independence, and yes, the second independence had been grander, but it was the same hope, the same intensity, and the same speeches. "Old wine in new skins, doesn't matter how you twist the metaphor—anything is possible. I just want my son back," he added.

"Soon . . . And what a surprise. You are right—this is a time of possibility. Even he cannot imagine the beauty he shall find," Sukena said happily. There were two big things she would cross off the list—Kalumba's return and the second independence. And with these two things happening, other little things in her list would fall into place.

December 10th

PREPARING TO GO BACK HOME!!!!!!

Last night, Comrade was inaugurated. I suppose now we have to call him President—can we call him Comrade President? President Comrade? E-mail message from Sukena telling me I should have been there.

I have just about 10,000 dollars. The talk at New York University brought me quite neatly to the five-figure mark. I suppose exile was worth a quantifiable something after all, all these talks financing my return. Would I gladly do it all over again for 10,000 dollars? Fuck no!

I have bought a ticket for January 3rd. Melissa is more excited than me. I suppose this is the big one, as the comedian Sanford used to say—she'll join me after a few days.

I don't want to think too much about returning and what it means. I have buried myself in the details—paying bills, packing, getting rid of clothes, cleaning, going through my papers and getting rid of the ones I don't need. Same thing with my books. It is amazing the amount of junk I have accumulated over the years. Even though I have never skated in my life, I found I owned a pair of ice skates.

December 14th

CALL ME DOCTOR WHO

I received the news that my dissertation was accepted stoically—with the same feeling as I do after a talk on exile. Who has fooled who? I now have a piece of paper that says I am a doctor of letters. Melissa spiced things up in bed by pretending to be a patient and I the doctor—not a bad by-product of all that work. I beguiled her with all the big words and the theories that I am an expert of—and she my student, eager to learn. I have to admit to myself the sex was quite enjoyable. But fair is fair; she has used me as a nude on many occasions, leaving me cold and shivering. She says that I do not realize the magnitude of what I have done—to survive and even triumph.

December 25th

XMAS AT MRS. SHAW'S!

I made a call to my father to wish him a merry Christmas—my first such call since I left—always easier to write than talk. We spoke briefly about my travel plans and that was that. I think we are more comfortable communicating through the pen; it's what we have been doing for so long. The conversation was brief and uncomfortable.

We cooked a lot of food and took it to Mrs. Shaw for a Christmas dinner. She ate, eyeing us with suspicion, especially when we sat down at the table with her as opposed to serving her. It was sort of funny in a tragic way. I could tell she was afraid, but she put on a brave face as if she was the liberal but cautious type that allowed this sort of thing to happen in her colonial world. We labeled everything; put some of the food in the freezer and the rest down below. At least she will have food for another week or so.

I am just marking time now. Time is moving so slowly. My life here is winding down and a new one is about to begin— the paradox of returning to a new life. I have been thinking of returning in the same way I thought of coming to exile— new beginnings.

But deep down, I know that it is a continuation. The difference is that in exile I did not think about continuation; otherwise I would have known of Melissa's father and other political prisoners, I would have thought about Puerto Rico, I would have thought about Native Americans, I would have continued the struggle, I would have found love earlier and continued to live. Instead I squandered ten years, my whole life, because in a way I was going back home to retire into teaching. Things are still hazy, but I know that even if I retire into teaching, I will not be blind. If nothing else, I will tell people in my country about Melissa's father. I will still be useful. I am a mess of hope, confusion, and doubt. But the anger is gone. I hardly ever drink now.

December 31st

NEW YEAR'S EVE AT MRS. SHAW'S

We went back to Mrs. Shaw and essentially had a repeat of the 25th. Even though we have been calling, it is obvious that she is not eating, or for that matter bathing. Melissa took her upstairs and bathed her. She was unable to stay up till midnight, and after we put her to bed we went to Eagle's Bar. It has been so long since we were last there. At midnight we kissed happy New Year and went home. We tried to have sex but were too worried about Mrs. Shaw and so we gave up.

It has been a year since I met her; she has brought me all sorts of luck, and now she is leaving me. How long after I was born did my mother live? Strange I cannot remember—one year? Two years?

January 2nd

ALL PACKED!

I am all packed and ready to go home. E-mails from Sukena and Ogum asking for my final itinerary. We haven't been saying much to each other—almost by agreement, the discussions, or should I say the fights, are being held off for the moment. Melissa and I went to see Mrs. Shaw again, and we couldn't help crying. There is a part of me that is mourning my own mother. Perhaps Mrs. Shaw was right after all, though I don't think my mother would have turned into a lipstick-lathering grandmother.

There is a part of me that has reconciled her to my mother, perhaps coalesced them both. I had been missing her all along without knowing. There is a part of me that celebrated the mother I did not know in the Mrs. Shaw I came to know. I found Melissa in the kitchen crying. I broke down too. After a while a tough-looking Mrs. Shaw walked into the kitchen to ask if something had at last happened to that *son of a bitch, her husband.* At last some laughter.

Yes, I am missing Mrs. Shaw rather terribly.

January 3rd

GOOD-BYES

I woke up at 6:00 a.m., sat on the bed, and called Mrs. Shaw to remind her to take her medication. I called her again at 6:30, and then at 7:00 a.m., again at 7:30 a.m. At 8:00 a.m., Melissa woke up to ask why I keep calling her. She saw I was crying, and she understood what was happening. She sat up with me on the bed and wrapped a blanket around us. I was very cold. I called again at 8:30 a.m. and then again at 8:45, 8:50, 8:55, 9:00, 9:05, 9:10 a.m., and each time she picked up the phone and each time I reminded her it was time to take her medication. At some point she asked me if I was okay and I said yes. At 9:30 a.m., I called and there was no answer.

At 10:00 a.m. I called again and there was no answer. I tried again a few minutes later and there was no answer. Then it was time for Melissa to drive me to the airport. We did not speak at all. I tried not to feel anything by concentrating on my return.

When we got to the airport, I called the police. "I have been trying to reach my mother since last night and no one is picking up. I am really worried. Can someone go over there and check up on her?" I gave them the address. I thought about the skull. Chances are they will conclude that it was a historical artifact. Once identified as belonging to an ancient African, it would be well preserved.

I don't think my parting with Melissa could have been any stranger. First, we now have the death of Mrs. Shaw between us, my killing her between us. Then we parted like an old couple, the way grandparents part at airports, no fanfare, just grumpy reminders to do this or that. Mrs. Shaw has aged us considerably. We would be seeing each other soon—same thing I thought about Sukena. But this is a more mature love; it has eaten a lot of salt in the one year.

After being stopped at every turn, frisked, and prodded, I was finally in the plane: destination—home. I was very tired. *I am so exhausted* is all I keep thinking to myself.

I am not sure if this should be the last of the journal. I suspect I will be too busy living to keep a journal, but we shall see. It has done its job, though. Here I am in the plane, return inevitable, barring some unforeseen circumstances.

January 4th

HOME—ARRIVAL!

Tourists with their pidgin Kyukato were simply walking in, waving a 50-dollar visa fee. But for me, it was hell explaining at the customs why I didn't have lots of luggage or something valuable like a stereo or computer to declare. "You have been gone for ten years and you are trying to tell us you are coming back with nothing?" the customs officer asked.

"I have a PhD, is that nothing?" I asked him.

But they insisted: they wanted to know how it was possible that I had been gone for so long and yet here I was with nothing. Never mind that I had been in exile. All the more reason why I should have more stuff, they argued.

"But I do have stuff. See?" I said, showing them the diploma and some of the books I had brought with me.

"What about money? You must be hiding some somewhere."

"What I have remains in a bank in the United States," I said. But they wanted to know how much I had on me. I had about 500 dollars on me. Not knowing the going rates for corruption, I left the customs officer with 200. I, a returning exile, had to pay a corrupt fee to enter back into my country. I was grateful, though; I did not have to deal with my own feelings of fear, panic, and longing. Customs official = expensive shrink!

But it was just as well, because the whole thing took my mind off Melissa, Mrs. Shaw, and my return. I was just about to meet with my ten-year absence.

At last I was home. Tourists and all. Hawkers selling roses, smokes, beer; taxi drivers trying to get me into their vehicle; criminals posing as taxi drivers; people yelling in joy as a loved one appeared from the mouth of the beast, others crying as they caught a last glance of a loved one; a thousand languages, tower of Babel, the smell of samosas and roast goat and in front of me the people I call my family. I was home. I was happy, the kind of happiness that is content, that has returned to its foundation.

The first person I saw was my father, then Sukena waving, and then Ogum. I tried to appear calm, but between nervousness and pure joy, a simple, childish, unmitigated joy, there was no way I would have succeeded. They certainly looked older, especially my father. His hair had grayed and he appeared more stooped, but his eyes were the same, shining, warm, but hard around the corners. Ogum was the same, reserved almost to the point of coldness, but those who know him well like I do understand he takes upheaval in small doses. He wants to remain standing, as he has for the past ten years.

And Sukena? She looked nervous, almost unsure of how to act. I had never seen her indecisive before, but she looked beautiful. Her dreads were much longer, down to her waist. She relaxed after we hugged, and she broke into a huge smile that put me at ease as well. I don't remember speaking until we got into the Datsun pickup that had driven me to exile. Mostly I remember looking and trying to commit everything to memory.

I was tired and hungry. "I would like some samosas," I said. Everyone laughed, remembering I could eat twenty at one sitting. There was this place that I remembered in Soweto, a slum area named after its counterpart in South Africa. They made the best.

"After all these years, your first request is a samosa?" my father asked. "Well, so it shall be," he answered his own question.

He revved the Datsun as if readying the car for the Safari Rally. I used to enjoy that a lot as a kid, and I laughed. And we were off, the four of us squashed into the dashboard. Ogum asked me a question about Harlem, and I answered that it was the only place that had felt like home. But was it home? Knowing what I know now, it was home, the place where I kept my eyes open to remember being home. It was warm to be surrounded by blackness. I don't think my answer was clear. How does one convey exile to one who stayed? He was just trying to make conversation, and I was thankful for it all the same.

I had forgotten just how bad things were in Soweto, especially when juxtaposed with Springdale Estate. A wall, about ten feet high, with barbed wire and broken jagged cemented glass on top of it, separates the two. Springdale is where the wealthy live, and from a distance one sees a sea of red-tiled rooftops. Soweto from a distance looks like a jagged rough black sea. The one entrance to Springdale is like a police post, designed to keep out the residents of Soweto. It makes me think of Icarus, though it seems that here it is the wealthy who are being locked in, as opposed to the criminals.

In the afternoon heat, I felt my stomach heave as the stench from open sewers hit my nostrils. There are little dead animals, and their predators are also dead: birds, rats, mice, cats, and dogs. There are piles and piles of garbage. I always imagine there are two kinds of poverty—urban and rural poverty.

Rural poverty seems humane while urban poverty seems cruel and excessive. But that is only in my imagination; they are both violent and unforgiving. It is strange that here in Soweto, I was reminded of the one time I visited Appalachian Ohio and was knocked senseless by the poverty I saw there.

Soweto is busy, like the airport but dirtier. There are people everywhere, each trying to sell something. "This kind of poverty is criminal," I found myself saying to no one in particular. "Well, welcome back," Sukena said. I didn't think they seemed bothered, but then again, why should they be? They had been here fighting. Finally we made it to the little kiosk. I did not recognize anyone, but soon I was salivating. Then the first bite, a second, and I was done with the first samosa. I was convinced that memory is in taste. That was the first moment when I felt I was truly back. I could even convince myself I never left. Ten more samosas and I was ready to continue with the journey home. Later in the night, I paid a heavy price for this.

But this much I knew, even though I did not think I did: Soweto and Springdale represent our country and all that is wrong with it; the new government that we had sacrificed so much for does not have the imagination or the will to tear down the wall. It requires an act of imagination. They had been driving through it too long—to them it was part of the landscape, like a mountain or a riverbed.

I didn't want to go on like this, for there was much to catch up on, more samosas to eat. I had to pay closer attention to how I was feeling and acting. I never imagined returning to be a simple affair, but I never thought it would be so complex either. I recognized the landscape, and all the talk about Soweto was just a valve—no one really wanted to talk about how they were feeling. After all, I couldn't get off the plane, punch Ogum in the nose, kiss Sukena, and find a wife for my father. So things would have to be taken easy—a day at a time, ease back into things.

We arrived home in the evening. I couldn't believe how tired I felt. It was weird being in the same house I grew up in. Everything looked and felt smaller. I wondered if I was more happy or relieved to be back. I was relieved to be still alive, that is for sure. I left my father, Ogum, and Sukena talking and went to sleep. They looked disappointed that I was so tired, but I imagine they talked way into the night.

January 5th

And . . . I Am Born Again!

I woke up to a lot of hustle and bustle. Ogum and Sukena were already up, and they offered to walk with me around the farm, but really I just wanted to be by myself. It was strange walking around the farm—memories were not yet dead. The pear tree I once fell out of, I was still up there eating fruit; a sisal plant where I wrote silly love poems for Sukena, even though it had outgrown them (as did Sukena), they were still there, love running faster than the river, brighter than the moon, love as deep as a volcano (waiting to erupt years later, I suppose, and what an eruption it was), etc., little notes.

At my mother's grave, I could see my father's guilt or love in the flowers, so many that I had to smile as I imagined her complaining that they were blocking out the sunlight. Jesus—I suppose I did find pieces of her in Melissa's mother and Mrs. Shaw—slowly I understood what it means to grow up without a mother. She would have taught me the best parts of myself; maybe I would not even have needed Mrs. Shaw. I think we want to do well in this world because of our mothers. I was being overly sentimental but fuck it, it's okay to be sentimental after ten years, no, a lifetime, of missing someone so deeply and yet never having known them, not knowing how. It was okay to sit there by her grave and miss her because I had seen pieces of her, finally. I sat there and cried, harder than I have ever cried, like a little kid, till I thought my eyes would bleed.

I lay there till little pieces of me returned and what before had been so fractured started to make sense. I had returned for a reason. The simplest of reasons. Because this is where I am from. And I owed this land the truth regardless. Nothing more, nothing less. This is why I was here crying by the grave of a woman I hardly knew, yet to whom I owed the truth. Ogum's father, my father—the whole nation should have the truths I was carrying in me. And the people I had met along the way in my exile were angels sent to guide me to this moment. Yep, very sentimental. Melissa would not recognize me like this, but whatever it takes.

I decided to walk back to the house. I ran into my father, who did not even ask me what was the matter. Instead he led me into a room and without a word ushered me in. Now, what I found, I had never expected. I had heard of the ceremony, but I did not think it was done anymore. In the old days, among the Kyukato, if a person lived in a foreign culture for a long time, he or she had to be reborn. Ogum's aunt and my aunts did it. I finally understand what it feels like to be taken over by a spirit—I did not speak in tongues or anything, just complete love, a spirit of well-being. Total love, this must be how it feels to be born. Being welcomed into the world in total unconditional love, a new beginning, a transition into a new stage, love that says we love you no matter what you become, and in my case what I was, what I became in exile. I was changed, left the room feeling rather weak, like a calf trying to find its feet.

I had to be helped by Sukena to the podium to address the people who had come to celebrate my coming back. There were hundreds of people. I awkwardly told them a story about the hunter whose house is taken over by the elephant and how he plots to get it back. Outside my exile story I was never a good public speaker, but I received much applause anyway. The action of return was the story—I could have just stood there.

Afterward I went for a walk with Sukena—a pleasant enough walk, I would say. I think we just might manage to save our friendship. I am hopeful. We did not talk much, just enjoyed seeing each other. Told her about Melissa and she told me about Ogum, their life together, marriage, etc.

Only a father could arrange such a ceremony. I am home. Like any newborn I have lost my eloquence, but damn it, I am back.

7
The Return

To Ogum, Sukena, and Kalumba's father, the first meeting after ten years was anticlimactic. After months and months of anticipation, years actually, it felt like the most normal thing in the world for Kalumba to be stepping off that plane. It felt like they had been picking him up from international visits every six months or so for the past ten years. *After all, a moment cannot contain ten years,* Ogum reasoned. And so they waited, talking about the weather, food, petrol prices, mundane things, and at times nothing at all.

Yet on another level the moment was a capsule, a grenade really, that in spite of a calm exterior was always moments from explosion. Inside, for those who were waiting and for the one arriving, it took all their will to contain the anxiety of anticipation. At this level, the amicable exterior of routine, the familiarity of just another day, was really the exterior of a grenade.

At first glance Kalumba did not look any different from when he left, except for adding a little weight. Kalumba, by way of explaining the extra weight, would later tell Ogum that while chicken at home was a delicacy, in the United States it was cheap and full of growth hormones. It was Sukena who first spotted Kalumba emerging from the long and chaotic line of passengers, and she excitedly pointed him out. He did not have the amount of luggage one would expect from someone moving back home, just a carry-on and one suitcase. He was dressed in jeans and sneakers, and in spite of it being January and hot, he was in a heavy sweater. His dreadlocks were much longer and unkempt. He had a short beard, and his eyes, in spite of the twenty-four hours of traveling, were not tired. He was smiling. That was the one thing that was different from his departure. He couldn't stop smiling.

Ogum wondered how he saw them: if they too looked changed and the same all at once. Kalumba's father was smiling too, and it struck him how they had the same features, how they looked more like brothers than father and son. They had the same spare, almost deprived, tall frame, except that Kalumba was bulging a little. Their jaws were set to give a face that was both reserved and at the same time welcoming. They had the same walk and the same voice, although while Kalumba spoke fast, his father spoke slowly, probably from his teaching days when every word mattered.

This was the first time Ogum had ever seen Sukena nervous. She seemed absentminded and spoke automatically. She held her arms across her chest as if she was trying to still something that was raging in her. She and Kalumba hugged nervously, for a few seconds only. Ogum felt panic welling inside of him as he saw Sukena emerge from the embrace with a huge smile on her face. Ten years ago, all four of them would have expected that Sukena and Kalumba would be reuniting as lovers. But now, they, like their nation, were standing on unsure ground.

When Kalumba left, he left behind a silence between Sukena and Ogum. Before he left, Ogum and Sukena had never really been alone together; whenever they had met, the occasion had always been Kalumba. On the drive back from the border, there was a silence between them, and sometimes Ogum felt that they had become lovers to fill this silence. Before, Ogum had told himself that the past would remain in the past and, just like nations, for lovers there is never going back. But he could not help wondering whether Sukena felt a twinge of regret and perhaps wished to reconnect with Kalumba. After all, she had loved him. Exile, in a way, had frozen their relationship, a ten-year-delayed heartbreak, and who knew if perhaps they would decide after thawing that they wished to remain lovers. Baba Kalumba felt the tension underneath the happy exterior rising and asked Kalumba if he would like something to eat.

"You know what I would really like? A samosa," Kalumba answered.

"After all these years, only a samosa?" Kalumba's father asked. "Well, I guess we have to make it possible," he added. He revved the car between gears, giving the samosa search a sense of urgency. He used to do this when Kalumba was young. There was one samosa spot that they all loved—in Soweto. Ogum thought that at some point he would like to study places and how they are named.

"Kalumba, did you ever make it to Harlem? Is it like our Harlem?" Ogum asked, by way of making conversation.

"Harlem, New York? I was there once. It was like being home. Other places I had to close my eyes to feel like I was home. In Harlem, I opened my eyes to feel at home. It's hard to explain, but it was such places that kept me sane," Kalumba answered. "Well, relatively sane," he added, trying to lighten the heavy mood the forced conversation was creating.

"Samosas?" Sukena asked.

"Nope, not like Soweto's," Kalumba answered. "You know, I don't remember eating in Harlem, the New York one, I mean. I remember sounds, blackness . . . the music."

"Billie Holiday . . ." he added after a second or two.

Ogum looked around Soweto and thought about the poverty all around him. Next to Soweto was Springdale Estate, where the wealthy lived. Like the local Harlem and Morningdale Estate, here the poverty existed to highlight the opulence. Soweto made Springdale possible. It was the labor from Soweto that had built Springdale, the houses, the roads, the sewers, and that dug the holes that carried electric and telephone lines. It was Soweto that supplied the maids to be raped by their new masters, and the old men, whom the new elites called garden boys, to keep everything manicured. The movement had appealed for Soweto's support, and Soweto had responded. Soon Soweto would be calling for the wall to be torn down.

The movement was committed to change, but it had to be gradual. The alliance might not last for long, Ogum thought grimly, but this was not discussed; among the four of them there was a silent agreement to put politics aside for the night. Therefore, no one mentioned that the new president had bought a home in Springdale, and if anyone had, Ogum would have said that the idea was not to make everyone poor but to make the poor better off. Hope, possibility—these were exciting times, and he wished Kalumba would lose himself in them and forget the past.

Soon after they ate, Kalumba complained of being tired, much to the relief of everyone. With the exception of sharing occasional details like new buildings, who was married to who now, and whose children were doing what now, they drove to Baba Kalumba's home in silence. Baba Kalumba showed Kalumba to his room as he would have a guest.

Ogum and Sukena slipped into the room next door. Finally alone, they too did not speak much, in fear of saying the wrong thing to each other. Mercifully, the day had wiped them out, and soon they were asleep. Everything was functioning, yet everything felt broken.

The following morning, Kalumba woke up to the sounds of pots and pans banging. He dressed and stepped outside barefoot. It was cold. Not the excessive cold he had left behind; here, it was cold because it was still early in the morning. He ran his feet in the grass to let the morning dew cool him into waking up fully. He walked over to the place where, before he left, there had been a pigsty and next to it a chicken barn.

They had been demolished and now only the foundations, overgrown by weeds, remained.

He walked to a huge sisal plant. Using a thorn from its tip, he used to chisel messages, proverbs, and thoughts of the day into its massive leaves. There was nothing on it now. He felt the rubbery green leaves, trying to read them like Braille for traces of things he had written. He felt nothing; not even his bold declaration "I love Sukena" remained. He walked over to the plum trees. It was January, and as he had expected, most of the plums had been picked or had fallen on the ground. The lone pear tree would not be ready with any offerings until April.

He walked farther down, to his mother's grave. He stood there for a while. He bent to pick a bright red flower and then decided against it. He tried to think of things to say, but nothing came to mind except that he was back. He walked over to the cow shed. He had been expecting to see the same two cows he left behind: one was named Funny because it had a funny face, and the other, an orphan, was named Abiku because its mother and twin had died during the calving. He later learned that both the previous cows had been sold to the local butchery soon after he left. Now in their place there were two healthy-looking Jerseys. His father's farm looked smaller than he remembered.

He walked back to the house feeling numb and disconnected. It was as if he was still in the United States looking at photographs someone had sent him. Madison's winter was still in him, Melissa's breath intermingling with his as they walked from place to place. What he had left behind in the United States would not become his past—this was his past. His real life was in a college town in Wisconsin. When he got to the house, he decided to trace the source of the noise that had awakened him. He wanted to remain distracted.

He found five women in the kitchen drinking tea, but he could tell that they were preparing for a big feast. Around them, in big baskets, were black-eyed peas, piles of green and ripe bananas and plantains, mounds of wheat flour, potatoes, cabbages, onions, and cilantro. Their faces looked familiar, but he could not place them, and he felt a sense of panic and shame at the embarrassment that was about to follow.

"Shame, shame . . . Why aren't you greeting your aunt?" one of the women said. As soon as she spoke, he saw traces of Ogum—it was Ogum's aunt.

"Of course I remember you, Auntie. It has been many years," he said as she hugged him. He reminded her how as a boy she had always given him a shilling for Fanta soda. From her happiness, one would have thought she was greeting her own nephew.

Kalumba's luck ran out, however, and he couldn't remember any of the other women, even though as it turned out they were close relatives and he had known all of them before he left. But if there was anything to be forgiven, it was not mentioned, and soon he was helping with the sifting of the rice as he answered questions about life abroad. And when he asked what all the food was for, he was told it was for him, to welcome him back.

"You know, I once met this British guy in a small city in the United States and the only thing we could speak about was tea. Any other topic would have led to war," Kalumba said in answer to a question.

"Did you tell him if he comes back here we will kick him out again? But at least I am sure you told him he had no business discussing our tea."

"But who taught us how and when to drink tea? They should come and take it all away," someone else was saying, to loud laughter, when his father came and called him. They had to go to someone's farm to collect goats for slaughter.

"Kalumba, of course I could have gone to get the goats by myself, but this is the only chance we might have to be alone for a while. There are so many people, some that you don't even know, who want to come and see you," his father said as they got into the car.

"I can't believe this car is still around. This is the boat that I rode to exile," Kalumba said.

"We are a lot like the Cubans, at least those of us who cannot afford new cars. Our mechanics will keep these things running on poached parts for as long as we want," Kalumba's father said. "How do you feel about Ogum and Sukena? That is what I want to talk to you about." Baba Kalumba felt like he was rushing his son, but he had been alive long enough to know that volatile issues, especially issues of love and heartbreak, are best discussed early. They would discuss his years in exile and his future goals later, but this was the most urgent issue for now.

"I'm not sure . . . I feel like a part of me is supposed to feel bad and let down, like I am supposed to react in a predestined way, the warrior protecting his turf. But the truth is, either way I look at it, my relationship with Sukena is in the past. Besides, I am in love with someone else. How selfish would I have to be?" Kalumba asked. "You will meet her soon." He reached into his wallet and pulled out Melissa's photograph. His father tried to steady his hands on the steering wheel as he looked at the picture.

"She is very beautiful. You said she is a painter?"

"You will get along well, a bit feisty . . ." Kalumba answered indirectly, his eyes for a moment looking happy and alive.

"As you know, I gave Ogum and Sukena my blessing and advised them to ask you for forgiveness—"

Kalumba interrupted his father. "But there is nothing to forgive . . ."

"That is exactly what I told them. But there is something else . . . something you should hear from your father so that you know how best to proceed." He was quiet for a moment, trying to find the right words. "I told Ogum that I think of him as my son. I told him that if it came down to it and I had to choose between the two of you, I would let both of you die. I feel like I betrayed you with those words." His father seemed to be feeling the conflicting loyalties tugging at him, and he looked tired.

"Ogum is my brother in many ways. Who has the right to choose who lives and who dies? To choose between two lives, that is what dictators do. Let it be on the conscience of the killer, not the victim. I would not choose between two lives either, even those between a brother and a stranger," Kalumba said passionately.

"I was worried I would not think of you as having grown up . . ."

"You know what I think: people like me die for strangers, strangers who are at the same time my brothers and sisters. It's silly when you put into words, but really that is what it is. So what is really bothering you?" Kalumba asked, attempting to make room for his father to speak freely.

"Every time I have spoken to Ogum in the past few months, he has spoken about how you don't remember your interrogation. He doesn't understand how you cannot remember and then mysteriously you end up with the List. But it is not his lack of understanding that worries me the most, it is that he seems to be looking for a sign that either exonerates or implicates you. He is looking for a way to judge you. Even though I said I cannot choose, I cannot let a wrong happen." His father sounded sad, even guilty, for having allowed Ogum to become another son.

"Father, I also worry that I don't remember. Most of my pain, my years in exile, were spent trying to answer this question. Should I say I didn't confess even though I know even the bravest of people crack under pressure? Or should I say I didn't crack, because there are many others who do not? I learned there is nothing I can do—I cannot torture myself to death for something I do not remember. I choose life. That is why I am back, to live," Kalumba said, speaking so animatedly that it looked like he was trying to break free from the seat belt.

"But with Ogum, there are things that you do not know about—from way back. From the early movement days," Kalumba said. "Things that make him feel entitled to how he feels," he added, looking straight ahead.

"So cryptic . . . I am almost afraid to ask," his father said, glancing at Kalumba before returning his eyes on the road.

"It all has to do with his father's death," Kalumba said.

"The truth always comes out," his father said absentmindedly. "Well, we are almost there, but I should wear mine as well."

"Wear what?" Kalumba asked, surprised that his father did not pursue the conversation, probably thinking that Kalumba only knew that Baba Ogum had disappeared.

"The seat belt," he said casually. "We all have to protect ourselves, especially you. You are most vulnerable," he added, and that was the end of the conversation.

His father had selected the goats months earlier. The owner of the farm, who remembered Kalumba when he was young, had given a fifth goat at no cost. Kalumba was beginning to realize that his exile meant more to his family and friends than it had to him. And with a degree of regret, he was beginning to wish he had known this. It would have made it easier to survive exile. He had felt forgotten, but everyone else had also been in pain. His coming back was a sign that things had changed; he was the proof of it.

<hr />

Kalumba's father had not expected so many people to show up. Certainly not the press, and now there were several reporters walking around asking people questions. In the old days, for weddings and funerals, one had to get a license from the local chief; no gatherings of more than five people were allowed. The government had calculated that it took five people to commit treason. With the new government, informing the chief of any event was a matter of courtesy. There was a group of homeless boys, bruised and beat up, who showed up for the free food. There were a few village drunkards there for the free alcohol, and then others for the drama and gossip that would ensue from what they called the "dangerous love triangle."

But the majority had come to support Kalumba. And all of them came with gifts, as if it were a wedding. Some brought food; others, like the next-door neighbor, brought Muratina beer; still others, pots and pans, lamps, livestock, mattresses, bookshelves, hoes, movie tapes from old Hollywood movies; one even brought a five-layer cake complete with a bride and groom on top. But the one that made everybody laugh was a huge box of clearly bootlegged Hunt's Ketchup, the idea being, the donor explained, that Americans loved ketchup.

There were so many people that the garden had to be converted into a standing area and seeds and plants were lost. But for Kalumba's father, who moved from one group of people to another welcoming them, it was well worth it. A child is born only once and returns only once ... hopefully. Tomorrow he and Kalumba would replant the garden to replace the lost seedlings.

By early afternoon the huge feast had been laid out on long tables. There were songs and dances, after which a local musician set up his band and began playing his most popular songs. He played a popular Kyukato song about warriors who raid the Samasi and return triumphant, and those who knew the song sang along. Between sets, people hijacked the microphone and recited poems, told jokes, or welcomed Kalumba back. More and more people kept coming until it resembled a festival.

It was in this festive mood that the local chief managed to get on the microphone, even though Kalumba's father had announced that this was a time of festivity and no factional politics were allowed. The chief smoothed a piece of crumpled paper and began to read, hands spread out to embrace everyone: "My people, some people went to exile and others stayed home and fought. But exile is not running away; they went because they had to. Who is better than the other? As one who stayed and fought, I say it does not matter. We have won our liberation. Let the past ..."

He did not complete his speech. He was yelled off the stage with shouts of "Tell a joke or get off the stage" and "Freedom from you." The musician was called back on stage.

~~~~~~~~

Kalumba, Ogum, and Sukena were sitting with other members of the movement, talking idly. Ogum thought Sukena was being unusually quiet, and he remembered the time her body had gone into mourning. He realized that she had not been alone with Kalumba since his return. Ogum did not want to leave them alone. Before he could decide whether this was a result of jealousy or a desire to catch up with his friend and brother, Baba Kalumba called his son. Both Ogum and Sukena knew why. It was time for the ceremony of the *one who has returned*. It was a ceremony that started being performed hundreds of years ago to cleanse the mind and body of one who had been gone a long time. It was done to ease the person back into society and rid him or her of bad spirits he or she might be bringing back. The ceremony had been abandoned for many years now, but Baba Kalumba knew his son would need more than a welcome back party. Kalumba had too many ghosts inside of him.

They walked into the main house, to a room that had been added on, and stood outside the closed door. "Kalumba, once you go in there I want you to listen to everything your aunt has to say." His father said this with so much authority that Kalumba did not try to ask what was behind the closed door. He looked back at his father as he opened the door, but Baba Kalumba was already turning to leave. Kalumba entered a darkened room. For a moment he panicked and almost ran out. His mind had flashed back to the school woodshed where he had met Ogum after witnessing the massacre. He could hear the din from the celebrations as he closed the door behind him. His eyes adjusted to find his aunt and three of the women who had been with her in the kitchen. They were sitting on the floor in a circle, and they motioned for him to join them.

"Kalumba. Do not be afraid. You are not yet used to being back with your people. Your father has told me about the terrible things that happened to you here and also in America. He told me that we forced you to a land where rivers and mountains are named after people the Americans killed, and those that survived were forced into reservations. He told me it is a land where slavery and death are part of life . . . and war.

If you had gone to the reservations and told those kind people that you were an orphan, because they understand suffering, they would have given you a home. They sound just like us. You didn't know. So you left a place of death to go to another place of death. If I had known this, I would have hid you in my womb. At home, we could have protected you with warmth and love. Who took care of our child in that land?" Ogum's aunt paused, and then she motioned for Kalumba to sit next to her. She reached for a bowl in front of her and washed her face, then her hands. The other three women did the same.

"These women you see here were present at your birth. In fact, we are very lucky that one of them, a mother of one of your playmates, was right there when you were born in hospital. But we cannot rely on the hospitals alone. The other two are midwives. We need two midwives, because we are about to perform a very difficult task. But we are unfortunate in other ways. Your mother is not here. And your grandmother, whose task I must now perform, is also not here. But they are here in spirit, and we must trust that they will be happy with what we do. My people and your people are one. That is why I am here." She took Kalumba in her arms and held him very tightly, so tightly that he labored to breathe. Small and thin as she was, Kalumba was lost in her arms and bosom. She continued speaking.

"If your grandfathers and grandmothers were here, we would have asked them for guidance. But they are not. You have lost a lot and yet you are so young. Without your father you would have had no place to go. You would have been an orphan. You will leave this room as a newborn baby who speaks and understands. You will not beat your wife or your children because of the things that happened to you in the past. You will not bring bad blood from America; we have spilled enough of our own. This is your home, and therefore you must claim it. Tell me, Kalumba, do you understand what I am saying to you?" she asked him.

Kalumba nodded his head. He was afraid to speak. She asked him again. This time he said, "Yes, I understand."

The mother he never knew, his flight, Ogum's father and his eyes, the massacre, his promise to never forget—his chest heaved more and more. But it was only getting worse. He heard moans and screams, some long and others short; he heard chants and war cries and accusations of betrayal for doing nothing. He thought about Rafael, about African Americans and Native Americans, how the lynching continued as he wallowed in his exile, and about Melissa, with whom he wanted to make a home, yet whom he had left alone in search of his return; he thought about Sukena and heartbreak, about his father, who was wedded to a grave, about his mother, who had died too young, who did not live to see her son grow up. He wondered how their lives would have been different had she lived; he thought about his grandfathers and grandmothers, all of whom he had never seen; he thought about those buried alive and hanged by the British, of the Mrs. Shaw who died when she killed her husband; he thought of this history that did not know itself and of the lives that he could have lived and had lived and had lost. He thought about Ogum's father and how he had failed him. He wailed.

As he wailed, his aunt held him between her legs. She was holding him tight against her naked vulva. The other three women were trying to pull him out, but she would not let go. He was screaming, but he did not have energy to push himself out of her arms and legs. The other three women were screaming for her to let go as they tugged and pulled. He fainted. He woke in the arms of his mother. He woke up again in the arms of Sukena. He woke up again in Melissa's arms. He woke up again to find his aunt rubbing his forehead with a warm towel. The other three women were gone. "How do you feel?" she asked him.

"Weak. I feel very weak. How about you?" he asked, eyes raised toward her.

"The same . . . very tired. You are a very large baby," she said. "Let us stay here for a while." She rubbed his hands and belly with castor oil.

"Do you know what you want to do?" she asked him.

"Yes. There are things that I don't remember. And there are things I can't forget. I must tend to those I cannot forget. The truth is all that matters," he answered with a long sigh.

She continued rubbing his head, hands, and belly with castor oil. She kneaded him back to life.

~~~~~~~~

Ogum's aunt ululated four times. It was a boy. Everyone joined in the celebration, women ululating and men whistling loudly. "Do you want the newborn to speak to you?" his aunt yelled to the crowd. Everyone hollered for him to step forward and speak.

He was so exhausted he thought he was going to die. What he wanted to do was sleep for a long time and wake up to find himself still there but with Melissa beside him. He missed her terribly.

"This was not your ordinary child. This one came out with a tongue and a mind. Do you want to hear what it has to say?" she asked again, and again the crowd yelled out for Kalumba.

Ogum watched, jealous, as Sukena helped Kalumba to the microphone. *The prodigal son has indeed returned,* he thought to himself. The sun was about to set. It painted the sky a bright yellow that became golden closer to the horizon.

Kalumba had not expected to speak. He thought how speaking about the pain of exile was much easier than speaking about the joy of return.

"When I got the airport, I was met by my father, my brother Ogum, and my sister Sukena. At that moment I knew I was home. But here, now, I really know I am at home. And more importantly, I know now, even though I didn't know it then, that I was never alone. That is very important to me. Having witnessed the treatment you gave the chief for trying to politicize something that is already political and does not need political words, I will not make the same mistake."

Here everyone laughed except Ogum. He was still thinking about how casually Kalumba had publicly called him brother and Sukena sister. It was good but not good enough; there were still many questions unanswered by Kalumba.

"But let me say the following. There are many things I do not remember. But there are many more I cannot forget. A people are not like a single human being. All of us have to remember those things others forget for each other. We have to remember for each other. And we have to help each other not to forget those things we wish had never happened." He paused and took a deep breath before continuing.

"Once upon a time there was a terrible storm. Lightning flashed so brightly that it could blind a small child. The thunder was so loud that the eardrums of small animals were shattered. The elephant came upon a house and begged the owners for shelter.

"The owners said, 'Okay, but since you are so big and we cannot all fit, let us shelter your trunk, since it is most crucial for your breathing.' The elephant agreed. But after a little while the elephant said, 'Look, my tusks are also very precious. If they get damaged, I don't know what will be become of me.' The owners thought about it and said, 'You're right, we are being very selfish. Bring in the tusks.' The elephant brought in its tusks. The elephant thought for a second and said, 'Look, why are we pretending? How can I shelter my trunk and tusks without bringing in my whole head?' The owners of the house were tightly squeezed. They refused. 'If we do that, we may as well let you have the whole hut,' they said, trying to appeal to the elephant's conscience. But the elephant said, 'My oh my, what a good idea,' and he threw them out."

Kalumba paused. Most people were familiar with the story. It had been retold a million times. But still, they had enjoyed Kalumba's tweaking of some of the facts. They applauded him to continue. And once he started again, his voice rose out of the receding applause.

"But the story does not end there. The elephant made one mistake. He did not kill the owners. For one thing, he needed them to continue tilling his garden. Secondly, he thought they were too weak to fight back." Here the people broke into cheers.

"The man gathered other men and prepared for war. They surrounded the house and said to the elephant, 'There are many of us, and if you do not leave now, we shall set the house on fire.' At this point the elephant thrust his head out and said, 'Let us be reasonable. If you set the house on fire, we all lose. In the process I will die and so will some of you. But I can be reasonable. Let me keep my head in and you can have the rest.' This divided the people. There were those who wanted to have the house all for themselves, there were those who wanted to run away to fight another day, and yet again there were those who wanted to accept the terms of the elephant.

"They argued that the elephant was already in the hut. What did it matter that the hut had formerly belonged to them? The fact was, the elephant was here to stay. Those who wanted to burn the hut were opposed by all the others. Even though they argued that from the ashes they could rebuild, the others argued that would take too long. In the end, the elephant kept its head in the house while some of the former owners were squeezed into a small corner. And those that wanted to burn the house were banished." Kalumba paused again. From this point he was not sure where to take the story, but it felt so incomplete that he could not stop there. And there was no applause. The people were waiting for him to carry on and bring the story home.

"So now, you see, the elephant got the bigger share of the house, some owners were squeezed into a corner, and others had been banished. It took a long time for those who had been banished to regroup. Every time they approached the hut to take it back, they were charged by the elephant and the owners. The banished people again threatened to burn the hut down, this time killing the owners *and* the elephant. The elephant said, 'This is even worse than the last time. You must be barbarians. Not only do you want to burn down the hut and kill me, you want to kill your own. But let's think about this for a moment. There is no space for all of us anyway. Why don't we give you a small piece of the garden where you can build your own house and also till? What we would like in return is some of what you grow in your garden. This way, we can all live together and prosper.'"

Some people from the audience started to boo the elephant, calling it a dog. Others quieted them down.

"Some remembered that the same trick had been played on them before. Others said that was a long time ago and it did not matter. Others said they should burn down the house. They were banished by the elephant, the old owners and the new owners. And the process began all over again.

"My question to you is this: How many independences can a country have? How many struggles for independence? How many generations of political prisoners and exiles? How many genocides and revolutions? I say there can be only one independence and one struggle. If the past is still here, why should we call it the present or the future? Let us remember, and let us not forget!"

Even though most people knew where the story was going, by the time he came to the end, none had expected those exact words. He himself had not expected those words; he had been led to this conclusion by the rhythm of the story. From the moment he had picked up its thread, it had been bringing him here. The people let out a huge applause. The musician came back on stage with his band. More beers and gourds of Muratina were opened. More goat meat was put on the grills. The birth had gone well; the child had spoken well.

It took a long time for Kalumba to make it back to where Ogum and Sukena were sitting. He stopped every two feet to shake the hands of guests who laughed appreciatively at the story he had just told. He ran into a reporter who wanted to do an interview on his escape to exile, but he declined. Speaking to the people gathered for his return had brought him back to life and at the same time exhausted him. He told the reporter to meet him the following day early in the morning. Finally he made it back to where Ogum and Sukena were sitting.

"That was a really good talk," Sukena said. "What is interesting to me is how we speak about remembering, yet I could have stood there and told the same story about women and our struggle. It's funny, isn't it? How you have been back only a day and you fall into the same patterns? Look around." She waved in no particular direction.

Kalumba looked around him. Women were in their own groups. Mostly they were sitting down on the ground, though some, like his aunt, sat with the men on chairs. It was women who were walking around serving food and drinks and collecting empty plates and dishes. It was they who were cooking. There were some men who were roasting goat and disbursing the meat, but the majority of them were having fun. True, there was happiness all around, but even then it was divided between the sexes, classes, ages, and education levels.

"Hey, do you want to go for a walk?" Sukena asked Kalumba. Ogum started to stand up, but she looked at him and he sat back down. Kalumba followed Sukena through the crowd. For those who had been waiting for some drama, this was the moment, and it did not go without speculation. *They would either come back as man and wife or a heart was going to be broken,* some whispered. They walked past the gate and took a thin path that branched from the road. They had taken this same walk hundreds of times before. It led to a small pond close to the lake that had dried up. They walked without saying much at first. It was the first time they had been together in ten years.

It was as if they kept passing themselves in different positions—sitting down, standing up, walking, kissing—and different moods, happy but also pensive. Each walk they had taken had remained, and they were tourists of their own relationship. Kalumba, as he had always done, picked up a thin stick that he beat against his leg to keep the rhythm of his steps. Without it, Sukena used to joke, he would waddle along like a duck in unequal steps.

"Well, why the walk?" Kalumba asked her. They had in the past always spoken freely.

"Just to talk . . . catch up," she said simply. And they walked along silently a little longer.

Then, all at once, Sukena said, "Marriage is around the corner. I want to do some research . . . I want to research the role of women in the independence struggle."

"Which one? Which struggle, I mean?"

"Didn't you just say there can only be one independence struggle?" she asked. "What about you?"

"I want to get a job teaching. Like you say, marriage is around the corner, then grow old and, if possible, quite fat." He was laughing lightly. "But I don't know if that is what I will do. There is a difference between what I want and what I am going to do." He added more seriously, "I don't know what I am going to do."

"What do you mean? If you can achieve what you want, isn't that all you need to do?" Sukena asked.

"I wish . . . Do you really love him?"

"I waited for a long time. I wasn't planning to. My body just wouldn't let me move on until I mourned you. It was a crazy time. I knew you were alive, yet I felt like a widow." She lost her balance in a pothole and bumped into him. He steadied her then let go.

"That life was taken from me. Perhaps that is the life you were mourning, because it was truly dead," Kalumba said bitterly. They could still hear the noise from the celebration.

"If the one who is left behind mourns, what happens to the one who leaves? Could you mourn your own death? Or in your world was it me that died?" She was looking at him as they walked. She did not know what to think; he was so familiar yet a stranger at the same time. She thought that perhaps he had held onto her a little bit too long when he steadied her.

"I think the one who leaves cannot mourn. If I had mourned, I would have healed, and I did not want to heal, because it meant giving up on you. For the one who leaves, things freeze . . . like watching the same movie over and over again through a soundproof window. You cannot touch, you are without senses." He was enjoying the conversation, the rhythm of it, how easy it was to talk about his pain to her.

"Yet you still found love."

"With another exile, an internal one, but yes I did. I made a lot of mistakes; there was no returning. I should have tried to find refuge among others like me. Struggle is what keeps an exile alive . . . She is coming to stay for a while." Kalumba was looking at Sukena as well. She really had not changed much, though he imagined that she laughed less—the laughter lines that marked her cheeks were not as deep as they were when he left. The past ten years had been hard on everyone.

"Melissa Rafael, that is her name," he added.

"I don't think the past matters much for old lovers. I mean, what would we do with it? Try to dig up the other life and give it mouth to mouth? We are lucky to have survived, that is all," Sukena said. "And even luckier to love, to have found more love."

They walked on until they got to the pond. Kalumba started laughing. The pond was dry, with dry mud along the walls and at the bottom muddy water.

"We used to sit by this little thing? This is more like a puddle," he said.

"It is better than a mirage," Sukena answered. She was also laughing. She hadn't been there for a long time. It looked much smaller than she had remembered. "Maybe nostalgia is not just for the exile," she said.

But they sat down anyway. Their eyes met, and suddenly they were kissing. They kissed, clothes hurriedly taken off. This moment, dreamt of for ten years, even when in the arms of other lovers, was finally here. Then Sukena pushed Kalumba away from her and started gathering her clothes. Kalumba did not say anything and started getting dressed too.

They had changed; their love was gone. There was no going back, for in the past ten years they had taken divergent paths. They hugged. The sun was almost gone and they waited it out. After it sent its dying rays from under the horizon, they began finding their way back. The party was still going on. A lot of people were leaving, but a lot more were arriving. So they each opened a beer and joined the guests.

Kalumba was woken by loud knocking. He opened the door to his room to find the reporter, accompanied by a cameraman from the national TV station. He washed his face and changed into jeans, sneakers, and a T-shirt. He offered the reporter and his cameraman some tea. There was a lot of leftover goat meat, and he heated some for breakfast.

"It's ironic, but if I remember, the night I left I was wearing the same clothes."

"The same clothes?" the reporter asked incredulously.

"No, not the same. Jesus, I wouldn't fit in those now," Kalumba said with a laugh. "I mean the same kind of clothes," he added, waving a rib bone at his clothes.

"Do you remember me?" the reporter asked. Kalumba looked at him but could not place him.

"No." Kalumba explained his abrupt answer. "At first I lied that I could recognize someone and just not remember their name. After a few mishaps last night, I have learned to just tell the truth and say no."

"My name is Oruka."

"Oruka?" And then recognition slowly sank in. "Jesus, how the hell are you?" Kalumba wanted to hug him. It had been so long, over twenty years. This could not be the same Oruka who had terrorized him when they were young. They were about the same size now. Oruka was laughing his old laugh; he had tricked Kalumba once again.

"I didn't want you to read tomorrow's paper and wonder. Besides it's been so long and we were so young that this is one of those things that do not truly matter," Oruka said.

"Did you ever wonder what happened?" Kalumba was laughing.

"I figured it must have been something you put in the food. Now I am just hungry for news and in some cases even the truth," Oruka said. "By the way, this is Ndau. He works for the national TV station," Oruka added by way of introduction. Kalumba and Ndau shook hands.

Kalumba knocked on his father's door to let him know he was leaving with his old school friend and would be back in a few hours. His father asked him if Ogum and Sukena were coming with him, and he said they were still sleeping. Outside Kalumba found dozens of people passed out in the yard. "It must have been a great party," Ndau commented. "It was a great ceremony," Oruka said, correcting him. Kalumba loaded some hoes and shovels in the back of the reporter's truck, and they were off.

The drive took about an hour. At first Kalumba had wanted to walk Oruka and Ndau along the same path he had taken, but he decided that the experience could not be replicated, it could only be told. He suggested they stop every now and then to take pictures.

―――――

Ogum realized the magnitude of what Kalumba had done the moment Kalumba told him where he had been. That their lives were going to change for the worse he knew; to what extent, Ogum wasn't sure.

"Kalumba, you cannot just do things arbitrarily. You know this. You are part of a movement and, whether you like it or not, part of the government. This . . . what you have just done is wrong," Ogum told him angrily. How could he? What gave him the right? And there were political implications. But also, importantly for Ogum, it was his personal secret as well. There was his mother to think about.

"You should have checked with us first. There is a good reason why the massacres have not been made public," Sukena added.

"I am only after the truth. I made a promise." Kalumba defended himself. He added, "Witnesses testify—otherwise they are haunted by what they have seen."

"It's my father, you idiot. This was my decision as well," Ogum said, shoving Kalumba on the chest.

"It was that decision that got us to where we are today. You are able to return because we made the deal. Besides, a coup is not a revolution. A soldier in government would have been just as bad as the Dictator," Sukena said, trying to get Kalumba to understand that the movement's decision had been well thought out.

"It was militarism versus people-powered democracy," she added. The SIDCF would have distanced itself from the coup, understanding it as the beginning of a military coup.

"What about the civilians? What about the movement people who lost their lives that day?"

"Keep my father out of this . . ." Ogum started to say.

"There were others too, many others." Kalumba cut him short. "This is about the truth."

"Don't make me laugh. You, the truth? How convenient can this be?" Ogum asked sarcastically.

"What exactly did you win from silence?" Kalumba asked, pointing a finger at Ogum.

"We got safety. The government knew that the story would finish it. Already the Americans and the British were distancing themselves from the stink of the dictatorship. Public knowledge of the massacres would do in the government, which in return was going to become more vicious. You understand? They were going to unleash the army on the people. It would have made Rwanda look like a joke." Sukena answered for Ogum.

"That is what the fuckers told you. That is what they wanted you to believe—the truth would have finished it off," Kalumba argued.

"You were in exile. You lost touch. Listen, the Dictator built an airport in his home province and an arms depot in preparation for civil war. If things turned out badly for him, he was going to secede. So the movement asked for a truce, no more political detentions and assassinations—it asked for civilized discourse. It got a leveled playing field for the most part," Ogum interjected. "It is not as easy as it seems," he added apologetically.

"You really believe that? That the playing field was leveled? Why was it that people like me couldn't return without threat of assassination?" Kalumba asked angrily.

"The movement traded those in exile and those already in detention for those already free. No more arrests, no more assassinations, but those in exile had to stay there. The government had to pander to its supporters. And the movement knew it was only a matter of time before we won. You are back, aren't you? All the detention cells are empty," Ogum said. "Isn't this what we fought for?"

"Nobody asked me," Kalumba said.

"You signed up for the cause of freedom—*victory or death,* we sang. What did you expect?" Sukena answered him.

But Kalumba was not satisfied. "We have over a hundred families wondering what happened to their loved ones. Is there anything that can justify that? Freedom worth that kind of a lie is a sham," Kalumba said, even as he knew he would never be able to convince them otherwise.

"Well, that is why they have the tomb of the missing soldier . . . for mothers and wives to weep for their dead sons," Ogum said sarcastically. "I gave up my father, didn't I?"

"I am not sure . . . I had to fulfill a promise I made." Kalumba did not say to whom, even though they all understood he was referring to Ogum's father. "I finally understand what I was trying to say to him. I was the witness who would mark his grave. I think he died easier for it," Kalumba explained. "I did it because I had to." But he could not be sure. Perhaps he needed to find something that would make sense of his life, his exile, the wasted life, the pain and tortures.

"Look, Kalumba, I understand the sentiment. But we all die. When we got into these politics, we understood that as a potential consequence. Ogum's father understood that," Sukena reasoned. "But for now, it really doesn't matter. The story is out. It's a question of what is going to happen next."

"You know, Ogum, I wished many times that I had died that afternoon with your father. But I am glad I didn't, because you, the movement, would have buried us right there," Kalumba said, sounding more bitter than he intended.

"You fucked up. You have been back for only two days, and look at what have you done. You have been gone a long time. I don't think you understand your actions. Instead of trusting us to guide you back, you run off and reveal things that can only hurt what we have sacrificed so much for. This is wrong. You should have talked to us. This is the same selfish you," Ogum said. He was angry. "If I stay any longer we will come to blows. Besides, I have to worry about my mother now."

Sukena hesitated for a moment and stood up to leave with Ogum.

At that moment, it felt like something broke to Sukena. Perhaps whatever it was had broken years before and this was the first time they were feeling it. In some strange way, exile had kept their friendship alive. There are political principles, and then there are revolutionary ethics. Political principles had won over revolutionary ethics. It was like praying to two gods—when commandments clash, the believers cannot reconcile. Kalumba had decided to follow his god of truth, Ogum had decided to follow his god of justice, and one had demanded a concession from the other. Neither could give way.

Kalumba opened a beer, both relieved and saddened that everything had been voiced out loud. He walked over to where a group of young men were sitting, drinking and arguing loudly about a soccer match between two national teams Kalumba had never heard about. Perhaps he had been gone too long. He thought about his scars and how they had caused him to give up soccer. He thought about what Ogum had said and wondered if Sukena fully agreed with him.

Ogum wondered the same thing about Sukena, for she had not been forceful enough with Kalumba. Usually in political arguments they took the same side. But she was there with him and that was what mattered. *Kalumba will understand what he has done when he sees the evening papers,* Ogum concluded. What worried him was how the movement, now in government, would take it. He could make his mother understand, and if not, time and maternal instincts would come to the rescue, but could a whole nation be made to go along? And everything was being complicated by the existence of the List and Kalumba's lack of memory about it. The irony that this might not be Kalumba's first betrayal of the movement did not escape him. He wanted to be wrong; this was his brother, after all. Yet even though he would not admit it to himself, he wanted to be right.

~~~~~~~~

Neither Oruka nor Ndau had expected it to be such a big story. Looking back, it shouldn't have been surprising; all the elements to make it the story of the year were there. Exile and return, discovery of a massacre site, questions of whether the new government knew about it and if so why it had kept quiet. The headline in the newspapers and TV news, *The truth that was buried,* was a sensation. By midafternoon the following day, the whole country was talking about the massacres. The new government denied all knowledge about massacres and went as far as thanking Kalumba for bringing the truth with him. But the new leadership was seething, trying to find a way to return the truth to its grave. Then the day following the revelation, Oruka published the story about Kalumba's rebirth and the celebrations and printed Kalumba's speech in its entirety. In the imagination of the people, Kalumba became a symbol of the nation, a return to truth and new beginnings.

Oruka and Ndau had taken turns helping Kalumba dig while the other took still pictures and filmed. When they struck bone, they brushed away the soil to reveal hundreds of human bones: skulls, hip bones, thigh bones, kneecaps, collarbones, and hundreds of hand and foot bones that from a distance resembled spilled rice. They took more photographs and filmed. They covered the site with plastic to protect it from the elements, crossed the stream, and went to seek refuge from it all in the baobab tree.

In the paper, Oruka called it the most exhausting thing he had ever witnessed, and following Kalumba's troubled eyes, he said he wondered what kind of strength it required to have been a witness to that massacre on that beautiful afternoon. It was late evening before they were done. They dropped Kalumba off and went to file their stories. There were still people, though not as many as the day before, celebrating Kalumba's return. They were mostly in small groups finishing up the remaining goat meat and beer.

In the course of the next few days, Oruka released segments of the film he'd shot, piecemeal. A dirty and out-of-breath Kalumba pausing every now and then to explain what he witnessed, the fear he'd felt, how his eyes had locked with the eyes of the soldier who had saved his life and the lives of many other activists, how his stomach had been ripped open—he lifted his shirt to show the long thick scar—and how he had hid in the baobab tree and thought about the sacrifices carried out there. The baobab tree became a national icon. The whole country laughed at the story of Kalumba disguised as a Samasi and cried as the three friends said good-bye and laughed again as Kalumba was driven through the border post by European tourists.

January 7th

Hi Melissa,

I am so glad we got to speak even though briefly when I arrived. You cannot imagine what the sound of your voice did to and for me. I wished I had never left and was of course filled with all sorts of guilt. I think knowing that I can return to you makes all the difference in the world and it somehow frees me enough to think of having a home away from home. So it makes me happy to be here—know what I mean? (last part I am using a Southern accent).

What a strange little life we have lived for the past year.

So many things have happened in three days to make it feel like a lifetime. The faster you move the slower time moves they say. I have attached some scanned newspaper articles which you can also access online but I think seeing the real paper, front page and all, makes a difference. Things have spiraled out of control. I am afraid I am in a mess as a result of it. My friendship with Ogum and Sukena has suffered a severe blow—but not to worry, friendships, especially the great ones, get tested from time to time. Factor in old and new lovers, exile, volatile political situations and one cannot expect anything less.

Simple truth arrived at on the road to Damascus: I understand my responsibility is to the truth and the truth only. Hundreds of bodies mourned for the past ten years, it was time for them to be buried by their loved ones. There is going to be a huge rally in two days which I am not planning on attending. I feel like I have done enough already. To say the least, things are not going as quietly as I had hoped.

I can't wait to see you, hear about how you arranged for Mrs. Shaw's funeral and see the photographs. I will tell you more about the ceremony then. Yes, I have been born again but not into Christianity. I feel freer from my past, less burdened, I feel lighter. I feel loved, a total embrace. But for now, just know that I know that love is being consumed and I am being consumed—I am always thinking about you. I hope this is the last time I leave you.

Love always,

Kalumba

P.S. What I have enjoyed more than anything is darkness. In Madison the night is not pure; there is never a complete absence of light. Here, I have enjoyed walking out into the farm in the middle of the night, letting the darkness, darkness so black that I can touch it, keep me warm. The stars sit in the sky, little hot plates that glow only to be defeated by darkness. It's amazing. But also imagine all the things we can do, me and you, in this darkness.

January 7th

E-MAIL TO MELISSA'S FATHER THROUGH A MUTUAL FRIEND, SUBJECT HEADING: MELISSA

Dear Rafael,

I hope all is well on your end. There are several things I wanted to tell you, mostly because I have a bad feeling about the direction the country is going and my place in it. I am enclosing newspaper reports so that you can see for yourself. If things worsen, and they will, I do not know what will happen to me. I just know that I cannot return to exile, so soon. The irony is that I find myself thinking more and more about returning to be with Melissa. I can leave and make a home elsewhere but I will not be forced out. Some stand . . .

I have received some death threats, some overt and some insisting that for people like me, traitors, suicide is the only option. I am taking the threats very seriously—I know my movement well enough to understand they don't joke about this sort of thing. I am curious; would you make the same choice that you made by refusing to make a choice between exile and imprisonment?

But here is my real reason for writing—Can you ask Melissa to hold off from coming for a while? In my letter to her, I did not ask her to, only because I am sure if I do she will try and get here the following day. But perhaps if you tried? I am worried that things might explode here and she will be in the thick of it by association. Besides, she does not know how to be silent, and I am very sure she will get herself in trouble.

I hope to see you someday,
Your friend and comrade,
Kalumba

January 7th

E-MAIL FROM MELISSA, SUBJECT HEADING: MRS. SHAW AND LAST LAUGHS

My not so dearest K,

My father called and of course told me the truth of what you are trying to do. It was a long collect call, so you owe me at least thirty bucks. What were you thinking? Did you think he could talk me out of coming? I am leaving and that is final. In any case it is too late for me to change my mind since I have closed my affairs, as they say. So consider the question of whether I am coming or not answered. In any case, the worst that can happen is being deported. I may be Puerto Rican here but the US government has to protect me when I am abroad—too embarrassing otherwise.

But on another note, I have some news that cannot wait even though I am coming in a few days. I was cleaning up Mrs. Shaw's house before the African Studies Department takes it over. I came across a large envelope addressed to me and you. It contained more money than I have seen in all my life. I guess she intended to give it to us and then forgot. Here is the letter that came with it:

> *My dearest Kalumba and Melissa,*
> *This little project of mine took over a week to plan. My moments of lucidity are becoming sparser and sparser. But finally through an intricate system of notes, feigned anger at bank managers (who are waiting for me to die so that they can try to steal my money) and taxi drivers who wanted to charge me twice I managed. This envelope contains 30,000 dollars. You are my only family. I want both of you to try to be happy. I want both of you to buy a nice little house on a*

*hill so that it's sunny whether the sun is rising or setting. We
should not give up on trying being happy. It is of course too
late for me but not for you. At least try. That is the least I can
wish for my children.*

*Kalumba, get that job teaching at the National
University, teach somewhere—and Melissa, you keep
painting. Each evening return to your little house on the
hill. Try to be happy.*

*Both of you added meaning to my life at a time when I
needed it most—for that, wherever this road finally takes us, I
will always be grateful. With as much love as can possibly be
squeezed out of these drying bones.*

Your mother, grandmother, fan and friend,
Mrs. Shaw

We did become her family after all. Now you see why I have
to come? In any case, I love you enough to want to be there
no matter what. We have chosen to live, how can we do it
apart? Do not try to protect me from life—it's silly.

Here is the funny part (I am laughing as I write this). I
found the skull and gave it to the African History Department at UW–Madison, explaining that it belonged to the
head of an African chief who resisted the British. I did not
count on them asking me if Mrs. Shaw knew whose it was
exactly. I remembered the story about the warrior chief who
was either buried alive or had his head chopped off. So I told
them that I thought it might have belonged to him. They said
that as responsible historians they felt that the chief's remains
(their words not mine) should be returned to his family for
proper burial. I figured Mrs. Shaw would enjoy one last joke.
So do expect the saga to continue.

I love you very much, as much love as can be squeezed out
of this youthful heart,

Your M.

P.S. I did a painting of you. I called it Kalumba but without
the title I don't think you would recognize yourself. I will
bring it for whatever little house on a hill becomes ours.

January 8th

E-MAIL FROM RAFAEL ROUTED THROUGH MUTUAL
FRIEND, SUBJECT HEADING: MELISSA

Dear Kalumba,

I received your e-mail via our mutual friend and have been
following the news with great interest and alarm. Your letter
sounded resigned. But remember as long as you are alive, you
can fight. At least that is what I tell myself here in prison. I understand that I could very well die in here but I am not dead yet.

In this sense, Kalumba, nations are like people, they act out
the nightmare they will not acknowledge. It is quite possible
to psychoanalyze a nation, only problem is how to get the
sucker onto the couch. You did a good thing and no matter
how it plays out I do believe your country in the long run
will be all the better for it.

I am afraid that my talk with my daughter did not go as
you had hoped. She was not happy that we were making deals
about her behind her back but that was to be expected of
her. But if I am worried about your safety, I am more worried about hers since whether she likes it or not she does not
know her way around your country.

More her father and less a revolutionary, I ask that from the
moment she gets there you introduce her to people you trust
who can in turn show her around. I would rather you didn't
do it yourself because that marks her right from the beginning.

You asked me if I would make the same choices today. At
times like these I do not know.

Your friend and comrade,

Rafael

January 8th

E-MAIL TO MELISSA AND HER FATHER, SUBJECT
HEADING: MINIMUMS

Dear Melissa and Rafael,

I do not expect to be able to write for a while. I have made
all the necessary arrangements for Melissa. You shall be met

by Sukena at the airport. She has weathered many a storm, and in this hurricane that is coming, you will be in seasoned hands. I think instead of staying at home with us, you should rent out an apartment in the city. They have some that are very secure so the little house on a hill will have to wait—is this our African version of the two kids, two-car garage, and a white picket fence American dream?

Things are coming to a head here. The hostility and death threats are becoming more vicious by the hour. My very own brother, Ogum, has been broaching the subject of my returning to exile once again as a way of keeping me alive. In my worst moments, I am not even sure I can trust him—the political always comes with a degree of paranoia so I am trying to keep that in check.

Here is an excerpt of an article I wrote for the paper which captures my minimum hope, but one which I am afraid might not even be met. The storm is on the date of your arrival (I hope you bring some good tidings) and if we survive the mass rally, it should give us enough as a nation to think about the future. For the most part, for me it feels like the days before I went into exile but then again I have never been known to be a great optimist.

> The minimum of a growing democracy is a guarantee of life. That the final solution of assassinations be outlawed. That the culture of detention and exiling and spreading fear be outlawed. If we can create a space in which all voices are allowed to speak without threat of sanction, in which there is a guarantee that we will not regress to those days when assassinations were a way of conducting government business, of kangaroo courts in which voices were criminalized then hanged, that would be a beginning of something beautiful where each voice contributes to the shape of the nation. That is my minimum hope for a beginning. It is an urgent hope. It is also a plea.

Am I being too naïve? Perhaps. There is so much work to be done, but without this minimum hope being made into a reality this work cannot be done. Anyway, tomorrow is the big day. Let's see what the new day will bring.

Rafael, did Melissa tell you about Mrs. Shaw's gift? It was good news but I wish she'd told me so that I wouldn't have had to do those horrible quasi lying manipulative exile lectures for money. Whenever I think about her, which is quite often, I remember how in the last days she would stare at Melissa and me and ask, "Are you my children?" At other times she would ask if we were her parents, cousins, etc. But that was shortly before she would rain invectives on us. It was a strange year, to say the least.

Melissa, I am very excited that in just another day we shall be together once again. It has only been a few days but I have hated them. Is it appropriate in a letter addressed to your father as well to say that I love you? Well, I do. And yes do bring the painting.

For you, Rafael, I offer you my solidarity greetings (and a warm manly hug).

Kalumba

January 8th

One More Day

I suspect I will not get a chance to write again for a while. Who knows what will happen after the rally tomorrow. Certainly my life will never be the same. Not that the past few days have been normal. But things like anonymity are over. Writing e-mails in a public café was a chore—so many interruptions, most with encouraging words, others pure disdain.

My heroic act? My crime? To tell the truth about a massacre that should never have been hidden by a movement fighting for democracy. My father hasn't been vocal about the latest happenings. I do not blame him—to have his son back for only a short time, then to see him spiraling into trouble must be hard. But I am a witness. The decision was made for me that day by the stream.

Ogum's aunt saved my life, and now I am about to send it down the rabbit hole of political protest. But thanks to her and my mother, this is the "wholest" I have felt all my life; not even before my exiling did I feel this whole. It is as if they returned a piece of me, the most important piece of me that had been lost for a long time. I feel like I have stopped mourning for my lost lives, for my years of exile, and for my future.

I feel ready for whatever crossroads my turn at the last one will bring. I have known true love and what it is to fight for the truth. Now I just need to survive tomorrow and Melissa will be here. I have survived worse—I survived myself. Staying alive for one more day; that I can do.

January 8th

E-MAIL FROM MELISSA, SUBJECT HEADING:
MOTHERS AND LOVERS

My Dearest Kalumba,

Now that I am leaving this cursed country of ours for the first time, I am behaving like one who is about to buy the farm, bite the bullet, kick the bucket, meet my maker—I admit that to be a very poor attempt at humor, but then I am not the funniest of gals as you say.

Yesterday, I signed a two-year contract with the gallery in New York—as long as I keep producing we are sure to have food on the table. Last week, I signed over my lease to a young artist friend—I don't think you ever met her but oh well. I gave my Imelda Marcos–like collection of clothes and shoes to the Salvation Army etc.

Then I flew went all the way to New York for some art business and then to see my mother. A stop-over before flying on to Nairobi. Don't I feel like I have been a bad daughter! Why have I been so angry at her and for so long? Do I really blame her for my father's detention as if for some reason she could be responsible for that? Or perhaps because she is not in prison and therefore not revolutionary enough?

I was doing my usual daughter visits mother for fifteen minutes routine. As I was about to leave she says to me that she is happy I have found love. For her the only man she truly loved is in prison—life has been a long heartbreak. "But you, you make me happy. If Rafael and I did nothing more than bring you into this world, that would be enough to get us into heaven." Well, she has a strange way of talking—*Latina metaphor speak* I used to call it.

I went back in and sat next to her. She took her hands in mine. We rarely touch each other and I started thinking how I have missed her hands. Her hands heal. They are rough, sandpaper-like—why a schoolteacher has hands like hers I don't know. But they are also warm, long fingers . . . very many veins. Almost like Mrs. Shaw's, only my mother's are brown and warmer.

"I have had several affairs," she said after a few minutes of us just sitting there. At that moment I saw my mother for the first time. I saw her naked, small herds of sweat starting at her graying hair flowing down the crevices of her wrinkles, her long neck arched back, her breasts heaving up and down, her untamed pubic hair, her thighs and legs making a Z, and beneath her some man believing he is in heaven. Is that strange?

I saw her late at night lying in bed letting the memory of her orgasm run through her body again after the man has left. I also saw her on some other night alone, all alone trying to fill the empty spaces with unnecessary cleaning or tears or laughter with a neighbor. I also saw her in front of her classroom teaching American history and trying so hard not to break down thinking about my father.

I saw all the things she wishes for me and all the grief my fifteen-minute visits cause her. I saw that my mother is a very beautiful woman and that I loved her more than I thought I did. I wished you had met her, I mean really, really met her.

But as she herself said, the world is smaller than it was fifty years ago. She can always get a ticket and 24 hours later, she is having dinner with us. I suppose all in due time.

I realized how much stronger I felt, how much stronger I always feel after seeing her. It is knowing that you are loved, even at your worst moments. So I ran all the way back to her.

I had to ask.

"Mother, do I give you strength?"

"More than strength, Melissa. You give me pride and love. That is why I am still here." And that was that.

"Are you going to see your father?" she asked.

"No—it's not like I am going to Kwatee to die," I answered.

"Good. Too many good-byes for one lifetime. And you know where to find him"

I think I am telling you this . . . well, because it is your job to listen. Do you remember that time in Harlem in that bar when you asked me about her—or did I ask you about your mother?—now I forget: This is what I should have said to you.

See you in a day or two. Love you very much,

Your rather pensive fiancée,

Melissa

January 8th

E-MAIL TO MELISSA, SUBJECT HEADING: RE: MOTHERS AND LOVERS

Dear M,

Yes, I saw that in her, that strength—extraordinary strength, yet able to carry it ordinarily because it's hers. I really don't want to imagine your mother having sex, hot though she is. Are you fuming at this joke? You are very lucky that you got to straighten out your relationship—some people never get the chance. I am also hoping to do the same with my father— you know, really talk, really see each other.

It has become imperative that you bring the skull with you. There are too many layers of untruths that we need to unpeel one by one. The best plan is to have the African studies historians certify it, as they are planning, as the skull of Shakara. This will help you slip it into the country. Be sure to promise them all the credit. You should have no problem at customs. Then we shall get the little sucker DNA tested and then tell the whole story. After that, people can begin to question everything around them—enough with the lies. And we just might be able to give Mrs. Shaw one last laugh.

I love you,

Kalumba (your co-conspirator)

P.S. This whole episode should have your imagination well fed for the next 100 years—so bring the brush—the country your canvas, truth your paint.

January 8th

WHAT TOMORROW MAY BRING . . .

I cannot sleep. Too much at stake tomorrow. Tomorrow is the rally protesting the massacres. Tomorrow I unveil the truth about Mr. Shaw and our history. Dementia had boiled (no pun intended) Mrs. Shaw's memory to the hardest of her truths. By evening, once known history will be history once again and the present can pick up today. I will honor her memory. Am I being too naïve?

I feel like one about to be guillotined and I want to re-member everything, feel it all one last time—but what's the point? It has been done and now there is tomorrow. What is going to happen? This much I know, the rest of my life de-pends on what happens tomorrow—and if I make it through the day, I shall be fine. Mrs. Shaw will have her last laugh or maybe find peace at last—she was haunted all her life by her husband's being buried in national myths. Tomorrow the truth shall be restored—Mr. Shaw and our history, the massa-cres and what they mean, everything will be brought to light in order to be buried.

We shall bury the part for the whole, the skull and Ogum's father, we shall bury them for whatever else lies beneath the earth, we shall bury the part for the whole.

Murmurs, but I can discern what is beneath them—helplessly. Whispers about Ogum, yes, he wants to find me guilty for all that I have forgotten. Oruka whispered to me that he has heard Ogum drunkenly declaring that I am guilty of his father's death and I must pay. Whispers. Rumors. Suspicion. Displacement. Projection. I understand how Ogum might think his life would be better without me around—but not in real terms. That I am sure he will see—he will surely see through this.

Thomas Sankara was warned that his brother was going to betray him. And he asked, "How can I protect myself against my brother?" Sankara, it is said, laughed when his brother pulled a gun on him. He thought it was a joke—a day later he was dead. How could he protect himself from those that he loved? I guess I can run away. I do have another home, whether I like it or not, even a parallel life in the US. I can go back. But how do you run away from your brother? And so I shall stay. Our bond is stronger than anything life can throw at us.

This past year, I have lived. Strange how I could have died in so many other places and in so many ways. Escaping into exile, what was it that made the police officer to let us go? We could have died that night; all he needed to do was point—but he didn't and we didn't and so we continued living. And so tomorrow shall come, and the day will pass and we shall continue living.

It is too late; our history is peculiar in this manner—it is like a train jumping rails—never happens—unless you plan for it. And we did not plan for any of this—the chaos. But is too much to ask that we survive just one day? Just one more fucking hurdle? Beyond tomorrow, there is me and Melissa, a little house, me teaching and her painting.

There is a nation with the truth behind it. Beyond a past of quick sand, tomorrow we can start to live, happy or tragic lives, ordinary lives, linear lives, lives not compounded by lies, lives without misdirection, where death is just that, natural, accidental, diseased, decay not through the barrel of a gun.

This past year, should I regret the last ten? Would have I been here, on this night, contemplating a tomorrow full of possibilities if it were not for the last ten? Would have I learned to love, to love so deeply that I would find belonging even in exile? To love so deeply that I can only wish for the best for those around me? Would I have met wounded Mrs. Shaw who decayed betrayed by her memory? Or Melissa walking with a limp, until we learned to hold each other up?

Tomorrow will be here. Sankara was once here. Maurice Bishop was once here. Patrice Lumumba was once here. Hell, our nation was once here. For fuck's sake, have we been learning?

Love . . . faith . . . hope . . . kinship . . . revolution—what is the difference? All or one of them shall see me through tomorrow. Tomorrow we win, tomorrow I will have truly returned!!!!

8
New Beginnings

It was rumored that right from the days of colonialism, a list with one hundred names always existed at any given time. It never went above or under, not even by one name. It was as if it had been calculated that in large populations, it did not take less or more than one hundred agitators to destroy social order. And so names were erased as agitators were detained and assassinated, and others were immediately added in replacement. For most people this did seem plausible: for three or four generations, there were always people being jailed, killed, or exiled.

The List, however, served one purpose—to keep each successive generation in fear. If in one family a parent earned his place on the List, the surviving parent tried to steer the children away from it, though not always with success. So each generation passed on a place on the List like a precious family heirloom. But some parents, like Kalumba's, had escaped the List, which had in turn latched onto their children with a vengeance. The List had become a god demanding human sacrifice in carefully measured quantity though every now and then it demanded a feast of human flesh.

After Kalumba's exile, within the movement, finding the origin of the List became an obsession that equaled in zeal the obsession with ousting the Dictator. The more the movement made deals with the Dictator, the more important finding the traitor became. *To enter the new era with a clean slate, with no hyenas in our midst* became the slogan. Comrades pointed to comrades, and the Dictator seized the opportunity to order doctored files from the Special Branch authenticated. Mutual suspicion and distrust infected the movement—brother turned against sister, wife against husband, son against mother, as families in the movement tiptoed around each other. And right at the moment when the movement was just about to break into two disorganized camps, the chairman of the movement gave the volcano release—he started the rumor that those in exile had created the List under torture. Some had turned informant and for cover had been sent into an exile of luxury, where they were given fat scholarships to study and during the holidays were wined and dined by the CIA.

No one came outright and claimed this, and if someone had done so, the movement leadership would have denounced him or her. But once the rumor was started it whirled and whirled, directing anger away from fellow comrades and misdirecting it toward exiled comrades. It made sense to some: How do some people end up in exile and others don't? Why is it that once they are in exile we never hear from them again? Why didn't they organize armed camps like other movements in neighboring countries to liberate their brothers and sisters? And why exile in the United States, the land with streets paved with gold?

It did not matter that the exiles raised money for the movement or that they gave talks demanding sanctions against the Dictator—once the rumor started, they were effectively orphaned. But the movement couldn't go public. In the people's imagination, the real heroes were either dead, in prison, or in exile. And so the movement privately blamed the exiles so it could survive and publicly heralded them as the spiritual fathers and mothers of liberation.

As the search for the origin of the List intensified within the movement, more and more fingers pointed at Kalumba. It did not seem likely that a soldier would give the List to him, a soldier who was then conveniently killed. *But if that was the case, why give the List to Ogum at all? Why not just quietly escape with it into exile? Well, perhaps his conscience had caught up with him,* others argued.

But if he helped draw up the List, why was his name on it? And here several opinions were offered—Kalumba genuinely did not remember drawing up the List under torture. Once he was released, he continued with his activism convinced that he had not compromised his comrades. This, as a consequence, saw his name added to the List since he remained a legitimate threat. In any case, the List was not drawn up by one person, it was from the collaboration of torture victim after torture victim, generation after generation, and the careless work of the Special Branch that looked for any excuse to add a name and then eliminate—*It made their future work easier,* they said.

The movement understood that someone had to pay for the List. Too many good people had died. Having made the deal with the Dictator not to reveal the massacre in return for immunity from detentions and assassinations meant that it could not place the blame on the real perpetrators. And so, as often happens when a movement betrays its vocation, it turned inward and started to eat its young, the defenseless— those in exile.

Ogum understood this—he knew that the movement manipulated the hysteria against the exiles. He, after all, prided himself on dreaming with his eyes open, of having the kind of revolutionary pragmatism that saw through the lies of friend and foe alike. So why was it that when it was hinted that Kalumba might have betrayed the movement he did not protest and say Kalumba was his brother? That he would die in his place if need be? Perhaps it was true that he felt threatened by Kalumba's return, as if Kalumba would take Ogum's place at home and in the nation, but then again he knew this wasn't true: Sukena loved him, and the movement would not allow him to be replaced.

What Ogum would not admit even to himself was that Kalumba was a threat because he was a witness. He had left with one version of history, that the first independence was a result of the ebb and flow of resistance until the decisive decision to kill Mr. Shaw. He had left believing that the British took the body of Shakara and many others to Britain to fill their museums so as to deny the people marked graves around which they could rally. In the United States, Kalumba had found competing versions that were now threatening to undo the very foundation of the nation. Kalumba, the witness to the massacre and the potential falsifier of the myths the movement was resurrecting, was a threat. Without being aware of it himself, Kalumba knew too much.

Ogum believed in the movement. What had been done was done. It had been done for the sake of political change. It had been done for the people. Freedom was here—and soon the fruits of freedom would begin to grow. And even though Ogum did not expect to raise his hand against his brother, they clearly had divergent views that might be costly to both of them in the end. And because he believed that they were both right, he hoped that Kalumba had indeed drawn up the List. That would make it easier. By sleight of hand, Ogum understood that he wanted or needed to substitute the real reason for a false reason.

And he now understood better than before that he wanted Kalumba to pay for his father's death. Kalumba, through no fault of his own, by virtue of being a witness, had robbed Ogum of his last moments with his father. Kalumba also knew that Ogum had traded his father's death for the nation. Ogum had forsaken his father, for without a burial and a grave his father could not have a legacy. Ogum therefore wanted, in fact needed, to find Kalumba guilty of having manufactured the List. The motivations were stronger than reason or brotherhood. In some ways, Ogum told himself in moments of honesty, they had both been overtaken by history. Worse than actors condemned to predetermined fate, he and Kalumba had refused to come to terms with this one fact.

And what did the truth of history matter? Could truth exist for itself? What could the truth matter for a tomorrow so close at hand? Man cannot live on bread alone, but neither can he live on truth alone—for the idea to live among the people, for the word to become flesh, it must alter its form. And even though Ogum was not religious, he understood that the idea of a perfect God found expression, once having taken the form of flesh, in an imperfect Jesus. The truth could exist for its own sake; it had to serve a purpose in order to become life. This Ogum believed fervently. In the same way that Kalumba believed even without knowing it that the truth was inviolable, truth at all costs, Ogum believed that a truth can be compromised if it brings a better tomorrow.

And so, for many reasons over which together they had no control, they were heading for disaster. When they recognized their brotherhood, history pulled them apart. And when they recognized what history was doing to them, the present and its demands tore them apart. And when they recognized all these, there was the List, Sukena, Ogum's father, and the question of who was the real son to Baba Kalumba. One of these reasons perhaps they could handle, but all of them at work at the same time was too much. The future had already been written by the past.

Ogum did not want to act against Kalumba, but something had to be done if the nation was going to survive his return. Because of Kalumba's action already there had been riots calling for the president's resignation. The United States and Britain were accusing the new government of corruption and lack of transparency and had issued travel advisories. The tourism industry was suffering. The World Bank and the IMF were withholding funds until a United Nations team investigated the massacres. The nation and the whole world, it seemed, had galvanized against the new government.

It was a confluence of several things: Western governments that did not trust the new government, which had revolutionary potential; a population that was legitimately scared about a second betrayal; a movement that had compromised itself into power and was therefore weaker than it thought itself; and national myths, which traditionally had held the nation together when all else failed, that were suddenly under attack.

The nation understood itself in the myths of colonialism and resistance and later in a movement that put the people before the politics of power. Kalumba was threatening to shatter both. Like Ogum and Kalumba's brotherhood, the nation's solidarity could take a threat to one, but it could not handle the myriad of things threatening its very foundation all at the same time.

So the lies had to be protected until the truth could be released in small doses. When pressed, most people couldn't articulate why a deal that had brought them freedom was so wrong. They did not argue against the movement's explanation, as offered by Ogum: that a coup was not a revolution and that had it succeeded, a military dictatorship would have been infinitely more brutal than a civilian dictatorship. Historically, it was okay that the coup had failed, for now they had real freedom. To some this seemed plausible enough. But there was something so unjust in the deal and yet so difficult to articulate that it made the anger toward the new government worse. It was the monstrosity of the government striking down those who were genuinely working for freedom, like Ogum's father, and then the movement striking a deal with the killers, that left the people angry. Yes, they wanted freedom, but not at the risk of their consciences. It was the secrecy, the backdoor meetings, the front of a bloodless democracy, and the self-righteousness with which the movement had negotiated this history away that made them angry. In a way the people had been made complicit with the murderers and the previous regime. Their name had been bloodied.

The people therefore took to the streets. *What else don't we know? Truth or death! Never again!*—were some of the slogans they adopted. And even though no one person in particular called for the meeting, it was agreed that they would march from the capital to the National Stadium. Unable to stop the "what else don't we know rally," as it came to be called, the new government did the next best thing: it offered to help. It offered cake, cold sodas and beers, samosas, and kiosks where the marchers could rest before continuing along the designated route. It hired bands to entertain people along the way.

And so, less than a week after his arrival, Kalumba and Ogum were on their way to a rally that Kalumba had ignited. As they drove inch by inch to the stadium, people recognized Kalumba and waved to him. Some wanted him to step out of the car and address them. But Kalumba signed to them that they would meet up at the stadium. Kalumba, like Sukena, had at first refused to go. "I have done enough already," he had said. Sukena agreed with him, saying that he could only make the situation worse, because the crowd would try to make a leader out of him. But Ogum suggested that having lit the fire, it was only he who could put it out. It was his responsibility, his one unselfish act.

Sukena could understand why Kalumba did not want her to come. He was afraid of being arrested and needed her to pick up Melissa from the airport. She could tell there was something wrong with the way Ogum wholeheartedly agreed with Kalumba. Normally, Ogum would have argued that Kalumba was giving Sukena a domestic role because she was a woman. She and Ogum always attended political events together. This time it was quite clear that he did not want her coming along with them; more than for Ogum, she worried for Kalumba. But she shook off the feeling that Ogum might, for jealousy or the movement, stand against Kalumba.

When Kalumba left to say good-bye to his father, Sukena pulled Ogum close to her. "I don't know what is going to happen, but I want you to promise to take care of him. He thinks he is home again, but he does not yet know his way around. If he doesn't come back, I don't want you back either," she whispered to him urgently. Ogum promised but not before saying bitterly that she ought to be concerned for him as well.

When Ogum and Kalumba finally arrived at the stadium, they found thousands of people already there. Again, as during the independence celebrations, there was a VIP section that had been cordoned off. But this time around, the amenities of food and drinks had been extended to everyone.

"It must be costing millions," Kalumba commented.

"Are you going to be writing the check?" Ogum retorted.

They sat down with youth movement VIPs who had been carefully selected by the government, those who were known as the most radical.

For the second independence celebrations, it was the moderates who sat at the forefront to signal the middle path of the new government. Here they needed movement members who were well respected. Thus, it was those who had called for the death of the former president, or who had spent decades in jail, that were being paraded to assure the people that a second betrayal was not in progress. They greeted Ogum warmly but all but ignored Kalumba. Ogum and Kalumba sat down and waited for the rally to begin.

A day or so before the rally, Ogum had received a call. It was from the president himself asking Ogum to come to his office in the morning—they had some urgent business to discuss. He would be picked up outside Livingstone Hotel in the City Center. "And Comrade Ogum, can you keep your visit quiet?" the president asked before hanging up.

Ogum was frisked in full view of the tourists eating a continental breakfast outside Livingstone Hotel, who instinctively started snapping pictures. Ogum did not care; he was both excited and worried about meeting the president. It was one thing to talk with him when he was a movement leader. As president, even though he wore power lightly, for those meeting him, it seemed to escape from his every pore. "The president hates having comrades checked for weapons, but we have to do our job," the Secret Service agents explained.

He had expected to be taken to the State House but instead was taken to the president's new home in Springdale Estate. They did not talk much in the car, not even when they drove by Soweto and passed an old woman being robbed by a group of thugs.

At the main gates of Springdale Estate, the driver flashed his badge and told the policeman guarding the gate that the president's guest had arrived. They drove through winding roads, past large houses with blooming rose gardens and expensive cars packed in driveways, past workers in yellow overalls with "Springdale Labor Force" printed on the back, until they came to a heavily fortified house. The president lived in a fort within a fort.

Ogum was escorted through long corridors. The walls were richly decorated with photographs of freedom fighters like Biko, Gandhi, Martin Luther King Jr., and Malcom X. He was led into a room that had even more photographs on the wall—Che, Castro, Cabral, Napoleon, Kimaathi, Marx, Lenin, Mao, Lumumba, Fanon—and a large oil painting of L'Ouverture.

Finally he heard a voice that got louder and louder, a rambunctious voice that was making jokes with the guards and that announced a confident owner before his physical entrance. Ogum found himself craning to peer into the corridor, and when the president finally came into the room, he could not but feel he was in the presence of a humble greatness. It was like meeting Gandhi, a simple man in a loincloth who led millions. But the loincloth was not just cloth, it was a symbol of freedom just like the salt on his table. Only this Gandhi was dressed in Samasi sandals, fading jeans, and a loose-fitting *kitenge* shirt. In the morning sunlight filtering through the windows, his graying hair, combed into a fierce Afro, seemed to glow.

"Hello, Mr. Ogum. I should call you Ogum or comrade. I hope you will not tell people what you have seen today," he said from across the room, as he walked toward Ogum with hand outstretched.

"About the photographs, Mr. President? They should be on the walls of each home," Ogum said, trying hard not to betray his nervousness.

"No, Ogum, a revolution gives people space to be individuals. Where would people hang their wedding photos?" He laughed heavily. "This room is my shrine. When I feel burned out, this is where I get reenergized. These were far better people than me and more deserving of leadership than I am. What can I say?"

By this time he had reached Ogum. "I meant, what you should not tell people is that the president was home on a weekday at this late morning hour instead of attending to matters of state. I tell you it is a very boring job. Sometimes I have to literally force myself out of bed. Boy, do I miss the rush of ducking the secret police," he said lightly.

"Well, Mr. President, I wouldn't dream of it," Ogum replied.

"Comrade, do call me Comrade . . . you know that . . . Comrade Ogum." He laughed at the number of *comrades* he had just uttered. "Have you had breakfast? John makes the best breakfast—eggs, toast, bacon, you name it. I love food." He called one of the guards in. "Has everyone else had breakfast?" he asked, meaning the guards and everyone else in the household. "Can you please tell John to make his delicious breakfast for two?" he requested when the guard answered that Comrade was the only one who had not yet eaten breakfast.

"Come." He beckoned Ogum. "Even though I said I love this room, it can become quite morbid for the living."

He led Ogum to the backyard, where he pulled two chairs to a wooden table. The backyard was beautiful, full of roses and carnations. They chatted about little things, like where Comrade grew up and how the press was always wrong about his birth date.

"I am actually four years older than they report," he whispered to Ogum. He asked Ogum if he was married yet. "Soon," Ogum replied. Comrade promised to come to his wedding.

"The work you have done has not been adequately appreciated. As you start your family I would like to be there to say thank you. Tell me; is your wife in the movement?" he asked. "But why should I go on like I don't know. Of course I know who she is ... very instrumental in making the country what it is today. You are very lucky, comrade. Me, my wife hates the fact that I am in politics. You and Comrade Sukena are the symbol of the new nation—united across ethnicity and class. Don't be discouraged by the animosity I am sure both of you are receiving from people on both sides; our people still have a lot to learn. Your wedding shall be the symbol of what we can become." For a moment, Comrade seemed to be envisioning a crowd of listeners before him.

"Love can teach us many things when we let it. But don't let me plan your wedding. As you can see, I will turn it into a political ceremony," he added, as if suddenly conscious that he had been addressing a larger audience.

He laughed as John, the cook, brought the breakfast. Comrade stood up and said like an announcer, "Let me introduce the best chef in the world. Meet John the Baptist. He takes an egg and baptizes it into the most delicious omelet. John the Baptist, meet Comrade Ogum."

John laughed for a long time and between gasps said to Ogum, "See, see, this is the side that people don't see about our president. He really should have been a comedian—our own Eddie Murphy. *Coming to Africa* ... Get it? Get it? Instead of *Coming to America* ... I am delighted to meet you, comrade," he said.

Ogum noticed that John, an older man about the president's age, was dressed very casually. In most homes the cook was dressed in a white outfit, but the way John was dressed, in brown khaki trousers, white sneakers, and a regular checkered shirt, one would have thought it was the president's friend walking away.

"Listen, Ogum; let me not insult your intelligence. I invited you here for a reason, a very delicate reason. Before I begin what it is I want to discuss with you, you must promise that whatever your answer, this matter shall die with you. If you say no, I will still come to your wedding, so don't be afraid to say no. And if you say yes, I will be all the happier . . . naturally. Actually, one of our senior comrades had offered to talk to you about this, but I said I wanted full responsibility." He paused, waiting for Ogum's reply. His tone had changed from one of joviality to one of serious collegiality.

"Comrade, I can assure you I will consider what you have to say, and I will take this conversation to my grave," Ogum said as he leaned forward.

"I will get to the point. You understand struggle. You understand what we have had to endure to get here. You understand we are on the cusp of liberating our people. We are close." The president closed his fist as if grasping something and brought the fist to his mouth. "Pfff," he said, blowing away whatever he was holding.

"You understand that we had to keep the massacre buried in order to make important political gains. You, perhaps better even than me, understand what the recent revelations have done to undermine our progress. It cannot continue," the president added emphatically, his now-empty right hand slicing the air and landing on the table with a thud.

"What do you want me to do?" Ogum asked.

"There is someone I want you to meet," the president said, instead of answering him. He walked to one of the guards and whispered in his ear.

Soon, Ogum heard the clinking of chains, and an old beat-up man was roughly pushed into the backyard. Comrade admonished the guard for being rough with an old man.

"The old man is human garbage," the guard answered.

Comrade shook his head sadly and asked that the old man's chains be removed. "We call him Judas—he betrayed our people," he explained to Ogum. "A most unpleasant fellow."

Judas, even with the chains removed, continued to shuffle as he moved over to the table. Comrade beckoned him to sit down and have some breakfast. He piled Judas's plate with food.

Comrade noticed Ogum eyeing the sharp knife that Judas was using to slice into his sausage and bacon.

"He knows he has done enough damage," he reassured Ogum. "Tell Ogum here what you did," the president ordered Judas.

"I worked as a torturer. I had a wife and children to feed . . ."

"Never mind about that." Comrade cut him short. "Just answer my questions." For the first time Ogum noticed a hint of impatience in Comrade's voice. He knew that this old man taking in the food in huge chunks was bringing him bad news, and a sense of panic overcame him.

"Why are you in jail now?" Comrade asked him.

"I killed my wife and children, sir," he said.

"How many?"

"One wife and two kids, sir."

"When did you kill them?"

"On the night of the second independence, sir."

"Why?"

"Because . . . I don't know . . . my world . . . finished." Judas laughed nervously. "Kaput! Finito! Sir," Judas said, pulling each word out through his remaining teeth.

"How?" the president asked. His voice shook slightly.

Judas cleared his throat. "I tied her to the bed as she slept. I split the young ones with an axe. Then her. The police said I raped and burned her with cigarettes." Judas dipped into his plate, rolled a piece of bacon into a neat roll, and popped it into his mouth.

"We had no place in this world," Judas added. "I was not drunk, sir," he said, as if to explain how rational a choice he had made.

Ogum stood up in horror.

The president reached out, put his hand on his shoulder, and gently pushed him back to his seat. "Comrade, I am afraid it gets worse," he said.

"Now, I want you to be very careful. I want nothing but the truth. You understand?" Comrade President asked him quietly but firmly. "Nothing but the truth. Do you remember a prisoner by the name of Joseph Kalumba Wa Dubiaku?"

"Yes, sir. I remember him very well. I remember all my boys," he said proudly and with no hesitation. He waited for further instructions.

"What did you do to him when he was brought to you?"

"He wouldn't talk. When he was brought to me, he was almost dead. I nursed him back to health. I fed him my wife's cooking. My fellow officers thought I was crazy. They said that he was near the breaking point, he just needed a push over. I had never thought of doing this before, but I knew I had to try something different. He was magnificent, strong, defiant, more intelligent than his previous interrogators, and full of conviction . . . Only new tricks would work on him. It was a stroke of genius on my part, really." Judas was speaking with newfound eloquence. It was almost as if he had become a completely different human being. He was not even touching the food that he had been greedily eating.

"One day after I brought him back to health, I found him in his cell doing push-ups, and I told him if he did not tell me what I wanted to know, the torture would begin all over again and if he did not talk, I would again nurse him back to health and work him over again. I described to him in great detail exactly what I would do. How I would flay his skin, pluck out his fingernails, electroshock him, smash his toes one by one, et cetera—really, just the usual. I told him if he had the energy for it, we could begin right there and then." Judas paused to reach for a scone.

"Well, to cut a long story short, he did not give me the names I wanted. The following morning the sessions began. I brought him to the brink of death without a word from him. Then force-fed him back to health. You see, that was my big discovery: driving the prisoner to the point where death becomes the Promised Land that he, and I should add sometimes she, can never reach . . ."

"Spare me the details. Just tell me what I want to know," Ogum whispered. He wanted to reach out and kill Judas for what he had done to his friend.

"Yes, of course," Judas said simply. "On the third try . . . Don't the English say the third time is the charm? About halfway into it . . . Let me just say we added ten names to the List." It was as if Judas was telling a story about his own hardship and triumph. Judas broke the center of a soft fried egg and dipped his scone into the yellow yolk. He made a hissing sound as he sucked it from the scone.

Ogum felt sick. "And my father?" he managed to ask.

Judas did not say anything for a second. "Yes, he was one of the ten. The last one," Judas said casually, as if describing the monotony of a tenth goal in a match that was supposed to be tight.

"You mean my brother gave you my father's name?" He asked, as he shook violently in rage and sadness.

Judas looked at Ogum—his eyes betraying no emotion, a gray impenetrable wall, behind it the madness and science of torture.

"Yes," he answered.

Ogum stood up and walked to a rosebush, knelt by it, and threw up for a long time, until only saliva mixed with blood was oozing out.

"That was the bravest of my boys," he heard Judas say somewhere in the background. He realized that the whole time Comrade had not referred to Judas by his real name. He felt Comrade's hand on his shoulder.

"I puked my guts out when I heard the story too," the president said, massaging his shoulders.

"It happens to all of us. Even I had to give them something. The only difference between me and Kalumba is that I gave them something they would have found out anyway," Comrade said as he led Ogum to the table. Judas was gone. The table had been cleared.

"Comrade, thank you for the truth. Tell me what you want from me," was all Ogum said to Comrade, who leaned back into his chair and let out a long sigh. And then he gave Ogum his instructions.

~~~~~~~

The stadium had filled to capacity. Chants of "Give us truth or give us death" filled the air. There were banners reading "What else don't we know?" all over the stadium. Some had changed it slightly to "What else should we know?" Across the walls of the stadium were pro-movement banners: "The Truth Shall Set Us Free: Trust the SIDCF," "SIDCF = Freedom," "Forward Now, Backwards Never."

"Kalumba, I want you to think very hard. When you were tortured, do you remember what happened?" Ogum said, leaning toward him.

Ogum's tone was measured, as if he wanted to make sure that he had asked the question in the best way he could.

"How many times do I have to say that I don't remember?" Kalumba said offhandedly.

"Go back into exile. Leave this mess to us," Ogum said. "I am begging you as your brother. Right now, let's go. I will drive you to the airport. You and Melissa, just turn around. Leave this mess to people like me and Sukena. There is no coming back for people like you. I am begging you," he added. He was wringing his hands desperately, very close to tears.

"If there is no coming back, there is no going back. I am staying here. I will not be forced out again," Kalumba said angrily. "This is my home. I can leave if I want to, but I am not going to get kicked out, not again, not ever again." He looked around him and then at Ogum. "You know me better than anyone else. This . . . do you really expect me to agree?"

This was not the first time he had had to explain to Ogum that he would not go back into exile. Not twice. Not for speaking the truth, not by the movement he had helped bring into power, not with all the sacrifices he had made of his life

225

and his relationships, and not with the promise he had made at the massacre site. It did not matter that it was a promise to Ogum's father; he could have made the same promise to a stranger. He was a witness.

"If I must die, I am going to die right here, on my feet, in my own fucking country." He noticed that Ogum was quietly looking at him. Ogum did not say anything in reply, just let out a resigned sigh, looked at him once, started to say something, then returned his gaze to the center of the stadium where the festivities were soon to begin.

Sukena left for the airport suspecting that something would go terribly wrong. She wanted to make a list to try to figure out what, but it was no use. Anytime she got close to naming it, it slipped away and she ended up making little nonsensical markings. There were too many things in the balance, and any of them unhinging spelled doom one way or another: that much she knew. Either Kalumba's truth that was dividing the nation now would become the foundation for an uncertain future, or the movement so set on preserving the present would triumph. Given the array of forces against Kalumba, the fatigue of struggle and the need for peace, his word against that of a whole movement, Sukena knew he would lose. But at least under the new government, which would guarantee freedom of speech and movement, those like Kalumba could continue speaking and acting, forever pushing the government in the direction of the people.

The days of the List would be behind them, and that at least guaranteed continued dialogue between opposed forces— hope would remain. It was not just Sukena who held this view; those in the movement who disagreed with the burying of history and the making of deals behind the backs of the people also believed that at least in the new era, there would be enough protections to guarantee the search for truth, no matter how gratuitous. But for now the new government had to be given full support.

As she drove to the airport, navigating through the throngs of people going to the stadium, she was thinking about Melissa. Even though they had never met and she hardly knew Melissa, only through Kalumba, there was a connection, there were roots that ran deep, and with time they would follow as many as they could until they were no longer strangers. They would, after all, be sisters-in-law, made so by a brotherhood of will between Ogum and Kalumba.

She arrived on time, only to find that the flight had been delayed. She bought a newspaper and a Fanta soda. The headline was not surprising—*Government Welcomes "What Else Don't We Know Rally."* This was the movement at its best—taking negative energy and using it to further cement itself in the people's imagination. For years, each assassinated person became a martyr, each funeral a recruiting opportunity, and the more the Dictator murdered and jailed, the more powerful the movement became. In this post-struggle era, it was using the same tactics. The minister of information was quoted as saying that the Truth Rally was in fact an indication of how far democracy had come in such a short time. "Our people are so free that they are free to say that they are not free" was his favorite quip when cornered by foreign journalists.

She finished her Fanta and walked to the baggage claim area. She did not have to wait for long before spotting a young beautiful woman with wild black hair, wearing a white T-shirt and jeans. It was Melissa. Sukena, for the first time in many years, felt old—she felt the years of struggling, fear and exhilaration, pain and love, the extremes of living weighing on her shoulders. It had everything and nothing to do with Melissa; she had simply made the occasion for reflection possible. They embraced. Melissa had not said a word—she looked scared as she laughed nervously.

"First time out of the US," she said. "Kalumba told me that people here might call me a white person . . . a *toubab?* I will kill myself if that happens," she said, making a sliding motion across her neck with her finger.

Sukena laughed. "Just like Kalumba. Better be prepared, I suppose. They will not mean anything by it. Probably after your dollar rather than your skin," she added.

"Yes, he said that they think it's a compliment—everyone wants to be white . . . more likely to give a dollar," Melissa said. The baggage claim belt began to whirl and the first droppings came through.

They waited for an hour, and still her luggage had not arrived. They walked to the Kwatee Airways counter. Even though the line was not long, Sukena offered to stand in line while Melissa watched the TV, where Kalamashaka, "the sensational Kwatee Republic hip-hop group" as Sukena explained it to her, was rapping in a language she couldn't understand. Then before the video was over the TV switched to what appeared to be a large crowd watching a soccer game. The words "Live from the Stadium," trickled through the screen, followed by "Comrade President to Address Nation," and Melissa yelled out to Sukena to come and watch. "The revolution is being televised," she added, laughing at her own joke.

Ogum knew from his meeting with the president that the stage had been carefully managed to make this rally a success. This was going to be a well-choreographed play. The crowd was getting restless, and just when it seemed they would rush the center stage, the first speaker made his way to the podium.

The radical chair of the youth movement, making his way to the platform, would call for an investigation into the massacres. He was also going to call for the dead soldiers and civil leaders to be reburied as heroes of the second independence.

The next speaker was going to second the call for the reburial and call for an investigation into why the people were not to be trusted with the truth. He was going to put the movement on trial and accuse it of vanguardism, a mentality that people can only be led like sheep. He was going to call for a democratic revolution in which the people were also the voice.

The third speaker was going to point to the progress that had been made—that people could assemble freely, criticize the government, worship whom and what they wanted, and be tried fairly in a court of justice. Instead of throwing out the baby with the bathwater, they should nurture the baby until it grew into a full democracy.

Food, beer, and music were to be in abundance, and when the crowd's anger was sedated, the president would appear and address the nation. But things did not go according to plan. The crowd booed the first speaker off the stage as soon as he said the word *investigation*. "Truth now. We want the truth now," they started chanting. They started calling for Kalumba. Kalumba looked unsure of what to do, but Ogum encouraged him to get on stage and quell the people. "Calm them, we have to keep them calm," he added.

The TV cameras picked him up and sprayed him all over the giant screens, and for a moment it seemed as if he filled up the whole stadium. Sukena and Melissa edged closer to each other and held hands, trying to stem the tension and palpitations that flooded over them.

Before Kalumba made it to the podium, sirens started to blare. Then the crowd let out a long roar as they glimpsed the first motorcycle from the presidential motorcade. The police officer, hearing the approval, lifted up the front wheel and with one hand waved the national flag. He spun around the podium, tearing into the grass until the soil turned into fine dust. Kalumba walked back to his seat forgotten.

Then one motorcycle after another shot through the stadium doors doing crazy stunts until the whole stadium was filled with smoke, dust, and flying pieces of grass. As the smoke cleared, a long line of black Mercedes limousines stretched into the stadium, making a circle around the racetracks that surrounded the soccer field. One by one the newly appointed ministers emerged dressed in neatly pressed black suits, with their wives dressed in expensive and colorful *boubous*.

The vice president was the first to emerge with his wife, and they stood by their limo. Then the defense minister in full battle regalia, medals dangling from all conceivable places, whom the crowd cheered wildly, the finance minister and his wife, the minister of education, they all emerged from the cover of their limousines, standing by their respective door until out of the whole government only the president was missing. A few minutes and still no president. An army jeep roared into the stadium, and the crowd raised the drumming and the cheers to a level such that it seemed as if the walls of the stadium could not contain the sound. But the jeep too was empty save for the driver.

The cheers broke into concerned murmurings. The ministers were not shaking hands; they were not embracing their wives in jubilation. As if on cue the crowd went quiet and the silence in place of the noise was just as loud. Was Comrade President dead? Had he been overthrown? Was he gravely ill? But before these questions, now thoughts, could be voiced and become blasphemy or reality, the door to the vice president's limo cracked open. There was a huge collective gasp. And then it fully opened, a second or two elapsed, and Comrade President jumped out dressed in simple green army overalls, a worn-out pistol strapped to his waist. He was laughing, as if he and the whole nation were all part of this joke. Pandemonium broke out. People rushed toward him. But the police kept them at bay as he made it to the podium.

He raised one hand. The crowd went quiet. He cleared his throat, gave a fatherly smile that held for a few seconds, and then started talking. "Each people, each nation, each generation, and each life at some point reaches a point where any step taken, forward, backward, or to the side, can only be painful. Any step we take today shall be painful. The question is this—how can we turn our pain into sacrifice? Which sacrifices will help us grow as a nation?" He paused. The crowd was still, spellbound.

"Today, I suggest we take a step back. Yes, sometimes we have to go back. I want us to go back and ask ourselves, 'Who are we?'" He paused. He let the silence turn into tension.

"Do you want to know who you are?" he whispered into the microphone. The crowd, unsure, responded quietly, "We do." "Do we want to know who we are?" he asked more loudly. And the crowd matched his tone so that it sounded like a loud indistinct murmur. "Do we care where we have been?" he asked loudly. Again the crowd matched him.

"Do we want to know who we are?" he asked loudly, angrily, so that Sukena and Melissa could see a fine spray of spittle escape his mouth. The crowd rose to its feet, shouting, "Yes, yes, yes." "Do we really want to know who we are?" He was standing on his toes, his frame taut, eyes slits, jaw set, hands held up as in prayer.

He beckoned to the vice president, and the vice president walked toward him on a red carpet as it was unfurled. As the vice president stood by him, he beckoned to the generals, who, as they walked toward him, were followed by soldiers who fell into a guard of honor formation. He raised his hand again, and the defense minister walked to the president's jeep and hopped in; the driver brought it to where the red carpet began. The crowd could not really see what was going on, but they cheered, still shouting to know who they were. "Yes, tell us, we want to know."

He raised his hands and the crowd went quiet. "To know who we are, we have to go into the past. We have to find those who made us. The truth is like a river; to find it we have to go to its source. We have to return to the source." The crowd was quiet once again, ears straining, standing on tiptoe trying to peer into the center of the podium, which was now blocked from view by the guard of honor and the VIPs surrounding the president. The only thing they could see were the raised hands, flailing as if in a trance. "For the last time, do we want to know who we are?" The crowd surged forward shouting "YES." The soldiers looked at each other nervously.

"We are lovers." The crowd surged forward. "Tell us! Tell us!" they shouted.

"We are lovers because we love freedom," he shouted into the microphone.

Tell us, tell us!

"We are warriors because our parents were warriors."

Tell us, tell us!

"They demanded!"

Tell us, tell us!

"They fought and they died."

Tell us, tell us!

"They bled into the water we drink."

Tell us, tell us!

"They bled into the earth where we grow gunpowder."

Tell us, tell us!

"They bled into the same earth where we buried our fallen comrades."

Tell us, tell us!

"They welcomed them into the earth."

Tell us, tell us!

"And the earth fed their children."

Tell us, tell us!

"Shall we sell this earth?"

No! No! No!

"We are warriors!"

We are! We are!

"We bury those that fall where they fall!"

We do! Tell us!

"Our nation is a burial ground!"

Tell us! Tell us!

"We are warriors!"

Tell us, tell us!

"I don't have to tell you!"

Then show us! Show us!

The crowd with each chant seemed to be taking a heave and a step forward in unison. Then the president stopped flailing his hands and froze them in the air. The crowd stopped. The hands dropped from view slowly, and just as slowly something rose from the horizon of the soldiers and VIPs surrounding him: a shiny white skull moving upward inch by inch until it was fully revealed.

"We have brought him back home. Comrades, Shakara our warrior ancestor has returned home to us!" the president shouted into the microphone.

The stadium let out one long roar as the people stampeded the podium. Some were crying; others spoke as if in tongues while others laughed wildly. For a moment Ogum sat transfixed by the spectacle. The president had pulled it off. The crowd was getting closer and closer to the president, who, holding the skull under his arm, was being ushered into his jeep through the protective guard of honor that was now facing the crowd.

Kalumba heard loud angry popping sounds that reminded him of Baba Ogum's assassination. He dove for cover. More gunfire, smoke, and teargas and it was chaos. People started streaming out of the stadium, some getting caught underneath thousands of moving feet. Kalumba stood up and started yelling for Ogum. Relieved, he saw Ogum emerging through the smoke a few seats in front of him. He started moving, readying himself to break into a sprint and join the fleeing masses.

He felt a violent efficient blow in his chest that pushed him back into one of the seats. Then pain began pulsing from its center until it filled his chest. He realized blood was filling up his lungs. *The soldiers, one of the soldiers shot me,* Kalumba thought. In his mind flashed the rifles raised into the air— they had been firing in the air to save the president from the crowd. *Was it an accident?* His face changed into one of anguish when he saw in Ogum's right hand a pistol so small and black that it seemed to be part of his hand.

He realized what the papers would say tomorrow: *Comrade Joseph Kalumba Wa Dubiaku Falls.* Perhaps Oruka would uncover the truth? His lips were moving rapidly, and his chest heaved as he gasped for breath. He looked confused, and then as his breathing became sparser and sparser, he calmed down. *There was nothing he could have done,* he thought; *all the crossroads had been leading him here.* To be killed, assassinated by his brother.

Then he realized there was more he could have done. He could have loved life a little bit more. He could have used the ten years spent wandering in his mind to better his life and the lives of those around him in exile. Even if, when all was said and done, he would have died here, he could still have lived a better life. The past year of living was too short. After the initial confusion he was not surprised that it was Ogum. He had known it since they were children. Melissa—she was arriving, she was here. That was the regret he would take to his grave and beyond. Like Ogum's father, he would be a buried secret. He turned his eyes away from Ogum. He did not want Ogum's face to be last one he saw.

Ogum made for the exit and was barely missed by a TV camera that panned to where Kalumba lay dying.

He had done it: he had avenged his father; no, he had saved Sukena from Kalumba; no, he had saved the nation from a counterrevolution led by Kalumba. Yes, this was his sacrifice; like his father's death, which had led to Ogum's sacrificing his relationship with his mother, now he was truly orphaned—he could not go to Baba Kalumba or Sukena. Even though the SIDCF, including Comrade President, would stand by him, those close to him would know it was he who had done it.

He knew he was truly alone now. He had sacrificed everything, and he had won his people their freedom. But no matter how he tried, he could not find solace, joy, or a sense of accomplishment. He knew his was going to be a long, tortured life.

At the moment Comrade hoisted up Shakara's skull into the air, Sukena and Melissa, still at the Kwatee airport, understood why the luggage had not arrived. Sukena thought about how only she and Ogum had known Melissa would be arriving with Mr. Shaw's skull mislabeled as that of Shakara. This was Ogum's doing; he could not let go. Ogum had betrayed his brother.

The soldiers started shooting into the air. People watching the airport TV with them were screaming: others ran for their cars while tourists tried to reboard their planes.

Then the camera panned to Kalumba, bloodied and pressed back against a seat, trying to breathe. Sukena and Melissa gripped each other tightly. Kalumba tried to keep breathing. He realized he was going to die. He stopped fighting so he could live out the last few seconds in peace. He tried to lift his head up to speak to the camera. "Melissa" was all he managed to heave out, but it came out jumbled. And the two women did not make out what he had said. They heard more gunshots and saw his body jerking from the impact. More shots, and the camera clattered to the ground. The last footage that Melissa and Sukena saw before the TV went dark was of empty stadium seats.

Sukena sat down on the airport floor and Melissa pulled her up. Melissa was laughing hysterically, tears running down her face. "Mrs. Shaw, she always said she had one more joke," she said as she embraced Sukena. Tomorrow a hollow feeling of pain and loss, one that would become her constant companion, would come. But for now they had to survive.

"I am a widow. I was always going to be a widow," Sukena said, to no one in particular.

"Yes, but we know the truth. There is no going back," Melissa said urgently but quietly to Sukena and held her even more tightly. Sukena, a pillar around which the world she had known and had hoped for had died, was now just standing there, arms hanging limply at her sides, looking into the distance with a numb fixed stare. Melissa more than anyone could tell that the Sukena of tomorrow would be more dangerous than anything Kwatee had experienced. But for now they had to keep moving.

Like wounded soldiers emerging from a battlefield, they leaned into each other and staggered out of the airport and into the new and old Kwatee Republic.